THE TROUBLE WITH EMPATHS

ELKE FEUER

DEDICATION

A huge thanks to my beta readers, Corissa, Cate, and Kim. This book wouldn't be what it is without you.
Thanks to my ARC readers, especially Charlotte Lynn and Lorraine who have been readers since my very first book
My fellow TSWAG authors whose support means everything to me!

Published by Elke Feuer

www.elkefeuer.com

Cover Design: Florida Girl Design

Editing: The Atwater Group | Deep Spark Editing

CHAPTER 1

Connor cringed as the noise from the party hit his senses, loud and booming in his head. He usually prepared himself for large crowds with heavy meditation or breathing sessions, but that didn't happen because his best friend Michael showed up early for a quick drink.

Connor should've insisted they didn't drink, but Michael was about to lose the freedom he had in university when he went to work for his father in the family business in a couple of months, so saying no wasn't an option.

Next came the mixture of emotions that swirled around and over him like multicolored ocean waves rolling to and from the shore.

Excitement.

Annoyance.

Anger.

Boredom.

And a bunch more Connor couldn't process. Didn't want to process.

Not if he was going to make it through this party tonight.

The happy ones he could handle, but the strong negative ones were like knives in his brain. Focusing on them only made it worse.

"You all right, mate?" Michael rested a hand on his shoulder, concern etched in his eyes.

Beyond the open doorway where they stood was Michael's sister Regan's eighteenth birthday party. The room was decorated like every other charity event they hosted, instead of a young woman's party. Their parents' doing, no doubt.

"All good." Connor's lips curled with a fake smile. Michael wasn't aware of his "gift"—or curse, as his parents preferred to call it. Although his father had no trouble using it to his advantage when needed.

Empath was the word he'd learned years ago, but to him, it was too simple a word to describe it, in his opinion. No one else knew. Not since he was a kid. The possibility of losing his only real friends, and in some ways a second family, in his mind, wasn't worth the risk. Or having them use him the way his father did sour his stomach.

He learned his lesson the hard way that relationships ended when you didn't fit the box they put you in, whether it was your friends or their parents. Being different wasn't appreciated, especially in their social circles.

Michael laughed and clapped him on the back. "Let's go in there and get this over with. I'm sure Regan wants it to end as quickly as we do."

"You go ahead. I'm heading to the toilet first." Not enough time to prepare himself for the barrage of emotions he'd have to deal with once inside, but it was better than nothing.

This was why he tended to avoid large events.

At university, it was easy to block out the noise with alcohol but that wasn't an option tonight. Not for Regan's party, and definitely not with her parents watching them. Being an adult didn't matter to them if he and Michael made a scene.

When he returned to the party, he tried inconspicuously to find Regan, but she was lost in a crush of her friends.

Regan. Just saying her name shot a thrill through him that swiftly shifted to crippling guilt.

Like an idiot, he'd complicated their relationship by kissing her on the lips on her sixteenth birthday. It was silly, really, and something he hadn't planned. He never thought of her that way before. But after she hugged him as a thank-you for his gift and gazed at him with those stunning blue eyes of hers like he was the moon and stars, he couldn't help himself. He regretted it the moment it happened. She was only sixteen, for Christ's sake, and he was twenty-two.

What made matters worse was she was no longer the skinny little kid who followed him and Michael around. For the past two years, he'd sensed her watching him like a girl with her first crush, which didn't help. Neither did the fact that she was Michael's sister and off-limits for more reasons than their friendship and her age.

The annoying part was she was the only person he had difficulty sensing. As a kid, she wore her heart on her sleeve and in her eyes, so it wasn't necessary. He only sensed when she needed him and what for.

The thrill that coursed through him when she watched him nailed him with guilt each time. She was just a kid, and they were friends. Close friends, even though it wasn't the same as the friendship he shared with Michael. Her friendship meant everything to him.

Being at university helped. Talking and texting was easy and comfortable and kept their connection in the lane it belonged.

His life was complicated enough between the strained relationship with his parents and leaving university soon to get out into the working world to find a job. One that paid him enough to get out of his parents' house. Being away from them at university made him realize distance from them was the best thing to happen to him.

The last thing he needed was to develop feelings for his best friend's little sister—his other best friend. And a kid. Although she wasn't a kid anymore. And that's what bothered him the most.

CHAPTER 2

Regan Doherty had been in love with Connor McGrath for as long as she could remember. They'd been childhood friends forever. Well, friends by association because he was her brother's friend, but in her mind it counted.

When she was sixteen, he ruffled her hair and kissed her on the lips for her birthday, and hugged her the way he always did. But unlike the other times, heat and goose bumps had raced across her skin, and her heartbeat stuttered before speeding up until she was breathless.

Thankfully, he didn't notice, but she did. From that moment on, Connor was no longer the friend who brought her favorite books, really listened when she talked, and wiped away her tears when her parents were being unreasonable.

He became Connor with hair that glistened in the sunlight when they were hanging by the pool. Connor with the muscles and six-pack that stopped her breath. Her friend with the piercing blue eyes that saw into her soul.

For the past two years, the way she felt about Connor had only deepened. The distance of him being at university didn't dim but strengthened those feelings, and she planned to tell him tonight. He and her brother Michael were home from uni. It was the perfect opportunity. Never mind that her heart was about to beat out of her chest, and doubt stabbed every pore on her skin. This was Connor. One of her best friends, who, other than her parents and brother, was the most important person in her life.

Pining for him was never going to get her what she wanted. Those were the words she'd repeated in the mirror several times as she was getting ready for tonight.

Confessing her feelings could work in her favor, if he felt the same way, or she could massively crash and burn and ruin their friendship. But it was a risk she was willing to take. When he kissed her, the sparks between them were mutual. She was certain of it. The shock in his eyes clearly said kissing her on the lips wasn't planned, but that merely convinced her the connection between them was real.

Sparkling lights from every color of the rainbow reflected off the walls of the ballroom her parents rented for her party. People of all ages, from her friends to business associates of her father, were cramped into the space like finely dressed sardines.

Regan hated that she had to invite so many people, but there was no other option if she wanted a party. Business before family. Always. No exceptions.

On one side of the room were friends from school and her social circle under the age of thirty covered in bold colors and fine-cut suits and dresses, while the other side of the party was anyone over the age of forty and friends or business associates of her family or friends.

"Is this a party or a wake?" Ciara Kelly sipped her champagne, her heavily made-up eyes moving about the room until they settled on Michael. "You should invite your brother and Connor over."

Regan rolled her eyes. Ciara was less than subtle about her interest in Michael. He never showed one ounce of interest, but that never stopped her. Ciara was closer to their age and only befriended her because she was Michael's sister. "They'll come around once they've made the rounds."

Her eyes devoured Connor once Ciara wandered off to a group of her friends. He was dressed in a dark-blue suit that hugged his frame. A frame she had watched fill out from the lean one he had in high school to the thicker, more solid one while he was away at school. The body of a man and one she now drooled over even more.

His hair was slicked back so it looked almost black instead of the usual shaggy sandy-blond locks she itched to touch for reasons other than ruffling it in annoyance. It was as soft as it looked, but she wanted to run her fingers along his scalp as she tugged his face to her in a kiss.

As if sensing he was being watched, he turned, catching her staring, and graced her with one of his sexy smirks. One that made her heartbeat gallop and her knees tremble since she was sixteen.

She returned his smirk with her usual goofy grin before remembering she wanted Connor to start seeing her as a woman and not his best friend's little sister. His eyes swept her from head to toe; his eyebrow rose in question when her grin turned into what she hoped was a seductive smile. Or maybe it was the dress she wore.

She was showing a lot more skin than usual with the off-the-shoulder, shimmering silver dress that reached her ankles, but with a split that went nearly to her thigh. Her mother had been appalled when she stepped out of the dressing room and then annoyed when Regan refused to change it to what her mother thought was a more suitable choice. Most of this party—her party—was what her parents wanted. Her dress was the one thing she wanted for herself. Her mother had relented when Regan reminded her how often what she wanted was sacrificed for the sake of business.

He glanced around behind him, as if looking for someone else the smile was meant for.

Regan took a sip of champagne and, over the rim of the glass, blasted him with the sexiest stare she could muster. *Would he take the hint?* Her heart sped up when he excused himself from the circle of people around him and strutted toward her with an air of confidence and yumminess that sent quivers to places on her body that were hidden, even in this revealing dress.

As he moved toward her, his gaze raked over her from the tips of her open-toe shoes to the tops of her exposed breasts, up to her lips and finally her eyes when he stood before her.

Shivers danced through her veins when his cologne hit her senses. The same one she gave him every birthday. Sandalwood with a hint of bergamot. "Connor."

"Happy birthday, Re."

She flinched at her nickname. "Please call me Regan. At least in public. I'm not a little girl anymore."

His gaze traveled over her face, which was covered in makeup. Not as much as Ciara, but more than what usually covered her face.

"No, you're not." His voice dropped an octave before he cleared his throat and graced her with a friendly smile.

She tugged his arm. "Let's go on the balcony. I need some air." Regan had scouted the perfect spot outside already. One where no one inside would see them.

Connor followed her to the balcony doors, leaving her champagne glass on the tray of a passing waiter. "You're too young to drink."

Regan snorted. "Did you miss that today is my eighteenth birthday?"

He held open the large French door for her. "I'm just looking out for you, so you don't drink too much and do something you'll regret later."

She released his arm and faced him, making sure to stay close. "Is that what happened on your eighteenth birthday?" Her eyes twinkled with mischief.

"No. But I'm not you."

Her face scrunched in question. "What does that mean?"

"I'm not my best friend's little sister who is wearing a very revealing dress and attracting more attention than she realizes."

"Am I?" Regan placed her hand on the lapel of his jacket. *Did he notice other men watching her?* She couldn't care less about them. It was his attention she wanted.

"You are." He scanned her face, pausing at her lips before moving back to her eyes. "And wearing too much makeup."

Regan chuckled, sidestepping his comment. "So where is my gift?" They usually exchanged gifts in private, because they were often ones her parents wouldn't approve of.

"For someone who's not a little girl anymore, you're sure eager for your birthday present." Connor's lips curled with a smirk.

She ignored his comment, not letting his teasing get under her skin. Not tonight. Tonight, she was on a mission, and the window was closing quickly. There was only so long they could stay on the patio before someone came outside. "I know you're going to give it to me. You want to give it to me," she whispered seductively, and watched with surprise and awe when his eyes darkened. Her breath hitched in her throat.

His mouth opened to respond but closed. His usual blue eyes were gray under the artificial overhead light on the balcony. Silence stretched out as vast as the night sky blanketing their backdrop. The cool Irish night air swirled around them, forming goose bumps on her skin.

Tension sizzled in the small distance between them. Regan's hand caressed the lapel of his jacket slowly up and down, imagining it was his bare chest until his hand gripped hers, stopping her movement.

"Regan..." His tone held a hint of warning.

She lifted her face toward him and moved in closer. When he didn't step back, she pressed her lips against his, a feat she couldn't normally manage without heels.

She'd kissed a few guys before tonight, not wanting to come across as inexperienced to Connor, whose lips had seen more than his share of women over the years. To her delight, his arms went around her, pulling her against his frame, his fingertips grazing the skin of her back. She moaned and gasped when his tongue slipped into her mouth and he took control of the kiss.

Regan's knees weakened with every stroke of his tongue against hers, every brush of his fingers against her skin. He broke the kiss and attacked her neck with kisses, then trailed down her collarbone. She was grateful for his tight grip; otherwise, she'd be a puddle on the expensive marble floor. She arched her back as his lips kissed the tips of her exposed breast. "Connor," she groaned. "I knew it would be like this."

"Did you now," he whispered hotly as he nibbled on her shoulder.

"Yes. And I want you to be my first," Regan breathed. Her head spun from the intoxicating sensations spiraling through her body from his mouth on her skin, the smell of his cologne, and his own delicious scent just below the surface.

Connor's lips stilled and his body tensed.

Regan met him with desire-filled eyes. "What's wrong?" *Why did he stop?* Everything was going the way she hoped.

"I can't be your first, Regan. A sexual relationship isn't in the cards for us."

Her grip on his jacket tightened. "Why not? I love you. I've always loved you."

His hand slid into her hair. "You think you love me, but you don't."

Is he serious right now? "I know how I feel, Connor. I've known it the moment I was sixteen and you kissed me on the lips."

"That was just a brotherly kiss."

Pain pierced her heart. *Why was he denying the attraction between us?* One that still had her skin and lips scorched from the heat of their kiss. "My brother doesn't kiss me on the lips, Connor." She yanked his jacket.

His hand caressed her cheek. "This is just a silly crush that will pass."

She pushed against him. *That's how he sees me? A silly little girl with a crush?* It didn't matter she was old enough to drink now and do everything adults did. "So why did you kiss me?"

His jaw clenched. "I was caught up in the moment."

"I felt how caught up you were pressed against my leg. You want me." If only she could get him to see her as more than just his best friend's little sister, then he'd change his mind.

"Of course I did. Look at you, Regan. In that dress, with your soft skin, how was I supposed to react? Any normal guy would have the same reaction."

"I don't want any guy, Connor. I want you," she whispered, beginning to crush under the weight of his rejection and the painful realization his reaction to their kiss was just one to any hot, sexily dressed woman. It wasn't because he was attracted to her or was beginning to see her as a woman. Someone he could be with. She could see it in his eyes. He regretted kissing her.

"Regan."

Him using her full name was a death sentence. He only used it when he was serious, or if she pushed the boundaries of annoying him.

"When time passes, you'll realized this was just a phase. You'll meet someone and we'll laugh about tonight."

He was adjusting his suit where she'd mangled it with her fingers and raked his hands through his hair to fix the mess she made. It would be like their kiss hadn't happened. Like what she said and how she felt didn't matter.

She was used to that from her parents and even occasionally her brother, but never him. He'd always taken her seriously, or so she'd thought. His reaction only proved he saw her the same as everyone else—a little girl who didn't know her own mind. Rage crept over her, starting at the tips of her toes, making its way through her body like a fire in her blood.

She met his gaze. "The only thing time is going to prove, Connor, is that you're going to realize this attraction between us is more than friendship, and it's going to be too late. You're going to watch me move on with my life, with someone else, and you'll be wishing it was you the whole time."

The sadness in his eyes angered her more.

"You, Connor, are a proper wanker," she seethed before storming back to the ballroom. It was her birthday, after all, and she'd be damned if she'd let him ruin the rest of her night. Never mind that her heart was shattering into a million pieces.

CHAPTER 3

Connor watched Regan leave and adjusted himself in his pants from the residual effect of their encounter and the sway of her gorgeous body. Shite! He was an idiot. When she said she loved him, it had shocked him right down to his toes before settling in his heart.

The words he said were necessary, but not the ones he wanted to say. What he wanted was to drag her to her room right then, or at the very least ask what time he should sneak in later. She was right. He was a right wanker. The woman he'd adored for the past two years had confessed her love and that she wanted him to be hers, and what had he done?

Belittled her feelings and her.

Something he'd never done.

Those words hurt her. He knew better than anyone there were enough people in her life doing that. She didn't need him added to that list.

Guilt had eaten away at him when he returned to uni, and he swore up and down that he'd never do it again. And what had he just done? Kissed her and more. The first time he kissed her had haunted him, and he was grateful he couldn't read her emotions. The last thing he needed was to feel how much Regan wanted him, as innocent as the emotion would be. But, on the other hand, not sensing her like everyone else was infuriating, especially when she was the person whose emotions he wanted to read the most.

A scuffling noise from the other end of the balcony caught his attention. To his dismay, it was Declan Kelly. He didn't dislike him, exactly...just wasn't a fan of what he sensed from him. He was a weasel just like his father and even his sister, who was as fake as they came.

"What are you doing out here?" Had he seen them kissing? Panic rocketed through him. Declan had a big mouth, and wouldn't hesitate to use it against him, or hold it over his head.

Declan lifted his shoulder. "Just taking in the night air."

Behind him came a giggle, and Connor thought a woman was with him until he saw one and then two of his friends come out of the shadows. From their eyes, he could tell they were not only wasted, but high.

"Are you crazy, bringing weed here? This isn't one of your uni parties, you idiots! The police commissioner is here."

This statement made them laugh louder. They were too gone to care.

"Don't let Shamus see you, or you'll be out on your asses."

Declan and a mate of his stumbled toward him. "We saw you out here with Regan and wanted a closer look."

Bollocks! He schooled his reaction with a shrug. "It's her birthday. I had a present for her." Never mind he didn't get around to actually giving her the gift.

"I bet you did." Declan laughed. "But she didn't look too happy."

"Don't be rude. That's Michael's little sister you're speaking of."

"She didn't look so little to me. Not in that dress anyway."

Connor gripped the boy who said it by his shirt, twisting it in his fingers. "Watch your next words, mate."

"Relax, Connor. We didn't mean to offend your girlfriend."

"Regan is not my girlfriend. She's a friend. Always has been. Always will be." Pain pinched his chest the moment the words left his mouth. He wished they weren't true, but as long as he and Michael were friends, he didn't see that changing anytime soon—no matter what she felt, or how much he wished it was different.

He released some of the tension in his body that they hadn't seen them kiss or hear what he and Regan were saying. Small mercies.

Declan clapped him on the back. "Come on. Let's go back to the party. You idiots stay outside until you sober up or your bleedin' eyes aren't the size of saucers."

The weight of Declan's hand on his shoulder irked him. He wanted nothing more than to yank it off and tell him to go to hell. He never liked Declan, who'd been a part of their circles due to their family connections. Since he was a boy, he and his sister Ciara were the definition of entitled, spoiled brats. Worst of all, they reveled in it in ways other kids in their group—himself and Michael included—never did.

When they were back inside the party, Connor scanned the room, looking for Regan, and found her in the middle of a group of her friends, laughing. She was enjoying her party again, something he was grateful for. He was worried he ruined her night after rejecting her. Something he was regretting, even though it was the right thing to do.

Taking his best friend's little sister's virginity was not something he deserved or was entitled to, even if he wanted it more than anything. Wanted her. But then what? It wasn't like they could have the relationship she wanted. He was headed back to uni to graduate in a couple of months, and she was about to start her first year.

Not only were they in different places in their lives, he was certain that once she got a taste of uni life, she'd see he was nothing more than a crush. Nothing more, despite what she said. Then why did that thought wreck him? Along with imagining her with someone other than him? He stuffed those feelings down to a place where they wouldn't and couldn't see the light of day. Regan was a bright star about to enter the world, and him in her life other than as a friend was the last thing she needed.

Connor grabbed a glass of champagne from a passing tray, instead of heading to the bar for a Scotch, where Shamus and Michael stood. He was afraid they'd sense his guilt over what just happened between him and Regan. Shamus already disliked him, but he disliked most people. Michael, on the other hand, would be upset and disappointed if he knew how he enjoyed kissing Regan and felt her softness beneath his fingertips and tasted her skin and heard her moans.

He took a deep swig from his glass and shoved a hand into his pants pocket in an attempt to stop his growing erection. Remembering the chaste kiss he gave her at sixteen was nothing compared to how their encounter tonight would haunt him.

Now he knew how soft and smooth her skin felt, that her skin tasted like honey and how her quiet gasps and moans sounded. He'd even caught a scent of her arousal. I'm screwed.

Connor had thought his obsession with Regan was bad before, but now that he had a taste, he wanted more.

The noise from people's chatter around him grew due to the free-flowing alcohol of an open bar. Connor ground his teeth when he saw Declan standing next to Regan. Too damn close, in his opinion—not to mention, he was openly staring at her exposed skin. Declan leaned down to whisper something in her ear, and her eyes widened in surprise before she laughed and bumped her shoulder with his.

Connor suppressed the urge to charge across the room and punch him in the face. When his hand made its way to her shoulder and then slid slowly down her back, Connor started to make his way toward them. There was no way in hell he was letting Regan anywhere near Declan. The man was a leech and was known for going through women like tissue paper. He was no angel, but Declan only saw women as something to check off his list. He'd never made a play for Regan before, but then she was never eighteen before. Before he could make his way over, he felt someone's hand on his shoulder.

"Enjoying the party?" Michael took a sip from his glass.

Connor shrugged noncommittedly.

Michael laughed. "Not exactly the uni parties we're used to, but at least it's not just a bunch of little kids like her earlier parties. And there's alcohol." He lifted his tumbler.

"Have you seen Declan over there with Regan? He's touching her inappropriately," Connor said with gritted teeth.

Michael's gaze shifted to where Regan and Connor stood. Sure enough, Declan's hand was still resting on Regan's back, although it was no longer moving. He stood way too damn close as he continued speaking with her, his mouth nearly touching her ear. Fricking hell!

"Are you going to do something about it?" Connor demanded.

Michael shrugged. "And be accused of embarrassing her in front of her friends? No thanks. It's her party, and she's known Declan for most of her life. Not to mention he's not about to do something stupid in front of his or my parents." Michael's blue eyes shifted back to him. "Besides, you know as well as I do that Regan can take care of herself."

Connor grunted. Not with idiots like Declan hanging all over her. But he wasn't about to say that out loud and have Michael question his sudden interest.

The sound of the music ending caused everyone to stop talking and turn their attention to Regan's mother, who stood in the middle of the ballroom, a spotlight creating a shadow around her. "Thank you all for coming to our daughter's special occasion."

Connor tuned out the rest of her speech, his gaze returning to Regan, who was now surrounded by friends—but thankfully missing Declan. Her eyes settled on him for a brief moment before returning to her mother. She didn't return his smile, not that he expected her to.

A fake smile, which she plastered on whenever she was at company or family events her parents insisted she attend, curved her lips. Michael stood next to his father, who was now next to his wife.

"Regan has certainly grown up quite a bit since I last saw her," Declan commented, slapping him on the back.

Connor resisted the urge to beat the shit out of him not just for his comments, but for having his hands on Regan earlier.

"Since you weren't interested in taking the gift she offered you earlier tonight, I thought I'd volunteer my services," Declan stated with a smirk, as if he were mentioning the weather.

If it wasn't for Regan's cake being rolled into the room and if this wasn't a big night for her, he would've dragged Declan onto the same balcony and thrown him over the side. It was only a couple of stories. He'd survive, although not without a few well-deserved broken bones and, if Connor were lucky, a concussion.

"Stay away from her," Connor threatened with a calm expression. He didn't acknowledge that Declan had seen them do more than talking on the balcony, even though his statement made it obvious he heard them. With Declan, you never knew whether he was bluffing or looking for ways to manipulate you.

Declan chuckled. "Relax, mate. I'm just offering what you didn't want to give. And I get it. She's off-limits to you but not to me, and it appears she's not picky."

Had he offered to take her virginity? He wouldn't put it past Declan. When it came to inappropriate behavior, he was the master and didn't care who saw, once it wasn't someone who could have leverage against him.

"I don't believe you."

Declan shrugged. "Believe what you want, mate. She's blossoming into womanhood and looking for someone to help her along the way, and that someone is going to be me."

Connor relived their interaction from earlier and remembered her moment of surprise. Had that been when he'd asked her? Why would she agree? Revenge? To hurt him?

The girl he knew wouldn't be so easy to hurt him or be callous in that way, but then he remembered Regan was no longer a girl and he wasn't around as regularly since being away at uni. She had grown up while he was away. Had that much about her changed? He didn't want to believe it, but then he caught the look between her and Declan.

Rage and hurt flooded his veins. He elbowed Declan in the ribs, not hard enough to make a scene, but he needed to injure him in that moment, even in a small way. "Go near her and you'll regret it."

Declan adjusted his suit and his posture after recovering from the blow. "You've got bigger things to worry about, mate."

"What are you talking about?"

"You'll find out soon enough," Declan said cryptically before leaving.

Connor cursed himself for not staying calm so he could read his emotions and know for certain whether he was lying. He'd been too upset after seeing their interaction and then Declan's words. He should've known better than to let Declan rile him up, especially about Regan. And what did he mean, I have bigger things to worry about?

Regan made the first slice of her enormous cake, and the servers were cutting off more pieces and taking them around the room for her guests. Connor took the piece offered to him, even though he didn't feel like eating the sugary confection that wasn't her favorite flavor but one her mother thought was the best option for the guests.

He was right. Regan took one bite, made a face, and then placed it on the standing table beside her and grabbed another flute of champagne.

Now that she was alone again, he took the risk of talking to her. Her posture stiffened as he approached.

"Go away, Connor," she hissed.

"I wanted to give you your gift before I left." He pulled a square box from his breast pocket and held it out for her.

She glanced around the room as if contemplating whether she would make a scene. Several seconds passed before she reached out tentatively to take it. "Thank you."

"Open it," Connor urged her.

A small gasp escaped her lips when she opened the box. Inside was a white-gold bracelet with a strawberry-shaped charm dangling from it.

Connor placed it around her wrist, his fingers lingering longer just to touch the softness of her skin. A lot of time would pass again before he could touch her, if ever, and he wanted a memory.

The expression on her face was one he didn't recognize.

"I love it," she whispered.

"Good." They stood in silence for several minutes, and Connor could feel eyes on them. When he glanced around, he found Declan watching, a hard expression on his face.

"Don't sleep with him," he blurted.

Her brows knitted. "Who?"

"Declan. He's not right for you."

Regan crossed her arms over her chest. "I see. You won't sleep with me and now Declan isn't allowed to either? Is there anyone I can sleep with, since you aren't interested?"

He was more than interested. That was the problem. But he couldn't say those words. It was better she was angry with him and thought he didn't want her in that way.

"You can sleep with who you want...just not him, okay?" Those words were a lie, but the truth was better left unsaid. The hurt that rolled across her face tore him up inside, but he couldn't stop. "You deserve someone who sees you as more than just another notch on his bedpost."

"And more than Michael's little sister," Regan added softly.

Connor didn't respond, no matter how badly he wanted to tell her that she'd been more than that to him since the moment he'd kissed her on the mouth and felt like the biggest pervert.

She'd always been a friend and someone he cared about who didn't fit into a compartment as small as "best friend's little sister." Instead of telling her the truth, he said, "Exactly. You deserve someone who sees you as the kind, passionate, loving person you are. For the person who's more than just a daughter and sister and what everyone in our circle thinks you are or should be."

"And that person isn't you. Is it?" Her voice croaked as she spoke the words and tears pooled in her eyes.

"No. I'm sorry, but it's not, Regan." More lies. He wanted to be that person for her more than anything.

Her head bobbed in understanding.

"Your and Michael's friendships means the world to me, and I'd never do anything to jeopardize them. Understand?"

"I really do, Connor. More than you know. I was just hoping our friendship could be more."

"I know, pet." He ached to touch her cheek, but this wasn't the time or place. Everyone's eyes in the room burned his skin, especially her parents, Shamus and Moira. Connor plastered a friendly smile on his face. "I hope you enjoyed your party, Re."

A gulp worked her throat before she nodded, returning his friendly smile and kissing him on the cheek. "Thanks for your gift." She touched it as if it were precious.

Connor nodded, the lump lodged in his throat keeping the words You're welcome from spilling. If he spoke, he was afraid he'd change his mind.

His phone buzzing in his pocket grabbed his attention. Unlocking his phone, he read a text from his mother, saying his father tried to kill himself.

His expression must've given him away, because Regan asked, "Is everything okay?"

Connor schooled his features before meeting her gaze. "Everything's fine, love."

The furrow in her brows told him she didn't believe him, but right now it didn't matter.

"I have to leave."

"Okay. Thanks for coming to the party and for my gift." The longing in her eyes was a combination of questioning and gratitude.

"Anything for you, Re." And he meant every word, even if he couldn't give her what she wanted—him. Their friendship was something he'd always offer and provide.

Connor left her standing by the cake and strode toward Michael to make sure he had a ride home, and to say goodbye to Shamus and Moira. He held it together until he left the hotel and got into his car. When the door closed, he banged his fists on the steering wheel before composing himself and dialing his mother's number.

"What happened?" he asked when her broken voice answered.

"He signed the contract with the Kellys."

"Bollocks! I told him not to."

For once, his mother didn't scold his use of foul language.

"He didn't have a choice, Connor," his mother offered, even though they both knew the truth. Connor's father was trying to get the business back to its former glory and into the inner circle, and he was willing to do anything to get there. Even sell his soul to the devil himself. Not the devil per se, but the Kellys were damn close.

"Which hospital is he at?" Connor asked, despite the doubt his father was taken there.

The long pause on the other end gave him the answer.

"He's in our bedroom. When I found him, I forced him to wake up and throw up. A lot of the pills came up but I'm not sure." Her voice trembled.

Connor clenched his fists, knowing it wouldn't do any good to argue with his mother about taking him to a hospital. His father would be furious, especially given the circumstances. Never mind leaving your family with the blemish of suicide because he couldn't face another financial mistake. One that Connor warned him not to take.

"I'll be there shortly, but I'm calling Dr. Wilson to visit the house to make sure he's out of danger." Dr. Wilson had been their family physician for years and could be counted on for discretion.

"Very well," his mother conceded.

"I'll be there shortly." He ended the call and yanked a hand through his hair, tugging at the roots before roaring his frustration at the empty car.

What good were his insights, financial or otherwise, if his father continued to ignore them? Connor had warned his father not to get involved in a business deal with the Kellys. Neither Declan nor his father were trustworthy, no matter their false pristine reputations. He'd tried to convince his father from a financial standpoint, but when that failed, he warned him about the emotional reading he'd felt multiple times around them.

His father became agitated as he always did when Connor mentioned the "feelings" he picked up from people. He argued those feelings weren't a valid basis for making important decisions. Never mind each time Connor warned his father before, he was always right. And that his father's own mother had the same gift.

From childhood, he'd shared the emotions he sensed from people, not fully understanding it as a child. His father had known what it was, but instead of telling him, he'd brushed his thoughts aside, claiming they were whims of a child. Connor's grandparents were the only people who believed him. His parents' reaction and those of parents of past friends stopped him from sharing the emotions he sensed with others, even Michael.

Connor came close to telling him and Regan a few times but lost his nerve. They were the only real family he had since his grandparents died when he was twelve and wasn't willing to risk losing their friendship, especially given his tense relationship with their father, Shamus. A past business deal with his father that went badly he seemed to blame Connor for, even though he knew nothing about it. Moira was kind to him and much warmer than she appeared in public.

Regan was another story entirely. Their relationship was beyond friendship, but the thought of her looking at him differently didn't sit well with him. Neither did imagining her being with other men.

Thoughts of Regan were pushed aside when he pulled into the driveway of his family home. Connor breathed deeply to calm his agitation at the situation and the fight that was ahead with his parents.

The doctor pulled up behind him, and they walked inside together through the door Arthur, their butler, held open.

Two hours later, the doctor left, leaving him alone with his parents. His father hadn't woken up but was, thankfully, out of danger. His mother sat on a chair next to their bed, worry etched in her face, making the age lines in her face even deeper. She was slumped toward her husband, his pale, frail hand on her own while she stroked it and murmured words too quiet for him to hear. The love she felt shone in her eyes even as they shimmered with tears.

Their relationship was one he never understood, considering they were so different from each other. She was outgoing and bubbly while he was sullen and reserved. Although she wasn't as vain as some of the women in their social circles, appearances mattered to her. Sometimes more than anything else.

"Do you need anything else tonight, Ma?"

"You're leaving?" Her curved posture straightened, and anxious eyes locked onto him.

"No, I'll stay in my room tonight if you or Da need me," Connor assured her. "I'll be gone for about an hour, but I'll be back. Call me if anything happens."

"It's late. Where are you going?"

"I left Regan's birthday party abruptly and she didn't get her gift." Not a complete lie. There was something else he wanted to give her.

"How was the party? Regan must be all grown up now."

Connor didn't miss the subtle hint from his mother. She'd caught him several times at family events, watching her for longer than he should have. And although she never said the words out loud, the knowing smile she gave him said everything.

"She's eighteen now, right?"

Connor nodded.

"Not too young anymore, Connor."

"Mum. She's Michael's little sister."

"True. But she's also an adult who can make her own decisions. You too."

"If it doesn't work out, it could ruin our friendships. Hers and the one I have with Michael. They're too important to me."

His mother's head bobbed in agreement, but her wise eyes said something else.

Connor was relieved when she didn't press him further. He kissed her forehead and left his parents' room. He wanted to insist she go to bed and rest but also knew his mother wouldn't pry herself away.

Connor went to the kitchen and pulled out a box from the refrigerator. Inside was the other present he bought for Regan because he knew her mother wouldn't allow her to make her own choice. He placed it in a small cooler, along with a few other items, and headed out the door.

Once in his car, he proceeded toward Regan's house, making sure to park far enough away so no one would see or hear him. He climbed up the trellis leading to her bedroom, the one she'd snuck out to wander the gardens alone more times than he could count.

Shaking it first to make sure it could handle his weight, he climbed up carefully, the small cooler hanging on his arm. He swung himself onto her balcony and eased the doors open quietly.

The outline of Regan's body was on the bed, her legs dangling off the edge. He exhaled softly, relieved Declan—or any other man—wasn't there. Her clothes were untouched and the bedding was undisturbed other than where she'd obviously plunked down.

He couldn't see her face clearly in the dark, but as his eyes adjusted, he noticed the trail of drool from the corner of her mouth. He was tempted to take a picture to tease her with later but decided against it and sat on the bed, close to one of her night tables. He pulled a bottle of painkillers from the cooler and the note he'd written from his pants pocket and smoothed down the note on the cooler.

"What the hell are you doing?" he whispered to himself, knowing he shouldn't leave the note he'd written her earlier. The last thing she needed was any kind of hope. She was leaving for uni in a couple of weeks, and they'd go back to only seeing each other during special family events—if she came back.

In a few weeks, he was returning home to start working. Doing what, he wasn't sure, given the state of his family's business. He'd worry about it when the time came.

Connor was certain she'd forget all about him once she immersed herself in the uni experience. That realization felt like a stab to his heart. Along with the image of her with someone other than him. He couldn't fault her, either, considering he was the one who rejected her. She was eighteen and just about to start her life while he...with what happened with his father's company, who knew where life would take him.

Being Michael's sister wasn't the only hinderance to their relationship. He couldn't imagine Shamus allowing his little girl to be with him. Shamus thought he was beneath his Regan. Connor clenched his fists. Shamus was the epitome of snobbery. If you looked up the word snob in the dictionary, his face would likely be there.

Connor carefully brushed aside the strand of hair covering her face so he could take one last look. An emotion he couldn't name tugged at his heart and made his skin feel tight. "Goodbye, sweet Regan," Connor whispered before he left the way he came.

When he was back in his car, he stared at her room window, remembering the softness of her skin beneath his fingertips and her moans when they kissed. Regan was eager for his touch, and the sound of his name on her lips was going to haunt him for years to come.

CHAPTER 4

The screaming pain in her head jolted Regan awake. "Ugh! I should've skipped those shots," she moaned when her stomach roiled, signaling it might toss out the lavish dinner from last night.

Leaning up tentatively, she glanced at her nightstand to find a bottle of painkillers and a glass of water. *Did I put them there last night?* She remembered saying goodnight to the girls in the limo and then crawling up the stairs to her room before passing out on the bed.

She sat up straighter and reached for them, swallowing a pill and guzzling down all the water before setting the glass back on the night table. She nearly jumped out of her skin when her foot hit a small icebox next to her bed. She pulled off the note stuck on top, her eyes tearing up when she read Connor's note.

"I do care, Regan. More than I should."

Regan held the note to her chest and sighed. Connor was right. Michael wouldn't accept them as a couple any more than her parents would—especially her father. Not to mention she was leaving for uni in a couple of weeks, and he'd be coming home to start working at his father's firm. The timing couldn't be more wrong.

She opened the lid of the icebox and grinned. Inside sat the biggest slice of strawberry cake she'd ever seen. The ice packs around it were no longer hard, but the inside was still cool, keeping the cake chilled until she could eat it. If her stomach wasn't so unsettled from too much drinking, she'd take a bite.

The cake was another sign that Connor saw her in ways her own family didn't. Her mother snubbed the idea of her strawberry cake in favor of the popular chocolate one. A flavor she hated. Never mind that it was her birthday party.

Her brother loved her, she knew that, but she didn't think he really knew her or even took the time beyond him being protective of her. She understood. He had his own issues with their parents, not to mention their six-year age gap. Michael was trying to prove his worth to his father while she struggled to find her own way.

The last thing she wanted for her life was to become a replica of her mother's—or worse, the women in their circle. A vapid, empty vessel they filled with meaningless charity, booze, and affairs. Although she didn't think her parents were unfaithful, she couldn't see her father resisting the temptation if the opportunity presented itself. Fear would keep her mother faithful. Fear of shame and the ridicule she'd receive if it came out.

She blushed at the image of Connor in her bedroom—and annoyed she hadn't woken up and caught him. The drool crust pulling on the edge of her lips told her it wouldn't have been a pretty sight and one she might never live down.

Sadness gripped her, thinking about Connor. It would be months before they saw each other again. She'd miss the upcoming charity events her family hosted as she'd be at school. Her mother had insisted she stay focused because it was her first year, claiming she'd have plenty of time in the future to attend their other charities.

Regan clenched when she thought of the life that lay ahead of her. Unlike her brother, who'd become part of their family's business, she'd be confined to running their charities. Not that she minded—she loved it, in fact, more than she thought she would—but what she resented was that she didn't have a choice.

Women in her family didn't join the business. They hosted charities and took care of their husband and the household. Regan cringed, thinking of the kind of man she'd eventually marry. If it was someone from their circle, he'd expect the same from her as all the other women. Her stomach protested, imagining that life. *No! Over my dead body.*

She eased herself off the bed and breathed a sigh of relief when bile didn't rise to her throat like she suspected it would. Although the pill would help with the headache, it wouldn't help her empty stomach. She took tentative steps toward the door and into the hallway, making her way down to the kitchen. As she got nearer, she nearly swooned at the smell of rashers assaulting her.

"Good morning, Ms. Regan," their housekeeper, Margaret, greeted warmly.

"What's good about it?" Regan grumbled, plunking down at one of the stools by the kitchen bar.

Margaret chuckled while she spooned a serving of eggs, rashers, sausage, mushrooms, and a thick slice of toast. No pudding, as Regan always thought it was disgusting.

"You're an angel, Mags," Regan cooed as she pulled the plate closer and dug into the food.

"I figured you'd need it after your party. Now that you're legally allowed to drink."

Regan snorted. She'd been drinking wine with dinner for as long as she could remember, but Margaret was right. She could legally drink now. Going on binges wasn't her, especially considering both parents had lectured her about being safe when drinking—and, most importantly, not embarrassing the family by ending up in the *Daily Star*.

"I did drink a bit more last night, but it was a special occasion." Not to mention she was nursing a wounded heart after Connor's rejection. Even though she understood his reason, it didn't stop her heart from aching as she remembered the disappointment in his eyes after she offered herself on a silver platter.

"I gathered from the noise you made coming in last night." Margaret grinned.

Regan slumped against the counter, shoveling more food in her mouth. "I'm sorry for waking you," she mumbled after swallowing.

Margaret rested a wrinkled hand on hers. "You didn't wake me, child. From the time you and Michael were teenagers, I've stayed up to make sure you got home safe."

For as long as she could remember, Margaret was the one who made sure she and Michael were taken care of. Although she wasn't their nanny, she kept them fed and out of trouble while nannies rotated in and out of their lives over the years. Margaret was the only constant, other than her parents.

"And we appreciated it. Especially those delicious meals that our mother wouldn't always allow."

Margaret's brown eyes twinkled.

"Speaking of more food I'm not allowed." Regan raced out of the kitchen, back to her bedroom, and returned with the slice of cake Connor left her.

"Cor, that's a massive piece of cake. Where'd you get that?" Margaret's eyes shifted from the cake to Regan.

"Connor."

"Of course. Let me guess. Strawberry with buttercream frosting."

"Is there any other kind?"

"Your mother didn't let you have it for your party?"

"She ordered chocolate cake!"

"But you hate chocolate!"

Regan shrugged. They both knew it didn't matter what she liked. It was about what was best for everyone attending.

"She could've had multiple layers with the one you wanted."

"Brilliant idea, right?" Regan wiped her breakfast off the fork and dug it into the cake.

"She didn't agree."

"Nope." Her eyes closed in bliss as the first flavor of the buttercream burst onto her tongue and then the cake with strawberry filling between each layer. "Best cake ever."

"Connor sure knows the way to your heart. Everything strawberry." Margaret chuckled, shaking her head.

Regan held up her hand with the bracelet he presented to her last night. "Birthday gift."

Margaret let out a low whistle while holding her wrist and inspecting it closely. "Are those diamonds?" The pitch of her voice elevated.

Regan looked closer and sure enough, each seed covered in the strawberry-shaped charm was diamonds. Not large ones, but diamonds nonetheless. This was the most expensive gift Connor had ever given her, and he'd given her a lot over the years. She shrugged. "I am eighteen now." She tried to sound as nonchalant as possible, even as her heart raced with joy. He'd never given her anything with diamonds before.

Margaret gave her a knowing glance. Regan was certain she knew about her crush on Connor. She had only realized what it meant when her heart beat a little faster each time she was near him, or the cause of the blush that flushed her skin whenever he touched her.

When his lips touched hers gently for the first time, she thought her heart was going to explode out of her chest. The shocked expression Connor tried to laugh off told her he'd felt something too. What, she wasn't sure of…until last night when he kissed her for real. And what a kiss. Heat rushed through her as she remembered.

"Did something happen last night?" Margaret asked.

"Happen?" Regan tipped her head.

"Between you and Connor. You're blushing."

Laughter bubbled out of her. "I kissed someone."

Margaret's eyes twinkled. "You've kissed someone before. Was it someone special?"

"The kiss was certainly special," Regan murmured.

"Anyone I know?"

Regan waved her hand absently as if to say no, and shoved another piece of cake in her mouth to keep from lying.

"Must've been some kiss." A grin pulled at her lips.

"It certainly was."

"I hope he was a gentleman."

"Not completely." Regan grinned, remembering Connor nibbling her shoulders.

"Regan Doherty!"

"What?! Nothing like what your dirty mind is thinking, Mags."

A strangled noise escaped her lips. "I hope not. You're still a child."

"I'm eighteen!"

Margaret snorted. "Still a child. Just one who's legally allowed to drink."

"Maybe."

Margaret took her hand and squeezed it gently. "Whoever you decide to bestow that gift to, just make sure it's someone you love. Promise me."

That was the plan. Too bad it didn't work how she hoped. Regan squeezed her hand in return. "I promise."

"Now that that's settled, are you excited about uni?"

"Excited to escape my parents' grip for a while, but honestly, I'm terrified. I've never been anywhere on my own before."

Margaret patted her shoulder. "You'll be fine. You're smart, strong, and it's a good school. Besides, you'll be back for holidays and special charity events."

"I know." Regan tucked a strand of hair behind her ear. "One friend from school will be there, but there will be a lot of new people there too." Everyone thought she was naturally outgoing and friendly, but the truth was meeting new people terrified her. New people who studied her like a bug under a microscope or who judged her if she said or did the wrong thing. They'd get angry or annoyed with her, the way her mother and sometimes her father did. This made it difficult for her to be herself. Did she even know who that was anymore? Yes.

When she was with Connor, she felt more like herself than any other time. He accepted all sides of herself that she showed him, whether it was a rambunctious kid or a broody teen. *Is that why I love him?* Maybe that was the reason for her attraction? The way he made her feel more like herself than anyone else? Maybe Connor was right and she didn't love him, but the idea of him and the comfortable way she was around him. She suddenly felt foolish and childish for the way she attacked him last night with her confession and her body.

"You okay, sweetheart?" Margaret's eyes filled with worry.

"I'm fine," Regan assured her, but the expression on her face told her Margaret didn't believe her. She'd known her long enough to tell when she was lying. "I will be," she added with a small smile.

"You will be, Regan." She squeezed her hand affectionately. "Getting out from under your parents for a bit and spreading your wings is just what you need. Promise me you'll be open to all opportunities and experiences, and really enjoy yourself and find who you want to be."

Regan nodded, but all she could wonder was what happened when she returned from school. When she was back with her parents and back in their world. She'd only lose herself again and any ground she might've gained. *I could walk away.* She almost laughed out loud at those words. What did she know about the world? Not a damn thing. Unlike most teenagers who were confident they knew everything, she wasn't one of them. She saw firsthand through one of her family's charities what could happen to women. Especially those who tried to escape.

She had none of her own money and getting a job wasn't an option. Her inheritance was hers when she turned twenty-five. But even then, the money came with strings attached. She'd seen it happen with her brother.

Regan took one last bite of cake before standing and putting the rest in the fridge for later. "Thanks for breakfast, Mags." She kissed her on the cheek and then headed back to her room.

Grabbing her phone, she scripted a quick text to Connor, thanking him for the cake, water, and painkillers.

He responded right away: *Anytime.*

As much as she wanted to keep texting him, she threw her phone on the bed instead. Picking up the note Connor left, she read it one more time before putting it in the drawer under a pile of random items inside. Like this note, she had to put what she felt for Connor aside and focus on her future.

CHAPTER 5

Connor glared at Declan and his father, who sat across from them at the conference table as he laid out the plan that would take away everything his family had built. He clenched his fists under the table. He couldn't even fault them, because his father had handed it to them on a silver platter. The sly grin on Declan's face made him want to stand up, grab him across the table, and beat the shite out of him.

Although his father lost their company, Connor could sense that Declan and his father had done something nefarious to make it happen. The deceit that rolled off them in waves was strong and unsettling. It was the reason he'd told his father not to make this deal with them, but as usual, his father dismissed his "feelings" and moved ahead. Weeks after the ink had dried on the paper, his father was still too weak—physically and emotionally—to attend this meeting and so he came in his stead. Although it was merely a formality considering they'd already taken everything.

As the Kellys continued going through the documents, Connor sat straighter when he noticed their family home was listed as an asset they were acquiring. He gritted his teeth, failing to hide his surprise and annoyance. "Why is my family's home listed?"

Declan grinned like the snake he was before his father answered. "Your father had nothing else for collateral."

The words were said so calmly, as if they weren't taking away the home that had been in his family for generations.

"The business wasn't enough?" Connor knew the answer and held back saying what he really wanted. He should've asked for this meeting—one his father should be attending—to be delayed so he had time to review the document with a solicitor himself. Instead, he'd gotten word a mere hour ago. "I'd like time to review these documents with a solicitor since I wasn't notified sooner."

Declan's father pursed his lips in annoyance. "The documents are already signed. This meeting is just a formality to make your family aware of what is required going forward." He flipped the page of the document. "Your family will have three months to vacate the premises, after which the home will be rented to cover your father's losses."

"We could sell the home and pay you back," Connor offered.

"That is no longer an option. Your father decided to waive that option when he offered up your home as collateral. And since the deal didn't make the returns he anticipated, the home now belongs to us."

And he made his decision without consulting Connor or his wife. *Bollocks!* "Surely we can come to some kind of arrangement?" Even as he asked, he knew there was no other arrangement to be made. If they were taking their home, which was worth millions, there was nothing he could do.

His fears were confirmed when he turned the page to see the amount of the debt glaring at him in bold black. Their family would never recover from this kind of damage. Even if he found a good job or worked with investments, it'd take him years, and he knew the Kellys wouldn't wait for that kind of money. His father had just gambled away their family's future. He knew their business was in trouble, but his father wouldn't let him anywhere near the books, even though he'd studied under him and his grandfather before he died a couple of years ago.

Another family would've worked with them so they could keep their home. Hell, even as much of an ass as Michael's father Shamus was, he'd never put them out of their home. They weren't the closest, but family was important to Shamus. Although Shamus wasn't crazy about his friendship with Michael, he knew what their friendship meant.

Not the Kellys. They went for blood and didn't give a shite who they slaughtered along the way. Being part of their circle didn't protect you. If anything, it made you a target.

Connor remained silent for the rest of the meeting, only nodding to confirm he understood what was in the document. He didn't care what Declan's father said about it being too late to have a solicitor look over the documents. He was going to do it anyway. He had three months before they had to move out of their home, and he planned to use that time wisely.

After the meeting, Declan's father left with their solicitor and other team members while Declan stuck around. Connor schooled his facial expression even as his insides churned when Declan approached him.

"No hard feelings. It's just business."

Connor remained silent, not trusting the words that would come out of his mouth. He knew Declan would feed off any outburst he made, and he had no intention of giving him the satisfaction. The smugness rolling from Declan in waves was all the proof he needed.

"It seems I'm destined to take everything that's yours." He sat on the conference table, watching Connor while he collected all the paperwork from their meeting.

"I guess so." He stuffed the papers inside the envelope, not caring some were getting crumpled.

"Even Regan."

Coldness settled in his chest before turning into a flame of heat that rushed through him. "What?"

Declan shrugged. "You weren't willing to take her virginity, so I took it for you."

"You're lying." Regan had made it home to her own bed. Although he didn't know what happened after he left her party, he was certain she wouldn't give herself to Declan. *Would she?* He hated the doubt swirling inside him.

"While it was just another night for me, I'm certain it's one she won't forget—or maybe it's she won't remember it." Declan shrugged nonchalantly.

Connor's eyes widened when he realized the meaning. "You bastard!" He punched Declan hard enough to knock him onto the carpeted floor. "You took advantage of her."

Declan laughed, knowing he got the reaction he wanted. "She was the one who took advantage of me, Connor. She wanted to rid herself of it, and you weren't willing. I was just her second choice. I'm the one who should feel used." His eyes twinkled with mischief as he stood up and wiped the blood from the corner of his mouth.

Connor resisted the urge to throw him onto the conference table and pound his fists at his face until both were bloodied from tearing into the flesh on Declan's face. He wanted nothing more than to knock that smug grin from his mouth. But he knew that's how Declan's mind worked. Poking and picking at you until you lost control—that gave him control over you.

Declan fed off the reactions of others like an emotional vampire—he evoked strong reactions and then sucked them from you until you were drained and he had you right where he wanted you.

Connor had no intention of letting him have that kind of control over him. His family had taken enough from him today already.

Connor took a calming breath to clear his head and that's when it happened. He sensed the lie. Whether it was from taking advantage of Regan or having sex with her he didn't know, but that was enough for him. For now.

Connor adjusted his clothing that had shifted out of place when he punched Declan, grabbed the envelope with the papers from the conference table, and stormed out the door. Declan's laughter followed him all the way out the room and down the hall.

As much as he didn't believe that Declan was with Regan, he couldn't stop the doubt and regret eating at him as he left the building and headed to his car. He slammed the car door and yelled as his fists pounded on the steering wheel.

Regan wasn't his, could never be his, but her with Declan made his gut wrench and his stomach hurl at the thought of them together. Losing her to another man was one thing, but Declan?

The sweet words of love she'd whispered to him while he kissed her turned sour in his brain. *Did she really mean them, or were they just the words of someone who wanted to lose her virginity as Declan had said?* Their relationship had always been close, but he remembered how she'd joked with Declan. *Was Declan right that he was her second choice after I rejected her?*

Connor ran a hand through his hair in frustration before starting his car and pulling out of the parking lot. He had more important things to focus on than worry whether Declan had been with Regan. He had to find a way to explain to his mother that the husband she loved and trusted had gambled away their family business and home. And he had to find a new home for his parents and a job to support them as his father wouldn't be working until he recovered. His mother had never worked and he didn't have a clue how she'd react to everything that happened.

Regan was the last person he should be thinking about. He had less than two months left of school before he graduated and returned home. Dropping out wasn't an option. He'd need his degree to get a job that would cover his family expenses. The pressure of his family pressed down on him in ways it hadn't when he thought he'd have to join the company and work with his father.

Although he was looking forward to working at the company his family had built, he wasn't looking forward to an office job with his father day in and day out. His grandfather had taught him about their family's business, how to make money and work with his father. His grandparents and mother had built up his confidence in himself and his abilities, while his father had made him feel like he didn't belong, and he could never understand why.

The reason didn't matter. What mattered was moving him and his family forward from the mess his father had left and navigating his way through the Kellys' deal. Connor snorted. There was nothing to navigate. The deal was done, and his family had to pick up the pieces and move on with their lives whether they wanted to or not.

Although he'd pay for a solicitor to look at the contract, the Kellys were solicitors themselves and likely covered their asses legally. They were ruthless but they weren't stupid.

As Connor drove back to his home, the weight of what lay ahead pressed down on him and the ache of losing Regan too was crushing. She wasn't his. Could never be his, he reminded himself again. Then why did the thought of her being with someone else make him feel like his world was ending even more than it already was?

CHAPTER 6

Two Months Later

The noises in the convention center drowned out the voices in his head. Today was graduation day, and his parents weren't in attendance—too embarrassed to face their former friends. Never mind it was their son's graduation. Thankfully, he wouldn't need to make excuses for them because no one other than the Dohertys had spoken to him. He could hear Regan's loud cheering within the silence of the crowd and graced her with a smile after his photograph was taken. She'd waved at him enthusiastically, despite her parents' disapproving glares.

Michael had given him a thumbs-up as he made his way off the stage and back to his seat. When Michael heard the news about his family situation, he'd been angry at the Kellys and then his parents for not offering to help them out. Connor pacified him, claiming no one could help them out of the hole his father had dug them into, not even the expensive solicitor he'd hired. But what the solicitor did point out was the bad deal the Kellys made his family and that it was set up in such a way to strip his family of their wealth and power.

Connor had gotten roaring drunk and confessed everything to Michael, who'd been even more furious. Although they weren't close to Declan, who was a conceited ass, they had grown up together and considered him a friend within their circle. But Declan was as ruthless as his father. Michael had wanted to beat the shite out of Declan, but Connor told him that would only create problems with his family and that was the last thing he wanted. At the end of the day, Declan was following his father.

Regan had reached out to him the same day she found out and offered him the emotional support he needed, for which he was grateful. She hadn't turned her back on him, even after he rejected her. He wasn't sure whether it was the note and cake he left, or that she didn't hold a grudge for long that explained why she had forgiven him so easily. *Maybe it was my family's financial fall?* Connor cringed at the thought that her kind messages were out of pity. *Or maybe guilt because she was with Declan?* His stomach churned at the thought of Declan touching her and kissing her the way he had.

Although he couldn't fault her if she had—he'd rejected her, after all—somewhere deep down, he prayed that Declan was merely trying to taunt him. And taunt him those thoughts of them together did. *Focus, Connor!*

He turned his attention back to the stage of the convention center before briefly glancing around the building. Elegant, themed décor was scattered around the stage and in key places in the building. On the stage, professors he'd met over the years sat on plastic chairs, looking as uncomfortable as the students who watched them from the other side of the stage. The only people smiling were family and friends who took the occasional photo or video. The students sat, quietly listening to the speaker on the stage, and if they were like him, desperately waiting for them to wrap up so they could get the hell out of the building and away from school for good.

The graduation ceremony was wrapping up, for which he was grateful. He and Michael were set to go drinking with friends, and he was looking forward to letting loose before reality set in and he returned home to finish moving his parents out of their home and into the small flat he'd found them. Connor had explained it was only temporary and once he found a job, he'd move them into a proper house.

He'd had several job interviews already and a couple of prospects, which he had to look at carefully before choosing. With his family's situation, job prospects took on a different meaning. Instead of joining his family's company like he'd planned, he was forced to choose the job with the biggest salary. As much as he wanted to believe his father would come out of the emotional coma he'd sunk into, Connor highly doubted it.

After the ceremony, Michael and Connor found each other just as the Dohertys strolled up. Regan's warm and friendly smile sent a rush of happiness through him, pushing aside all the heavy thoughts weighing on him.

"Congratulations, you two," she said to them both, but her eyes never left him.

She hugged her brother and then put her arms around him.

Connor held on longer than he should have before giving her a quick squeeze and releasing her.

Her eyes were twinkling when they met his. "I took lots of pictures. I'll send them to you later." She didn't say the words *for your parents*, but they hung in the air between them.

"Thank you."

Shamus shook their hands firmly while Moira gave Michael a long hug and a shoulder squeeze for him. "We are so proud of you."

"What will you do now?" Shamus inquired coolly, as if it were his fault he wasn't joining his family's business after graduation.

"I've had several interviews with prospective firms and a couple of offers."

"That's great!" Regan declared happily.

"Have you found a new place to live?" Moira asked quietly, as if not wanting anyone around them to hear their conversation.

Connor didn't know whether to be grateful or annoyed. Not many people knew about his family's situation, and he'd prefer it that way. The last thing he wanted was pity from his friends and peers.

Declan was at the graduation but thankfully kept his distance. Seeing him anywhere near Regan would set him off. The last thing he wanted was to make a scene and have people question why. Connor snorted. No one would wonder. Declan was a known arse in their circles. Thrived on the title.

Regan gave him a quizzical look. He shook his head to indicate it was nothing.

"Is there a party later?" Regan asked.

"Absolutely not!" Michael and his parents said all at once.

Regan pouted. "But I'll be with Connor and Michael, and it'll give me a chance to meet other students."

"Are any of your friends going to be there?" Moira asked.

"No," Regan grumbled. "But Ciara will, right?" She gave him and Michael pleading eyes.

"Probably," Michael responded, with a hint of an annoyed moan after.

"Only if Connor and your brother keep an eye on you and you stay close to Ciara," her father stated, his meaning clear. If anything happened to Regan, they would pay for it with their heads.

"And I want the names of two new students you met tomorrow," her mother added for good measure.

Regan rolled her eyes, but not before excitedly bouncing on the balls of her feet.

So much for a careless drunken night. There was no way he could enjoy himself with a bunch of rowdy, horny uni boys swarming around Regan, who would be considered fresh meat.

"I don't think it's a good idea," Michael voiced, likely thinking the same as him.

"Of course you don't want your sister tagging along, but I promise you won't even know I'm there."

I highly doubt that. Connor didn't want to agree with Michael and ruin her obvious fun, but he lifted his shoulders, as if saying *why not.*

"Fine. But no heavy drinking. And no drinks from anyone. And I do mean anyone. You make and drink your own drinks or ones that Connor or I have made for you. Understood?"

Regan's expression said she clearly didn't understand why Michael was so adamant, and he made a mental note to explain to her later so she wouldn't just think it was an overprotective brother thing.

Although he wasn't crazy about Regan out partying, he was glad she'd be there and they'd spend time together now that their relationship seemed to have returned to the easy friendship it'd been before her confession.

Being around her would be simpler with a crowd of people and no dark spaces for them to get lost in alone. His eyes wandered to her lips, remembering how soft and willing they were, along with the rest of her body when it was pressed against him. He yanked his eyes away from her lips to glance about the room to find Declan waving at Regan, who waved back, albeit a little less enthusiastically.

What the... Connor resisted the urge to flip him off, considering the Dohertys and other parents were around.

"The nerve of Declan," Regan whispered.

"He's a wanker." Michael shrugged.

"Michael Doherty!" Moira admonished, quickly glancing around to see whether anyone had heard him.

"Well, he is," Regan agreed. "He put Connor's family out of their home and now he's waving as if they're still friends."

"It is not Declan's fault Connor's father lost their family business and home," Shamus said calmly, as if he were stating a fact about the weather.

"He was there, Da," Michael said with conviction. "Even if it wasn't his fault, they could've done something to try to help, not rub Connor's nose in it. Did you know his father was too ill to show up to the meeting?"

Connor flinched, realizing he'd lied to his best friend, but he couldn't handle the pity that Michael would surely express if Connor had told him the truth. That his father tried to take, in his mind, the coward's way out.

"How is your father now?" Moira asked, a hint of sympathy in her tone. Their parents weren't close friends, but they were in the same circles and had socialized over the years and were more than just acquaintances.

"Better," Connor mumbled. *Another lie.*

"Don't mind Declan. He's just like his father. Competitive and ambitious to a fault, no matter who's in his way." Shamus's tone was one of admiration, as if they were traits he wanted for Michael.

Connor merely nodded, afraid he'd say words he couldn't take back. His gaze met Michael and then Regan. They understood, as they were holding their own stories about Declan that would make the hair on Shamus's head curl. Or maybe not, because Shamus could be just as ruthless.

"Brunch at our house Sunday. No excuses." Moira pointed at all of them.

Being hung over or busy with school was no longer an excuse they could use. Although Connor had the best reason of all—looking for flats so he could move himself and his parents from a home his family had known for generations.

"Let's get going." Michael interrupted his thought. "I'm not going to a party in this suit."

Connor, Michael, and Regan headed to the exit, weaving between the slowly thinning crowd in the room.

Keeping his distance from Regan when they weren't close was easy, but what about when they were at the same party? He was beginning to think that agreeing to one last party was a bad idea.

CHAPTER 7

Regan frowned when another woman approached Connor, touching him in a familiar way that made her both angry and jealous. She was trying to listen to what the guy who stood next to her was saying, but the loud music made it difficult to understand him. She rolled her eyes when she found him staring at her breasts again. “Eyes up here, mate!”

He met her with glassy eyes and a wobbly grin. *Why the hell did I think coming to this party was a good idea?* Because she wanted Connor to see her as an adult. She’d even flirted and chatted with the boys who approached her and asked her to dance, but took her brother’s advice to heart about drinks when he explained on the drive over. She’d been horrified and almost changed her mind.

Time with Connor was what she’d hoped for, even with being surrounded by so many people. In her mind, it was the perfect opportunity for her to drool over him without him noticing. Boy was she wrong. Although he and Michael kept her in their line of sight, they were too busy with all the girls—or rather, women—at the party.

Michael and Connor were more popular than she realized. Not that she should be surprised. Ciara and her friends were constantly hovering around them. Her stomach dropped, imagining all the women he’d been with while at uni. What would he want with his best friend's inexperienced little sister when he had his pick of women?

That's not the only reason, Regan tried to assure herself. Connor was loyal and took his friendship with Michael seriously.

A woman with jet-black hair and legs for miles was pressed against his side as she whispered in his ears. Seductive words, no doubt. Words not meant for her virgin ears. Regan knocked back the rest of the liquid in her glass and headed toward the kitchen for another, leaving behind the boob glarer. Flickering lights led the way through bodies of students who clung to each other while dancing in tune to the music or were lip-locked with hands in places they shouldn't be in public. *Is this what's waiting for me at uni?*

Regan was certain this was not what Margaret had in mind when she told her to enjoy all the experiences school had to offer. Or maybe she did, thinking it would get her mind off Connor.

Opening the kitchen cabinets, she found another bottle of liquor, not caring what it was, and poured it into the cup she had pressed tightly against her chest—another bit of advice from her brother.

"Do you really need another drink?" Connor said right by her ear.

Regan jumped and screamed, "Connor! You feckin' scared me." Her elbow connected with his ribs, and she pushed against his frame.

A chuckle rumbled deep in his chest, sending shivers through her, especially the sexy smirk tugging at his mouth. His large frame was practically pressed against her side and the kitchen wasn't as loud as the other areas of the house where the party had trickled into.

"I'm here for the uni experience." She took a sip from her cup, ignoring the way Connor's gaze moved over her face before settling on her mouth.

"Hmm. Not all the experiences, I hope." His fingers brushed her face, moving aside a strand of hair.

Sparks shot through her when his fingers trailed from behind her ears, down her neck, and along her collarbone. "Connor." Her voice was a thick whisper in her throat.

"Regan."

The sound of her name, low and sexy, turned her knees to mush, and she leaned against the counters behind them. "What are you doing?" she croaked. Not that she didn't want his hands on her. Speaking of hands, thankfully they had returned to her neck, where his fingertips rested against her pulse that was erratic from his closeness and touch.

"Regretting making friends with Michael and wishing I could take you somewhere we could be alone."

Regan inhaled sharply. *He wants to be alone with me?* Her gaze met his eyes, and the way they glazed, she knew the alcohol was starting to affect him. "You're just saying that because you're drinking."

"Yes and no, pet."

Her eyebrows knotted in confusion.

"Yes, I have been drinking," he clarified, "but I'm not that drunk."

"Maybe you should find one of those girls who were hanging all over you."

Connor chuckled and leaned closer, so his lips were by her ear. "Jealousy looks good on you."

The sound of his deep voice and his playful laugh sent her body into a tizzy. Not to mention his solid frame pressed against her so his chest grazed her silk blouse. Heat radiated from his body and shot into her fingertips when her palm touched his shirt to put distance between them. As much as she wanted Connor's body on her, she couldn't take the sting of his rejection again. "I'm not jealous," she said firmly, pushing harder against his frame, but he didn't move.

"Liar. If I left with one of them tonight, how would you feel?"

Regan shrugged noncommittedly.

"Really? So you wouldn't mind me kissing them. Touching them." His fingertips ran along her bare arm, sending shock waves of electric pulses through her. "Licking them." His tone dropped and his tongue ran along the side of her neck.

Words lodged in her throat as Connor sprinkled small kisses to her neck and then along her jawline.

"My fingers inside them, the way you want them inside you."

Heat rushed over her cheeks and then down to her core from his words. *Get a grip, Regan. This is what you wanted.*

"I do, Connor. I've made it very clear I want your fingers and you inside me." *Oh my goodness. Did I say that out loud?*

Connor's breath was a sharp intake and his eyes darkened, and she felt him harden against her stomach.

"You're playing with fire, pet."

"So are you." Her voice was breathless as her hands ran along his shoulders until they were around his neck. "I meant what I said. I want you to be the first." She rolled her hips so she rubbed against his erection.

Connor hissed and his hand reached for her hips to still them. "Regan." His voice was strained, and creases marked his face. He gripped her arms and dragged her toward the stairs.

Regan's heart beat in time to the loud techno music as Connor linked their fingers and they walked up the stairs. The two doors they opened were occupied, but the last one was empty. Connor locked the door once they were inside. She wrapped her arms around his neck and kissed him when she saw the glimmer of doubt in his eyes. The last thing she wanted was for him to change his mind. When they kissed and her hands were on his body, he lost control, and she wanted him to remain in this moment with her.

Connor's hands ran down her back, his fingers digging in, making her knees weak and a moan escape. He turned them so she was pressed against the door and moved his mouth from her lips to kiss her jaw and then along her neck. "You smell so good."

Regan almost said it was the perfume he gave her, but somehow it didn't seem to matter in the moment. *This is it. It's happening.* She clawed at his clothes, wanting to touch the gorgeous skin that had taunted her when he was shirtless by their pool. The skin she'd drooled over behind sunglasses so he and her brother couldn't see what she was looking at.

His polo shirt came out of his jeans easily, and she sighed when her fingertips grazed along his chest and down his abs. He was hard and soft at the same time, and his deep groan in her ears sent a multitude of tremors over her body. She yanked the shirt over his head, dropping it on the carpeted floor by their feet, and attacked his belt buckle and pants.

Connor unbuttoned her blouse, shoved it from her shoulders, and threw it on the floor next to his shirt. Her skirt followed, until she was in her bra and underwear. She was grateful it was a sexy navy-blue set, especially when Connor's eyes darkened. His lips descended to the tops of her breast; his one hand slipped a bra strap from her shoulder while his other hand unsnapped her bra bearing her breasts. "Beautiful," he whispered as his lips captured her nipples.

Regan arched her back into his mouth and dug her hand into his hair. "That feels so good, Connor." *Holy crap! I'm half naked with Connor and we're about to have sex!* She would've burst into girlish laughter if Connor's mouth didn't feel so good. His kisses trailed from her breasts down her stomach while his hands slid her underwear down her legs.

"You're so damn sexy, Regan," Connor murmured as he lifted a leg onto his shoulder and put his mouth and tongue on her core.

"Oh my God, Connor." Regan moaned, her weight sinking onto his shoulders as he devoured her, his tongue licking and teasing her. Her orgasm barreled down on her embarrassingly quick, but the man's tongue was amazing.

"As much as I love my name on your lips, pet, you've got to be quieter." Connor raised his head to look up at her before slipping one finger inside her. "You're so tight," he groaned and slipped another finger, curving them so they hit her sweet spot as his tongue continued his torture. "Look at me, Regan. I want to see your gorgeous face as you come apart for me."

Regan lost her breath when she glanced down to see Connor on his knees, looking at her as if she were the sexiest woman who he worshiped, mixed in with a healthy dose of panty-melting lust. Her fingers gripped his shoulder to steady herself while she moved her hips to get closer to his mouth.

"That's it, sunshine. Ride my fingers."

The deep rumble of his voice and his words send her tumbling over the edge as she was hit with the strongest orgasm that sparked white light behind her eyes. She bit her bottom lip to keep from screaming out his name.

Connor released her legs but held his body against hers as he kissed her. The shock of tasting herself on his tongue made her gasp, but it was exhilarating. His erection pressed against her, and she grasped it and found out why Connor was so cocky. The man was not small. A tremor of fear ran through her at the thought of trying to make it fit.

"It'll fit," he whispered, as if reading her mind. He lifted her, and she wrapped her legs around his waist. "Are you sure this is what you want, Regan?"

She'd never been sure of anything more in her whole life, but words escaped her from the gentle way he caressed her cheek, so she merely nodded.

"I've got a condom in my pants pocket."

Regan shook her head. "I'm on the Pill. I don't want anything between us, Connor. I want to feel all of you."

"I've never been bare with anyone before, Regan." Doubt filled his eyes.

"Then it's a first for both of us." Regan held his face in her hands and kissed him softly at first, but the feel of his tongue against her, stroking and sucking, built a longing heat in her she knew only having Connor inside her could quench.

She reached for him and guided him to her core. Connor pressed her further into the door and used one of his hands to gently push himself into her. He pulled back a little each time, coating himself in her wetness, so he slid in easier. Regan swiveled her hips and arched her back. It was uncomfortable but not unbearable, and she wanted to feel all of him inside her.

"You feel so good."

I couldn't agree more. The feel of his skin beneath her fingertips, the warmth of his body pressing into her...it was amazing. "Go deeper, Connor."

"I don't want to hurt you," he groaned. "Tell me if I do."

Regan nodded but knew she wouldn't because she didn't want to risk him stopping for any reason. Connor was about to be hers, and she'd do everything to keep it going. She flinched when he was finally seated fully inside her, the burning sensation catching her by surprise. Her legs tightened around Connor to keep him from moving, and she rested her forehead against his shoulder. "Give me a minute," she whispered.

"Take as much time as you need, Regan. I need a minute myself so I don't embarrass myself by coming quick."

Regan chuckled and her body moved against him, and he moaned.

"You feel so damn good, Re. So hot and tight."

His words sent a shiver down her back. She put her hands in his thick hair and pulled his lips to her and slowly rotated her hips. A jolt of pleasure replaced the earlier sting, especially when Connor gripped her thighs and moved with her. "Connor," she moaned, and tightened her grip on his hair and arched her back.

"That's it, sweetheart, move with me. Jezzus, you're so sexy." Regan opened her eyes to find Connor watching her in awe. She was certain she looked a mess considering she could feel her hair in shambles around her shoulders from his fingers and being pressed against the door. But Connor looked at her as if she were the most beautiful woman in the world, and her heart clenched, knowing he'd never love her the way she loved him.

She shoved those thoughts aside and held onto him for dear life as pleasure raced through her body and another orgasm made its way up her trembling legs.

"I can't hold on much longer, pet. Tell me you're close."

"Yes."

Connor's strokes became harder and deeper; she lifted her hips to meet every thrust until her body exploded with pleasure. She released a long, deep moan instead of shouting out Connor's name like she wanted.

A rumble of curse words tumbled from Connor's mouth next to her ear. "Jezzus, Regan." He kissed her roughly before his lips slowly softened as their breathing returned to normal.

"That was..." Regan couldn't find the right words to say, because there were no words.

"Yeah," he agreed with a smile that lit up his whole face.

Their moment was interrupted by a loud knock on the door and someone calling out, "Regan?"

They both froze. Michael.

"Regan, are you in there?"

"Yes. I just wanted a minute to myself to get away from a guy who was harassing me."

"Why didn't you get me or Connor?"

They scrambled for their clothes, getting dressed as quickly as they had undressed.

"You were both busy," Regan offered as an explanation.

Michael groaned. "I'm sorry, Regan. I shouldn't have gotten distracted and that's not like Connor."

"It's fine. I'm safe in here." She buttoned up her blouse and tucked it into her skirt, trying to return it as close to its original state as possible.

"Why is the door closed?" Michael turned the doorknob.

"I was trying to keep that creep out."

"Open the door, Regan."

Her eyes went to Connor's frantically. "I'll meet you downstairs. I just need to use the toilet."

"I'm not leaving you alone again."

"Why don't you look for Connor? I'll just be a couple of minutes. I promise."

A frustrated sigh came from the other side of the door before Michael grumbled, "I'm going to give Connor a piece of my mind. We were supposed to cover for each other."

Regan didn't speak until she heard his footsteps far enough away that he wouldn't hear them. "That was close." She chuckled.

"Damn it! This shouldn't have happened, Regan. Your first time should've been better than a quick ride against a door at a uni party. It should've been special. With someone your own age. Not me."

"What?"

"I knew better." He raked a hand through his hair to fix the mess she'd made of it earlier and in frustration. "Michael is my best friend, and I just defiled his sister against a blooming door."

"I wanted this," she said quietly, trying to reassure him.

Connor snorted. "You're eighteen. You don't know what you want. I'm the adult. I never should've started this."

His words made her feel like she was a child he'd taken advantage of. "You're only six years older than me, Connor."

"Six years older to know better. What the hell was I thinking?" Connor jammed his shirt into his jeans.

"We weren't thinking," she offered, trying to lighten the mood with a joke.

"You're right. This was a mistake."

The only words she heard were *This was a mistake*. Being with her was *a mistake*. Pain stabbed her heart in a way his rejection and words at her birthday party hadn't. There was nothing and no one she wanted more than Connor, and he'd once again just expressed she wasn't what he wanted and that being with her was a mistake. She choked back a sob.

He was never going to see her as anything more than her best friend's little sister. He'd never be hers the way she wanted. Although he cared for her and wanted her physically, being anything more was never going to happen. Regan swallowed the lump of sorrow making its way through her body and up her throat, along with the tears burning at the back of her eyes.

"I'll go find Michael," she whispered, barely able to keep from vomiting emotions from her eyes and mouth.

"I'll be out in a bit. I need to think of an excuse for Michael that doesn't include screwing his little sister."

Regan didn't respond but rushed out the door, leaving her urge to cry and her shattered heart in the room with him. She'd given everything of herself to Connor—her heart and her body—and it still wasn't enough for him. She wasn't enough for him.

CHAPTER 8

Bloody hell! Connor wished he could punch a hole in the wall or the door in the room, but that wasn't an option. He had just willingly taken his best friend's little sister's virginity and had loved every minute of it. Guilt nailed him in the gut and his stomach roiled as he remembered all the moments they'd shared as kids and how she'd looked up to him like a friend and how everything changed when she turned sixteen and he became the biggest perv. One who'd kissed her on the lips and given her hope there could be something between them. Tonight, he'd taken advantage of her in ways he never should have. He was the reason she'd been so bold on her eighteenth birthday and again today.

Regan never would have looked at him as more...if he hadn't shattered that boundary with that kiss. Another man would've been with her tonight who was age appropriate and made her night special. *You're only twenty-four, mate.* Hardly an old man, but that didn't make him feel better.

Bullshit! What eighteen-year-old boy was going to do that for her? He certainly wouldn't at that age.

Connor yanked the door open and stormed downstairs in search of Michael and Regan. He found them arguing by the front door.

"What the hell were you thinking, going upstairs by yourself?" Michael scolded.

"I already told you the reason. I locked the door. I was safe."

"I never should've agreed to you coming here."

"I'm eighteen, Michael. Technically, I don't need your permission to do shite!"

"You do if Ma and Da have any say."

"They're my parents. You aren't."

"You're right, but I'm your big brother and it was my and Connor's job to keep you safe tonight. Where the hell were you?" Michael asked when he finally looked up and saw Connor.

"Same place you were, probably," Regan offered.

"You left my sister to get laid?" Michael roared, taking a step toward him.

"I went to the bathroom and when I returned, I couldn't find her. I was looking for her. Like you were." Shame from the blatant lie burned a hole in Connor's chest.

Michael was his best friend, and they always swore to tell each other the truth, no matter how painful, and he'd just broken that vow. Again. Once with the lie about his father and now with Regan. No, he'd obliterated it the moment he stuck his tongue in Regan mouth the night of her birthday.

He could've explained their kiss with the excuse of too much alcohol if the truth came out. Michael would be hurt and angry, but he'd move past it. What Connor did upstairs to his sister—what he wanted to do again, if he were honest—Michael would end their friendship and likely kick his arse too.

The Kellys had devastated his family financially, but the Dohertys? God only knew what Shamus would do to him. He'd be blacklisted from the financial industry anywhere in Ireland. Any hope of restoring his family's wealth and home would be destroyed. He'd lose more than he already had, along with his only real friends.

After tonight, he'd lose Regan's friendship too. The heartbreak on her face from his words hurt him. He could've explained that he didn't mean what they shared was a mistake, just how he'd gone about taking her virginity, but the words became hurtful vomit he couldn't stop flowing from his mouth as the guilt and shame slammed into him. Not to mention the fear of Michael finding out and him being crushed by the betrayal.

Her thinking less of him and maybe even hating him was for the best. Then she'd stay away from him. They couldn't escape each other's lives completely, but being distant would help. He was returning home soon and thankfully she wouldn't be there. Time apart would help him stay focused on the challenging times ahead.

Distance and the university experience would show Regan she was better off with someone else. Then why did his chest hurt thinking of her with another man? Why did imagining her kissing someone else and having another man's hands on her body strike him with the urge to break bones? She wasn't his. She'd never be his, even with her confession of love and hot sex moments ago. Regan was his best friend's sister, and that was never going to change.

"Connor? Where'd you go, mate? Are you that drunk? I was hoping you'd drive us home," Michael interrupted with a shove to his shoulder.

"I'm sober as a judge, mate. Let's get the hell out of here." Connor strolled through the open door, away from the loud music and the dull buzz of emotions from people at the party.

The quiet of the night and the cool, damp Irish air engulfed them as they headed to the car. Thankfully, most people at the party were in a good mood, so their vibes weren't needles to his mind, the way strong, negative emotions usually were.

Regan slid into the back seat, her hands clasped tightly in her lap and her eyes on the floor.

"Aren't you going to fight me for the front seat?" Michael turned in the seat to look at her.

"No." Her voice was soft and low.

Michael shoved her knee. "What's gotten into you? Did you guys have another fight?"

Connor and Regan usually got along, unless it was a topic they didn't agree on; then the gloves came off, along with all bets on their close friendship. Regan was known for going for the throat and not holding back. Something she could only do with him and Michael. When it came to her parents, there was no fight.

Their eyes met in the rearview mirror, hers filled with sadness and his with regret. Her gaze jerked back to her hands. "Not exactly," she mumbled.

What could they say? We're not talking because we just had the best sex of my life? And I told her it was a mistake. Not exactly words he could say out loud, much less to his Michael about his sister. "I wouldn't let her drink more."

Michael shrugged and then buckled his seat belt. "Smart, with all the guys at the party. Besides, you need to learn to pace yourself when you get to uni. Drinking here isn't like drinking at Ma and Da's parties," he lectured.

"I know that! I'm not stupid," Regan blurted defensively.

"We know that, Regan." Connor captured her gaze in the mirror. "We just want you safe."

Regan snorted and adjusted herself in the back seat, so she leaned against the leather interior instead of her previous stiff posture. "You made it very clear what you want."

Connor's heartbeat stuttered in his chest with fear. *What the hell are you doing?* He glared at her in the mirror, his eyes pleading.

He didn't dare look at Michael, terrified he'd see the look of horror in his eyes and know something was up.

"No guys anywhere near you?" Michael added, guessing that's what she meant.

Connor released the breath he was holding and relaxed in the seat, starting Michael's car and pulling onto the road toward their house where he left his car before driving together to the party. A car he would soon have to downgrade to something cheaper. Another reason for him to keep his distance from Regan. His financial situation was a dumpster fire he needed to fix before he could bring any woman, let alone someone from a family like hers, into his life. He couldn't even afford to take her on a proper date. His parents would be living with him for the foreseeable future, not exactly making him a catch.

Regan wouldn't care about those things.

Those words mocked him, and they were true. Although she enjoyed a lot of things about her family's wealth, Regan wasn't like most of the girls in their circle. She wasn't caught up with the latest fashion or had the need to impress her friends with expensive handbags and shoes. That was all her mother.

Then there was his wonderful gift—or, rather, curse as he liked to call it—sensing the emotions of the people around him.

Connor wound down the window and let the crisp night air flow through the car and ran a hand through his hair. How he wished the circumstances in his life were different. The months and years ahead of him were going to be a nightmare on so many levels; the last thing he wanted was to drag Regan down with him—even if she wasn't his best friend's sister. She had her whole life ahead of her, one he was certain she'd make amazing, despite her parents' endless pressure.

She was a rising star, and he was merely a shooting star on his way down—at least for the next few years while he rebuilt his family's business and integrity. The last thing she needed was someone like him in her life. Even their friendship would be tenuous now. Michael had assured him nothing would change with their friendship, but Connor knew better. While Michael and Regan would continue to get invites to the usual charities and social events, no invitation would be sent to his family or him. They would be ostracized. He'd seen it before, and he couldn't blame his friends if they left him behind. As far as he was concerned, he was now just dead weight.

When they reached their home, everyone climbed out of the car. Before Connor could head to his car, Michael grabbed him by the shoulder. "It's late. Stay the night. Margaret will make us breakfast and we'll hang out by the pool all day now that there's no school."

Regan's posture stiffened, making it clear being near him was the last thing she wanted.

"Another night, mate."

"Come on. How many more times like this will we have before real life catches up with us?"

You don't know the half of it. Was this Michael's way of spending final moments with him before their friendship fizzled to the realities of work life and adult obligations and, in his and Regan's life, family commitments that didn't include him anymore?

"Convince him, Regan. You're the only one who can make him do things he doesn't want to."

In more ways than you can imagine, mate. Except he'd wanted it. Wanted her. Badly.

Regan shrugged noncommittedly. "Whatever."

Michael observed them before saying, "She's sure mad at you for cock-blocking her, mate." He laughed when Regan blushed.

"Don't worry, Re." He put his arm around her shoulder. "You'll get lots of opportunities when you get to uni, and we won't be there to stop you."

Michael was drunk, which was the only reason he'd say those words.

"Enough, Michael. You're embarrassing her."

Michael kissed her forehead before releasing her and stumbling to their house. He hadn't seemed that drunk earlier but the alcohol must have finally caught up with him.

"You okay?" He followed her to the path leading up to the front door that Michael had left open.

"No, but I'll get over it," she murmured, her small frame hunched over as if trying to make herself smaller.

It was something she did with her parents, and he hated it. Hated that he was the cause of it now when he'd always encouraged her not to shrink herself for anyone, especially him. "Let me walk you to your room." Connor placed a hand in the middle of her back, but withdrew it when he felt her tense.

"I'm fine, Connor. You don't need to babysit me anymore."

The words pricked his heart. He'd hurt her more than he realized. Part of him wanted to make everything between them better, but then what? He couldn't ask her on a date or visit her at school to spend more time with her and explore their relationship. Even if she wasn't his best friend's sister, they were at different stages in their lives.

She was just beginning to start hers, and he was trying to fix his crumbling world. Not to mention their relationship would change—and not just because they had sex. Their families were no longer in the same circles, and they wouldn't be at the same events anymore. Their times together would grow further apart, like his friendship with Michael.

A sharp pain pierced his chest, thinking about losing their friendships. They'd been such a huge and vital part of his life for so long, thoughts of losing it was like losing a limb. A deep ache spread through him, thinking of not hearing Regan's laugh or seeing her face crinkle when he and Michael did something to piss her off.

Silence followed them up the stairs and down the hallway to her room, which was across from the guest room he usually stayed in. He hadn't stayed there as often since he and Michael were at university, but on the recent occasions he had, he always found himself waiting in the room until he heard her door open so he could meet her in the hallway and talk while they walked downstairs either to the kitchen for food or to the pool to swim.

When they reached their rooms, Connor lingered too close to her. So close he could smell the heavenly scent of the perfume he'd bought her years ago. One that mingled so well with her own smell and drove him crazy whenever she came close to him. Like earlier tonight. And now.

Don't think about it! screamed in his mind. *Don't remember the way she clung to you, her legs wrapped around while your hand gripped her ass and you moved inside her hot, tight body.* He was going to burn for creating those memories and worst of all for wanting to make more with her. Right now.

As if sensing his thoughts, those breathtaking blue eyes of hers zeroed in on him. Reflected in them was the same desire that was there earlier tonight, along with longing and the pain of his rejection.

"You deserve more than I can give you right now, Regan." His finger brushed against her lips when she started to speak. "I know you don't believe or understand it, but eventually you'll realize the truth."

Simmering blue eyes locked onto him. "I know you think you don't deserve to be loved because of what's happened to your family, but that's a lie, Connor." She traced her hands through his hair. "You are worthy of love, Connor. No matter what your financial situation. The feelings I have for you have nothing to do with money. But I understand. You think I'm just a child and I don't understand, but I do. I know how important it is for you to provide for your parents and the people you care for, and anything less just isn't good enough for you. I know that I'm not what you need," her voice broke, "or what you want." She stood on her tiptoes and pressed her lips against his lips and then his cheek. "Goodnight, Connor."

She backed into her room, and closed the door, not sparing him another glance.

The silence of the hallway pressed down on him the longer he stood there, part of him longing to go to her room and hold her. But his feet turned to the door behind him, and he walked inside, leaning against the door when it closed. He raked a hand through his hair when he realized he'd just shut the door on the woman he cared for deeply. A woman who loved him. The person who saw him in ways no one else did. Who saw his fears, doubts, and every trauma that burned within him. Her words dug deep into him, making him realize his belief that her emotions for him weren't the childish crush he originally thought and knew in his soul to be a lie. The passion and love she experienced for him was as deep and meaningful as those he had for her.

He was an Eejit, but there was no turning back.

The memory of the feel and taste of her skin was still on his tongue, and her sweet smell pinged around in his brain, reminding him of the moment they shared. One he couldn't repeat no matter how much his fingers longed to touch her again and how badly his body burned for her. And for once, it wasn't just because she was Michael's sister. At this point in his life, he wasn't worthy of her. Probably never would be. *Feck, I'm screwed!*

CHAPTER 9

Connor stared at the woman who sat down at his table, dressed in a rainbow of colors and jet-black hair that didn't match her aging face. Her arms had tracks of tattoos that were a range of constellations. "Can I help you?" He didn't want to be rude, but he certainly didn't have time. A strong inquiring vibe rolled over him, which was no surprise, but when that vibe changed to knowing when she met his gaze head-on, he shifted uncomfortably in his seat.

"You are gifted." Her grin lit up her whole face, causing her wrinkles to bunch to the edges of her face.

"Umm. I'm not sure what you're talking about?" Connor glanced around nervously to see whether there was anyone in the café who knew him. Thankfully, there was no one because most people left school right away after graduation or went home to spend their time with family. He'd stayed behind to pack his and Michael's room before returning home for good.

Honestly, he'd been hoping to catch a glimpse of Regan; she'd be starting uni here soon. Not to mention he was avoiding going home to face the nightmare of moving his parents out of their family home. While his mother was helping with selling what she could and packing only what they'd need, his father hadn't come out of his room other than to eat and complain about the move.

The woman's deep-brown eyes twinkled knowingly. "You do, but I understand your hesitation since you haven't gotten any support in the past." Her small, frail-looking hand covered his.

Connor longed to remove his hand, but she held him with a gaze. The depth of her stare peered into his soul, reading his thoughts or about to put thoughts into his head. The emotion of her humor rolled over him strong and clear. When she squeezed his hand tighter, the feeling strengthened, nearly overpowering him so he wanted to laugh himself. "What the hell was that?"

She released his hand and eased back into the chair, continuing to study him but not as intensely. Every emotion pulsing through her hit him in waves, until he realized it wasn't just her emotions he was sensing, but the other people in the café around him. It shot excitement and dread through him all at once. Sensing the occasional strong negative emotion from others was one thing, but sensing everyone's emotions all at once was a gift he'd happily return.

"What did you do to me?"

"I showed you how strong you could really be if you embraced your gift. A gift you can use to help people."

"Lady, I can barely help myself right now," slipped out before he could stop the words. Heat rushed to his face.

"You'll find your way, but you must continue to embrace who you were meant to be and not let anyone—not even family—keep you from growing your gift. Your grandmother was a wonderful woman who bestowed this gift to you. Don't break her heart and waste it through neglect. Like any skill, if you don't use or develop it, it will fade."

The mention of his grandmother sent a shooting pain through him. His grandparents' death still left a hollow place his parents could never fill. Connor grit his teeth. "My gift doesn't bring me anything but pain and being disregarded since no one believes me or listens." Hence how his family had gotten into this financial situation to begin with.

"The right people will listen. Find ways for them to understand you and your gift."

Connor glanced at the woman seated across from him, who was revealing things about him and his life no one else knew. Doubt rippled through him. *Was someone playing a trick on me? Had someone sent her? For what reason?* "Did you know my grandmother?"

The woman pushed a stray lock of midnight hair from her face and leaned forward, resting her elbows on the table. Her wise eyes glowed. "Not exactly."

Connor's eyebrow rose with skepticism. *Who the hell was this woman?* Someone must have sent her. His gaze shifted about the café, looking for Michael or one of his uni friends. But then he realized none of them knew about his gift, so the chances of them pranking him this way was a long shot. "What does that mean?"

"I didn't know your grandmother while she was alive."

It took a moment for her words to sink into his brain and digest them. "What?"

"One of my gifts is I see and talk to dead people."

Connor laughed. He couldn't help himself; the notion was ridiculous. That laughter continued until he realized her expression hadn't changed. *Wait. She's serious!*

"Your grandmother asked me to talk to you. She knows things are difficult now with the mess your father put you into and believe me, she's not happy about that. But she also wants to make sure you don't go down the road of living a life where you're neglecting your gift and making yourself even more unhappy. She's encouraging you to use your gift in ways that will help you. To see it as an advantage instead of a curse."

Connor didn't know whether to start laughing again or leave because the woman was crazy. What kept him immobile was her statement about their family situation. That wasn't public knowledge—not yet, anyway. The amount of digging required to uncover those details would take time and effort, and he couldn't fathom what benefit she'd gain. She wasn't asking him for money to learn more or offer solutions. The advice she offered was free.

"She's telling the truth, garmhac." The woman's brown eyes narrowed quizzingly. "What the heck is a garmhac?"

Connor grinned. "It's an endearment my grandmother used for me." *I'm going crazy because I'm starting to believe her.* And why not? His grandmother knew more about spirituality and gifts than anyone else he knew. Although a little strange, it wasn't farfetched she'd find a way to reach him. And in a way that was truly unique. Her.

"Thank you," Connor whispered with a croak in his voice.

Her hand covered his. "You're very welcome, son. It's not often I find someone who believes or understands me."

The flicker of happiness vibrating from her was subtle, but strong enough for him to sense it. He breathed deeply into it, embracing it until it became stronger and more emotions trickled through.

When their eyes met, they shared a knowing smile. One that was born from recognizing they weren't like other people. Never had been and never would be. And for the first time in his life, Connor was happy about that. This experience with her was deeper than any he'd shared, other than with his grandmother.

In that moment, he knew with certainty she was there with them, expressing herself through this woman like a channel. One that was more than just sharing the thoughts of dead people. The gift of this experience was one he'd never forget.

His other hand covered their hands. "Thank you for giving this moment to me."

A warm smile tugged at her lips. "You're welcome. And thank you for seeing parts of me and allowing me to share them with someone who isn't dead."

Connor grinned when her mouth twitched.

They sat there for what seemed like several moments before they unraveled their hands. "What now?" Connor whispered, asking not just her but himself too.

"Learn how to develop your gift, believe in yourself, and the rest will fall into place," she assured him as she stood. Her hand rested on his shoulder as he looked up at her. "You are stronger than you think. Your father knows that and that's why he's always tried so hard to show your grandparents he was as good or better than you. He never embraced who he was meant to be. Don't make the same mistake, Connor."

My father thought I was better than him? Those words didn't make sense to him, but Connor remained silent, nodding in response. The woman left the café, her vibrant clothing and hair swaying like her full hips, leaving Connor with his own thoughts.

CHAPTER 10

The atmosphere in the room was tense as Connor and his parents sat at their dining room table. It was one of the few rooms that still appeared normal and wasn't stripped of its furniture and other items that were sold off for their value. Connor had arranged an estate sale quietly to save his family embarrassment from selling the items themselves or his father trying to interfere. The money from the sale would go toward their new home—or, rather, flat because they couldn't afford a home right now.

A man who claimed to be his uncle's solicitor was seated across from them. An uncle only spoken about in hushed tones since he left the folds of his family years ago to follow pursuits outside of finance, much to everyone's dismay and shame. Even his grandparents refused to talk about him.

"Your uncle, Oisin McGrath, left you his bookstore."

His father snorted. "A bookstore."

"It's small, but it's surprisingly profitable since it is the only one in the community and your uncle was a very popular man. He created diverse services for the writers and artists in the community."

"What is the value of the building?" his father asked.

"There is one stipulation, however. The building can never be sold. It must be handed down to each generation of family. This ensures the existing tenants remain in the building and are not pushed out for profits."

Connor flipped through the paperwork the solicitor handed him with the monthly profit of the bookstore. Although it wasn't a lot of money, it was enough to help sustain his parents so he could spend his own money on restoring his family's wealth. The words of the old woman echoed in his mind at that moment, reminding him to center himself so he could get a read on the emotions of the solicitor. Trying to become centered in front of people was something he had to master as he felt his father's glare scorching his skin. Right now, he didn't give a damn. They were in this situation because of him.

The solicitor's emotions were thankfully neutral except for being slightly uncomfortable, which was probably normal. They weren't about to sign any rights away, just claim the inheritance his uncle left him. An inheritance that thankfully didn't come with any debt. Connor schooled his thoughts when he saw the money in his uncle's bank account.

The last thing he wanted was his father getting wind of it. Although he had no rights to it, that wouldn't stop him from trying to get his hands on it. Shame burned his chest, thinking negatively about his father, but he was still bitter about the situation he'd left them in. One he tried to escape from and leave them no better off if he had died.

"Thank you for your time." The solicitor packed up, standing to leave. He handed Connor his card. "Call me if you have any questions."

"Thank you." Those words meant more than a simple thank-you, and he wished he could repay the man in some way because he couldn't repay his dead uncle.

"You're welcome. Your uncle was a fine man to work for, and he will be missed."

Connor nodded. "Let me see you out." He grabbed the envelope with the papers, knowing he couldn't leave them with his father.

When he returned, his parents were drinking—his father whiskey and his mother wine.

"Are you going to give us more information about the bookstore and the papers you signed or are you going to treat us like children?" His tone was sharp and cutting.

An equally cutting comment burned his tongue before Connor swallowed it and sat. "There is nothing to tell, except it will make it easier for me to help support you and Mum, unless you plan on going back to work?"

His father's jaw jumped, but he didn't say anything.

If only he'd been silent about the choice of flats they'd looked at. Each one was not good enough for him.

"I have another job interview tomorrow and another flat to look at. I'm hoping to hear from one of the companies soon. I want to make sure the place we find is close to work."

His father grunted while his mother responded with, "Yes. That will be nice. Hopefully we can find a home with a small garden." She loved gardening, and it was one of the reasons she never fit in with the other wives. They didn't get their hands dirty and were horrified she knew so much about gardening, and not just the types of flowers based on how they were used for hosting events.

"Perhaps I can help by getting a job at a florist—part-time," she whispered, her eyes avoiding her husband.

"Absolutely not! No wife of mine will work."

"You don't need to, Mum, but if you want to for the joy of it..." He ignored his father's narrowed eyes glaring at him.

She blushed and nodded. Connor was pleased to see she was stepping outside her comfort zone; otherwise, his father would have her at home, catering to his every need, now there was no housekeeper or chef. Letting the staff go was the hardest thing, especially without being able to offer them a significant severance. Everyone was understanding but sad about leaving. Connor longed to tell them it was only temporary, but that would be a lie.

"When you go to the bookstore, I'm going with you," his father stated.

"Hmm. Perhaps."

"What do you mean, perhaps?"

"I have no idea what to expect there. I'd rather go alone."

"I don't care what you'd prefer." The glass in his hand hit the table loudly.

Connor schooled his expression; he breathed deeply through his nose to center and calm himself but didn't keep his eyes focused on his father. He didn't need to read his father to know anger was radiating from him, but what Connor wanted was to dig deep below the surface.

Since his encounter with the woman who told him to explore his gift so he didn't lose it, he'd been making a conscious effort to read everyone he met. The payback was worth the extra time he took.

Beneath the surface, a turmoil of emotions whirled within his father, making it difficult to focus on them. Mingled with anger was curiosity and uncertainty. His father longed for control but with the recent events, that control was yanked from his fingers and he was clawing to get it back in any way he could.

"You can come with me next time," Connor assured him. "I have another interview, so I won't have time to drop you back home."

His jawline rippled, but he nodded and retreated into the amber liquid he swirled in his glass.

"How is the job hunt coming along?" Maeve asked, a bright smile on her face.

"Really well. I have two offers right now, but I wanted to have my final interview before deciding. I want to make sure I choose the job with the best location, money, and benefits."

"That's smart. You don't want all your money eaten up by commuting."

"And I don't want to burn out before I'm thirty," Connor added with a teasing tone, but it wasn't far from the truth. He'd rather spend his time investing, but that wasn't the best option because he had to take care of his parents. Although Connor was hopeful his father would come around and perhaps find a job, he couldn't rely on that possibility. At least with the income from the bookstore, some of the financial pressures would lessen.

"Once I get a job, I'll set up a card you can use for expenses."

"Why can't I use the cards I have now?" Rory asked with a hint of anger.

"They'll be canceled at the end of this month and all our bank accounts affiliated with the business closed."

"What about the personal ones?"

"I'm canceling them once they're paid off from the funds we made from selling everything in the house."

"I don't understand why I can't keep them."

"You can, if you find a job to pay off anything you charge on them."

Rory shifted in his seat, his posture stiff.

"You and Mum will have a card to buy groceries and other necessities once I get a job, but the amount will be limited to the budget I can afford."

Maeve rested her hand on Rory's. "Whatever the amount, we're grateful."

Connor nodded and smiled in gratitude at his mother's attempt to keep the peace. "Hopefully it won't be for too long." In addition to his job and investing, he was going to explore more ways to monetize the bookstore. Whatever it took to make their lives better.

Later that evening, Connor stared at his phone, longing to reach out to Regan. He missed her. Michael continued to call or text him, for which he was grateful. Their friendship meant everything to him. A friendship he'd need in the years ahead because that's how long it was going to take to recover financially. Shorter now with the bookstore his uncle left him. An uncle he'd met only a couple of times and one he barely knew.

Connor wanted to ask the lawyer why his uncle left the bookstore to him, but when he mentioned his uncle didn't have any other family, he understood. Well, partly. He could've gifted the library to his community or a charity, but perhaps his uncle, who was related to his father, knew he'd need it. Whatever the reason, he was thankful.

Staring up at the ceiling of his childhood home, sadness pressed down on him as he realized he'd be leaving it for good soon. The Kellys had given them three months, and the end of the last month was fast approaching. He'd found a couple of places that were a good fit for his parents, but he wanted to make sure wherever he picked, it was close to his job.

His final interview was tomorrow and then he'd make a job choice. Although each company was exceptional, he chose them because of the salary and not necessarily because of the work. Whatever happiness he had to sacrifice in the short term was worth it until they were financially stable again.

After his interview, he planned to swing by the bookstore. Finding more ways to monetize the store was his top priority and hopefully the manager had their own suggestions. The more monthly income he had for his parents, the more of his own money he could invest. Maybe after his meetings, he could visit Regan at university.

Bad idea, mate!

Connor was trying to give her space, although he secretly hoped she'd text or call him like she usually did. But his phone had remained silent, with him checking it with every little ping. But why would she reach out to him when he'd rejected her advances, even though he wanted nothing more than to go into her room, throw her on the bed, and do all the things to her body he hadn't been able to against the door? Like kissing every inch of her body, hearing her moan and maybe even scream his name, and stay inside her until the sun came up.

Her words still haunted him, along with knowing he barely deserved her friendship, let alone anything more. It didn't matter her saying he deserved love. Everything up until this point in his life said otherwise, making it hard for his heart to accept her words. Calling meant opening himself up to her in more ways than he already had.

He tucked an arm behind his head. Who was he kidding? Being with her again wasn't going to happen any time soon—if ever. By the time he got his life together financially, she would've moved on with someone else. Or worse, married to some rich bastard her father approved of who would never cherish her the way she deserved, and he'd be forced to watch it from the sidelines while another man kissed her. Wooed her. Married her.

As strong-willed as Regan could be, when it came to her parents, they had a way of pushing her to their will whether she wanted to or not. She wanted to pursue event planning and interior design, but her parents had pushed her to business. More practical to her future responsibilities managing the family's various charities, they claimed. Never mind that she'd single-handedly decorated almost every room in their family home. If her mother released the reins more for events, Regan's talent would shine more. They only saw her talents as something to use for the family and nothing more.

The memory of their conversations about the disappointment in her parents and herself for not standing up to them rolled through his brain, reminding him of the special moments they shared after.

God, he missed her. More than he imagined. He sincerely hoped Michael was true to his word about keeping their friendship. That was the only way he would be able to see her. At family and, if he were lucky, company events. Although it would be torture to watch her move on, at least he'd have her friendship, even if that status changed slightly because they had sex. Mind-blowing sex, for sure, but it changed things between them.

She was no longer the little girl who tagged along with his and Michael's crazy adventures, or even the sixteen-year-old he'd kissed. She was a student and would be stepping into her family role with charities once she graduated. She'd been out of his league before, and now, she was leaving him behind. He only wished she were headed in a direction she truly wanted.

Connor rolled to his side and hugged his pillow. A long day awaited him tomorrow and he needed to sleep. He closed his eyes, but all he dreamed about was Regan.

CHAPTER 11

The noise of the party around grew dim when Regan caught sight of Connor walking into the room with her brother. Her pits sprung a leak while her heartbeat thundered in her ears as they walked toward her. Michael was smiling, while Connor's gaze remained solemn. *He doesn't want to be here. Doesn't want to see me.*

Why would he? With everything going on in his life?

Their physical encounter a couple weeks ago had gotten hot and heavy quickly, and he couldn't help himself; he didn't want more sex with her because he didn't want her the way she wanted him. The other conclusion was too painful to think about—that she sucked and he didn't want to sleep with her again. She had enjoyed it and thought he had too, but what did she know? She had nothing to compare it to.

Regan thought about sleeping with someone else to get a comparison, but that reason seemed like a poor excuse, not to mention she hadn't found anyone she was attracted to that way at uni. She thought of Eamon, whose annoyingly friendly smiles quickly became part of her life at school. Their connection was built on tons of coffee, a common family dynamic they both wanted to escape, and being there for each other. Eamon promised he was a good listener and was true to his word. She never told him about Connor, but he knew she was nursing a complicated heartache.

His friendship filled the void that Connor left, becoming a dear friend. But the thought of sleeping with him didn't appeal to her, even with his striking light-blue eyes, stunning red hair, and muscles for days.

Connor had ruined her for other men with their quickie against the door. *Pathetic!* She had to snap out of it. Connor was never going to see her as anything other than Michael's sister, and she had to make peace with that and move on. Even as the words left her brain, her insides protested profusely, not ready to let go of him just yet.

"Connor. Michael." She put a hand up. "Muss up my hair, and Mother will kill you!"

Her brother grinned before becoming serious. "Look at you. All grown up."

Regan rolled her eyes. "I've been grown up for a while now, brother."

He threw his arm around her shoulder and kissed her forehead. "You'll always be my little sister."

"And you'll always be my pain in the arse big brother." She couldn't help smiling, realizing how much she'd missed him. They texted regularly, but it wasn't the same.

"At your service."

"Hello, Connor." She finally greeted him, needing time for her racing heart to recover and her pulse to calm down.

"Hello, Regan." His smile didn't reach his eyes as he glanced around the room, looking everywhere but at her.

Her heart sank. *He couldn't even look her in the eyes? Was this going to be their future interactions? Small talk and avoidance?* Her heart ached at the thought. She'd hoped they could at least retain a smidgen of their past friendship, but she'd guessed wrong. It was probably for the best. Time alone with Connor was the last thing she needed, along with pretending their relationship was the same after having sex. It wasn't and never would be.

Michael's gaze shifted between them. "What's up with you two? You're greeting each other like strangers."

"I've just got a lot going on right now, Michael."

Her brother's eyes dipped in sadness and understanding. "Right. Sorry, mate."

Regan studied his face. The face that was etched in the crevices of her mind since she was sixteen and started to notice him as more than just a friend and her brother's best friend. The strong jawline that was covered in a thin beard, the sharp edges of his nose and face that made him more handsome and continually devastated her when she looked at him for too long.

But his eyes were what made her weak in the knees when they focused on her alone. They were a shade of blue she'd never seen on anyone else, going from a bright brilliant summer sky to a stormy sea when he was angry or turned on. She remembered the texture of his sandy hair beneath her fingertips, soft despite a little bit of product holding it in place. The taste and weight of his lips against her skin haunted her dreams at night and caused her to wake up tangled in her sheets, panting and heated.

Regan grabbed a glass of champagne from a passing waiter and took a big gulp.

"What's your excuse?" her brother asked.

"Uni is a lot," she said carefully, her voice barely a whisper.

"Not partying too much, I hope." Michael's eyes narrowed in concern.

"I've been too busy for parties." That certainly wasn't a lie. "Unless you count study dates at the coffee shop partying."

"Who are you having dates with?" Michael asked.

For the first time since she walked over, Connor's eyes snapped to hers.

She rolled her eyes. "Did you miss the part where I said study, M?"

"So, it's only girls?" Connor asked.

Was he jealous? The way his jaw jumped made her wonder, but he no doubt asked for the same reason her brother did. "No." She didn't elaborate. *Let them both stew and wonder—especially Connor.* He was likely making his way through his share of women, the way her brother was.

"How is the job hunting going, Connor?" Changing the subject was the safest way to avoid telling them about Eamon. Trying to explain their relationship, and that it was just friendship, would make them roll their eyes while claiming that he wasn't interested in being just her friend. Although that might be true, Eamon had been nothing but a gentleman and a true friend.

"Feck! I'm out of here," Michael mumbled as he hurried away.

When she saw Ciara headed in their direction, she understood her brother's sudden departure. "I can't believe she's still chasing him."

"He made the mistake of going out with her. Now he can't get rid of her."

They chuckled, easing the tension between them for the first time since he came over. Regan was relieved and had every intention of cultivating it. "I can't believe he agreed. Didn't he know he was opening Pandora's box?"

"He thought a few dates would make her see they weren't a good fit." He shrugged. "No luck."

"Where did Michael disappear to?" Ciara's gaze shifted about the room.

"He left. Early meeting tomorrow," Connor said with a straight face.

Regan nodded in agreement, biting back a grin at the annoyance that etched Ciara's face.

Thankfully, she strode away once she realized her prey was gone.

"She doesn't even like Michael that much. Her parents are trying to put them together and she's trying to get into their good graces."

"How do you know that?"

"I overheard her talking to her parents. Sadly, our parents think it's a good connection too. Good for business."

Connor snorted. "No way Michael will marry her. No matter how much your parents want it."

"You don't know that. Our parents can be very persuasive," Regan whispered, taking another sip of champagne. She knew that better than anyone. Their parents adored Michael. He was the favorite child who was living out the dreams they had for him, while she was the difficult one who fought them at every turn. At least until they bulldozed over her, which was often.

Connor's hand rested on her shoulder. "You do fight them," he reassured her, a smirk tugging his lips.

"Not hard enough," she murmured, her gaze on her feet.

The pressure of working on multiple degrees, and her mother pulling her back into hosting events when she promised to give her this year to settle, was weighing on her. Unlike other students at uni, there was no luxury of parties and having fun to unwind. Not if she wanted to pursue what she loved by carving out something for herself outside of what her parents demanded from her.

Every time she took a step in the direction for what she wanted, her parents seemed to sense it and yanked her back into the folds. Not only was it draining emotionally, but it was weighing on her physically too: The late nights studying. The long days in class.

Her only friend at the moment was Eamon who, like he promised, turned out to be a great listener. Coming from the same world, he understood the pressures of parents and their expectations.

Being away from everyone she knew and loved was harder than she thought, especially Michael and Connor.

CHAPTER 12

Connor's last intention when he agreed to come to this event with Michael was to find himself alone with Regan.

Even with the crowd of people surrounding them, their emotions swirling around him, her presence was intoxicating, like a drug he shouldn't expose himself to. The moment he stepped into her sphere, he smelled her sweet perfume of vanilla and spice. The same one he gave her every year. Knowing she wore something he bought her was intoxicating to him. As if a part of him was on her body. *Jezzus! Coming tonight was stupid.*

But as her face morphed into heartbreaking emotions she couldn't hide, Connor knew instantly coming to this event was the best thing. They were avoiding each other, but he still wanted to be there for her, and right now he could sense she needed him, needed his comfort. And nothing would keep him from giving her what she needed.

Connor's hand moved to her chin to lift her face so he could see those eyes. Their blue depths haunted him for weeks whenever he slept. The vulnerability in them knocked the wind out of him.

He wished he could wrap her in his arms and tell her the truth: that he was crazy about her and wanted nothing more than to be with her in every way. Wanted to take her out on a date, hold her hand in public. Kiss her in front of her family. Have her in his bed and worship her body for days to make up for her first time being against a door at a uni party.

To tell her how much he missed being near her, even if only to hear her complain about her parents. Missed her laughter and the way her eyes sparkled when she talked about planning the latest event.

When a glimmer of hope sparked in her eyes, he dropped his hand. The hurt reflecting back at him tore at his heart but he knew he couldn't give her hope. The only thing he could offer her in that moment was comfort.

Regan's eyes caught sight of something beyond his shoulder, and she took a step away from him. Moments later, a guy placed his arms around her waist, pulling her close.

"There you are, sweetheart." He kissed her cheek.

Regan glanced up at him in question before smiling. "Here I am." She leaned into his tall frame.

Connor clenched his fists at his sides. *Who the hell was this wanker?* Whoever he was, the way he touched Regan was too familiar for his liking. *What did you expect, Connor? That she'd wait around for you? Wait after you rejected her?* She was having the uni experience. One he'd encouraged her to have because he couldn't offer her what she wanted. She obviously found someone who could.

That didn't mean he had to like it. The urge to wipe that smug grin from the boy's face was strong. Even stronger was his need to pull Regan away from him, throw her over his shoulder, and take her home.

Home? To live with you and your parents? He winced, thinking about it. "I'm Connor. And you are?" He didn't extend his hand. The last thing he needed to do was touch this wanker. There was no guarantee he wouldn't yank his arm from his body. Although he'd feel better, he doubted Regan or anyone at the party would appreciate it.

"I'm Eamon."

The boy didn't extend his hand either, as they glared at each other like two bucks in a field. Eamon didn't offer who he was to Regan or his last name, which told him a couple of things. He wasn't as arrogant as Declan, who threw his name around to impress people, so he probably wasn't from a wealthy family. He didn't claim Regan was his girlfriend, which meant they were either friends or just sleeping together.

That last one didn't sit well with him. He'd rather him be her boyfriend than just some bloke she was sleeping with. *Would I. Really? Hell no!* But the thought of him using her that way churned his stomach.

"I've heard a lot about you." Eamon pulled Regan even closer to him.

Connor's gaze shifted to Regan. "Really? I haven't heard anything about you." His heart raced. If she mentioned him, then it probably meant they were only friends. Relief rippled through him.

"She said you were her brother's best friend. That she's known you since she was a child."

Connor flinched at his indication he was nothing but a family friend and making him feel like a complete perv because they'd known each other since she was a little girl and he was a grown man who'd taken advantage of her. The odds of Eamon knowing the depth of their relationship were unlikely, but it didn't stop the guilt and shame that rushed through him in waves.

"Aye. We've known each other for many years. I consider Regan a dear friend." Connor noticed her visibly stiffen next to him. He hated having to use those words, but what more could he say? That she was special and meant more to him than anyone else? Would that make her feel better or just make the current moment even more awkward?

"Yes. Friends," Regan mumbled.

"How long have you two been a couple?" Connor asked, the urge to know if this boy meant something to her overwhelming him. His insides tightened as he awaited their answer. No matter the answer, he had no claim on Regan other than she was someone he couldn't have for himself.

They glanced at each other, as if asking the other how to respond before they broke into laughter.

Anguish ripped through Connor as he watched her smiling. A real one and the kind she reserved for her family and limited friends. The kind she used to share with only him and Michael. This boy had just yanked Regan away from him, and there was nothing he could do but watch. *Only yourself to blame, mate!* It was true.

His life was a mess, but Regan wouldn't have cared about any of that. She would stand by him because she cared about him and was fierce about protecting the people she loved—especially Michael and her parents, even with their complicated relationship. She would have stood by him and been a part of his life as his girlfriend, the woman who loved and adored him if he'd given her the chance.

What had he done?

Pushed her away for reasons he rationalized were for her own good, but the truth was he was scared. Terrified she'd pity him, like he needed saving, and the loving and adoring way she'd looked at him over the years and the night she confessed her love would evaporate. He convinced himself pushing her away was the right thing to do, but he was wrong. So wrong. And now he'd lost her.

Regan glanced up at Eamon the way she used to gaze at him, with adoration and affection. Something pinched his heart at the thought she might love him.

Sorrow surrounded him, squeezing his chest until he couldn't breathe. He had to get the hell out of here and away from them. "Nice meeting you, Eamon. Regan. Good to see you," he said with a weak smile. He flinched at the pathetic tone of his voice.

"See you, Connor," Eamon said.

Connor couldn't hear whether Regan responded, too busy heading to the nearest exit to get away from them and what their relationship meant. He'd lost her and it was his own damn fault. He couldn't stay and watch them together. Watch him touch her, dance with her, and make her laugh again. Even if they weren't dating, he'd lost that special position of friendship he treasured.

The cold, crisp night air cut through his lungs, and he breathed deeply, pushing aside the rush of emotions clogging his senses. He'd been so focused on Regan and the whirlwind of sensations she always made him feel, he hadn't thought about reading Eamon and learn his true feelings and intensions about Regan.

"Stupid Eejit!" he hissed, knowing the opportunity was gone. Who knew when he'd see them again and what damage he could cause Regan in the meantime. If he read him, he could've... *What, Connor? You haven't even told Michael about your gift. What could you say to Regan without having to tell her the truth? And then what? Are you really wishing to risk her reaction if she learned who you really are and what you can do? If your parents couldn't accept you, what makes you think she will?*

It was the reason he hadn't told Michael. Another thing to be scared about when it came to Regan. He knew he couldn't handle seeing that look in her eyes. That look of shock before it morphed into something that would make her either be disgusted or terrified of him.

He'd already lost her on so many levels. He couldn't handle losing her forever...and in that way. Or worse—having her use him for his gift. No matter how much he wanted to believe she and Michael would be different, that they were true friends who would love and accept him no matter what, fear and experience told him otherwise.

As much as it hurt losing Regan in this way, he still had Michael's friendship. And in a small way, still had her friendship too. They were still a part of each other's lives. Having a part of her was better than having nothing of her. It hurt to see her with another man, but he only had himself to blame.

She offered him her body and her heart, and he decided not to accept it but remain friends. It might take time for them to return to the relationship they had before being together, but he hoped with time, they could have some kind of relationship, even if it wasn't the one he really wanted.

"Everything all right?" a worried voice called by the doors he had just come through.

Turning, his gaze locked onto Regan, whose eyes were filled with worry.

He released the tightness his body was holding. "Fine. What are you doing out here? Shouldn't you be inside with your boyfriend?" The word *boyfriend* burned his tongue. They hadn't confirmed it, but their interaction screamed they had something special.

Regan wrung her hands in front of her. "He's just a friend. That's why we were laughing." Her eyes were downcast, unable to look at him.

Connor strode over to her, standing so close he could tip her face to meet his gaze. "I wish I could say I wasn't happy about that." He took a deep breath, wishing his own emotions weren't in such turmoil. "But, honestly, I have no say in whether you want to date someone or not, Regan."

Sea-blue eyes scorched him, filled with longing and regret. "You could if you wanted to," she whispered.

"I couldn't for all the reasons that are still an obstacle for us, Regan." His hand caressed her cheek. Sparks shot up his arm from the warmth of her face resting deeper into his hand. *Coward!*

He stiffened when her lips pressed against his palm, and her heated gaze singed him. Her tongue came next and then her mouth closed around his thumb and sucked as she met his gaze.

"Jesus, Mary, and Joseph!" Connor hissed, hardening instantly. The fingers of his other hand found their way into her hair before he pulled his hand away from her mouth to crash his lips against hers.

Her deep moan ricocheted through him. "You're going to be the death of me, Regan," he rasped, his lips making a trail along her jawline and down her neck.

"Hmmm. The feeling is mutual," she whispered, her fingers raking along his scalp.

He backed them up to the nearest wall and in a corner, away from the eyes of the people at the party. The last thing he needed was Michael or anyone else seeing him kissing her. The right thing would be stepping away from her and taking them back inside. But when his gaze locked on her and he saw the longing in her eyes, he froze. He couldn't stop himself from touching her; his hands grazed along her bare arms and down her back, her smooth, soft skin beneath his fingertips feeling like a dream.

Just one more time.

Liar!

"Connor," she moaned, as her hands pulled his frame closer to hers and yanked his mouth back to hers, their tongues hot and eager to suck and run along each other.

Unable to help himself, he pulled her dress up her legs, pressing his hard length to her core until their groans mingled. "God, I missed you," he murmured against her mouth as his hands slipped between them, tugging her panties aside so he could touch her. "So wet for me."

"Only you." Regan whimpered.

Connor's gaze met hers. "You haven't been with anyone since me?"

She shook her head, tendrils of her hair tumbling over her shoulders.

He tucked a stray strand behind her ear. That knowledge should scare him and convince her even more to move on, but somehow it made his heart race with happiness. It had been almost six months since they were together.

Her shy gaze met his. "Have you?"

"No. I haven't been able to stop thinking about the feel of your skin beneath my fingertips. The feel of being inside you." Connor groaned before kissing her hotly, wishing they were alone, but knowing it was his worst idea ever.

"Come to my flat later," she whispered, her tongue running along his bottom lip.

There was nothing he wanted more than to bury himself in her again. *One last time*, echoed in his mind like a traitor to convince him.

"I'm leaving here in an hour."

"No. Let's leave now." Connor knew if he had more time, he'd talk himself out of it and he wanted this time with her. Needed it before their lives pulled them apart again. Although guilt nailed him in the gut, in this moment, he didn't care. He'd take whatever time he could get with her.

"Together?"

"Yes. I'll offer to drive you back to uni."

"But I came with Eamon."

Shite! He'd forgotten all about him. "Can you convince him to leave now?"

"Yes." She kissed his lips softly. "I'll text you when I get back to my flat."

"I'll be waiting." *And hoping like hell I don't change my mind.*

They untangled their bodies, and Connor watched her return to the party, remaining outside to calm his erection. The cool night air prickled his heated skin. "What the hell are you doing?" he said aloud. The last thing he needed was to keep seeing Regan. If they got caught, it would be the end of his relationship with Michael, and her parents would likely destroy his career and any hope to restore his family's reputation. Being with Regan was a bad idea on so many levels. He'd be risking her relationship with her family too. Who knew how they'd react if they found out?

Connor raked a hand through his hair in a weak attempt to fix what her fingers had mussed before heading back inside. His gaze shifted around the room, looking for her. She stood with Eamon before returning to her parents, chatting with them for a moment before she and Eamon left. Her gaze didn't search for him, but he didn't mind. Her eyes would be all his later tonight. He'd make sure of it.

Michael was nowhere to be found, no doubt still hiding from Ciara. He'd text him later. The Dohertys were still polite, if not more aloof than usual when he said goodnight, but at that moment he didn't care. In just a short while, Regan would be in his arms, his hands and mouth on her skin. He ignored the guilt gnawing the back of his spine as he made his way to his car and Regan's flat. Losing her again wasn't an option.

CHAPTER 13

Regan's hand shook as she texted Connor to let him know she was home. On the drive to uni, Eamon plied her with endless questions, but she diverted him with lame responses. Explaining her relationship with Connor wasn't something she wanted to discuss with him and for more reasons than they weren't that kind of friends.

They didn't talk about dates or the opposite sex in that way. Trusting people didn't come easy for either of them, so they had—without saying it out loud—not spoken about their dating lives. Not that she had one.

Did she get asked out? All the time. But she was either too busy with classes or wasn't interested in the guys asking her out. They were boys compared to Connor. A five-minute conversation was all it took to convince her she wasn't interested.

Not to mention the lack of a spark. Connor had ruined her for other men. *Give yourself some slack, Regan.* He was more than just a simple crush that wasn't going away easily. It meant moving on wasn't going to come easy. And she wasn't the type to go through men as a remedy for a broken heart, no matter how much her classmates and even Eamon suggested it. Although Eamon didn't know about Connor, he guessed she was nursing a broken heart. Regan hadn't corrected him or offered an explanation. After tonight, Eamon would likely guess it was Connor, even with her avoiding answering his questions.

Being attracted to Eamon would be easier, especially considering he seemed to get along with her parents, who were thrilled to meet him even though she insisted they were just friends.

Inviting Connor to her flat was probably not a good idea. Maybe the worst, because she knew it wouldn't mean anything to him. But she didn't care. She missed him and if her only way to have him was sex, she'd take it.

She was the reason they weren't friends. The one who pushed for a physical relationship and then made things awkward. After their night together, going back to their previous relationship wasn't an easy option. No matter how badly she wanted it. She missed their conversations, his teasing, and the occasionally funny photo of him and Michael and their antics.

Their lives had changed since they left university and were now out in the working world. Michael was knee-deep in the family business, learning even more than he had during the summers, and Connor was working and trying to restore everything his family had lost. She didn't know the details, except what she overheard her parents talking about. The people in their circle weren't easy to forget, and losing your money was the worst crime you could commit.

Although her parents hadn't ostracized Connor, his parents had all but disappeared. Likely because they wouldn't be welcomed.

A light knocking on her door set her heart racing. *He's here!* She smoothed down the simple short silk pajamas she'd changed into before taking a calming breath and opening the door. Connor took up the entire doorway with his frame, making her realize he'd filled out even more since he left uni. The intoxicating smell of his cologne hit her like a wave, and her insides quivered, along with the heated way his eyes locked onto hers after they seared her from top to bottom.

"Are you going to invite me in or leave me standing in the doorway?" His deep voice was laced with a hint of arousal and teasing.

"Since when have you needed an invitation?" she shot back playfully.

Stormy blue eyes darkened before he pushed her farther into her room and kicked the door closed with his foot. He pulled her against his frame, and she gasped when his erection swelled against her stomach. She traced her hand along his chest, up his neck and into his hair. His lips smashed against hers; she welcomed his kiss and opened her mouth to let his tongue dance with hers. Their moans filled the room as the kiss deepened.

"I missed you," Connor groaned hotly in her ear.

Those words were the sweetest balm to her wounded heart, even though he said those same words earlier tonight. She'd never tire of hearing them because they meant he missed her as much as she missed him.

He pulled the sweater over his head, while her hands gripped his shirt underneath, and she yanked until the buttons flew across the room while she roughly pushed it off his shoulders. His own hands tore at her silk pajamas until she heard them rip but, in that moment, it didn't matter. Their clothes ended up in a tattered pile by the door. Regan sighed as their naked flesh touched when they landed on her bed.

Connor's large frame didn't leave much room, but she didn't care as her hands traced his skin. She wanted to memorize every inch, because she'd likely never have him here again. "I want everything," she whispered.

His bottomless blue eyes studied her silently before he chuckled. "I don't think we have enough time for that."

"It's Friday. We have the weekend." Her hands framed his face and sunk into his hair.

"I'll see what I can do in that time." Connor smiled, his hands caressing her cheek before making a trail down her neck and breasts.

Regan's breath stuck in her throat.

"When I saw you standing in the doorway in those sexy shorts, I wanted nothing more than to rip them from your body and ravish you, but then I remembered that's what happened last time." His hands traced her stomach. "I wanted this time to be different. To savor every inch of your skin and do all the things I've been dreaming about and wished I'd done."

Regan's heart fluttered in her chest, filling it with a deep ache. *He dreamed of me?*

Connor leaned off the bed to pull a pack of condoms from his trouser pocket and threw them on the nightstand.

Regan's eyes bulged. "Are we going to use all of those?" There was more than she expected. Her insides trembled. He was planning to stay longer than just tonight, but he couldn't use them all in one night, could he? She suddenly realized she had no idea, but she was eager to find out. They didn't use protection the last time because she was on the Pill. But after he broke her heart, she didn't see the point.

Connor chuckled. "I sure as hell plan on it. We've got the whole weekend, and I plan to use all that time in this room with you."

"You can go that many times?" Surprise lit her eyes.

Connor let out a boisterous laugh, pulling her against him. "I have no idea, but I'm going to try. You're worth it."

Her eyebrows quirked. "I didn't think men your age could go that many times in a short period."

"My age? Why, you cheeky..." Connor rolled them, so he hovered above her, caging her with his arms next to her head. "I was going to take it easy on you, but after that comment, I'll have to torture you a little first."

Regan glanced at him with a sweet smile. "Can't we do both?"

His hands gripped her wrists, holding them above her head. "You're going to be begging me for mercy by the time I'm finished with you."

His words and heated gaze shot tremors through her in the best way.

One of his hands held both her wrists while his free hand traveled achingly slowly down her neck and shoulders, his knuckles skimming over her pebbled nipples.

"Connor," she moaned.

He chuckled as he continued to torture her with a combination of his fingertips, lips, and tongue until she was arched against his mouth, trying to get closer. Wanting more from him.

"I want to touch you too," she pleaded, her voice rumbling.

"Not yet," he whispered, right before his mouth and tongue teased her core.

"Omigod." Regan's back arched as his hand pushed her legs farther apart. He finally released her wrists, and her hands found themselves fisting the sheets next to her head as he devoured her with deliberate leisure.

Just as her orgasm was creeping up her back, he stopped his assault and climbed up her body, leaving a trail of kisses with his lips and fingertips before reaching her mouth.

She groaned in irritation. "Why did you stop?"

A wicked grin pulled at his lips and sparkled in his eyes. "Because, pet, I want to be buried deep inside you when you come, so I can feel you squeeze around me and see if it's as good as I remember."

A shiver raced up her spine at his words. One of the many things she loved about him was how open and vocal he was when describing her body and how it affected him. She didn't know what this weekend meant and if it would go any further but right now, she didn't care. The only thing that mattered was she was with him.

She wrapped her arms around him, kissing him with everything swirling inside her that consumed her when it came to him—his eyes, his mouth, the feel of his mouth and skin beneath her fingertips. The energy between them pulsed and radiated everywhere, from her heart to her body and somewhere deeper.

After he rolled on a condom, he gazed down at her. "I forgot how beautiful you are up close. Blinding," he whispered as a hand caressed the strand of hair touching her cheek.

Her breath caught in her throat at his words and the intensity behind his eyes as he eased inside her leisurely, as if she were something precious he wanted to savor.

They both groaned but kept their gazes locked when he was fully inside her. "Is it as good as you remembered," Regan teased, despite the fact that the myriad sensations vibrating through her were far from humorous.

No words left his mouth, but his eyes spoke volumes, along with the lines that etched his face that screamed, like her, he was in heaven. This time, there was no sting of pain. No pain at all, only searing pleasure that rippled through her with every thrust.

"Connor," she groaned, arching her back and meeting his hips with hers.

"I'm here, pet. I'm not going anywhere." His penetrating stare held her as their fingers interlaced tightly. "Nothing can tear me away from you."

The words hit her somewhere deep inside that she didn't realize needed to be soothed with those very words. She didn't know what tomorrow would bring, but they had right now. This weekend.

As an orgasm barreled toward her, fierce and all-consuming, Connor murmured, "That's it, sweetheart. Come apart for me."

"Only you," she whispered at his words as her orgasm ripped through her like a shock of white light.

She watched him find his own release moments later as hers crested. Their fingers remained linked like their bodies, and she clung to him, not wanting to let go. Wanting the heat of his skin to remain pressed against her, even with the sweat that covered them.

This time, not just the hunger and urgency of the first time but connecting with him again sparked something deep and vibrant. Touching not only her body, but every part of her soul. She was his, and nothing was ever going to change that.

Regan caressed Connor's chest, reveling in the warmth beneath her fingertips.

"We'll hit the shower next. Is it big enough for the two of us?" His hand made a lazy trail down the middle of her back until it settled on her butt.

"It's a large tub. I chose this place because of it."

"Hmm. A tub. Even better. I get to watch you ride me while I lavish some love on your breasts."

Heat rushed to her face and other parts of her body at his words. This side of Connor was one she'd never experienced. She was used to his teasing, playful side, but one that was more best friend vibe than the lover vibe radiating from him now. She didn't hate it. The way he spoke during sex thrilled her in ways she didn't expect

She'd never considered herself shy, but the words coming out of his mouth made her blush right down to her toes.

"Are you like this with every woman?" Regan regretted the words the moment they left her lips. *Why are you trying to ruin the moment?*

Connor's hand stilled his caress of her back. His blue gaze burned her for what seemed like several minutes. "Honestly?"

She nodded slowly, her heart in her throat, waiting for his answer. *Could my heart take it if I don't like the response? What did it matter?* Connor might be her first, but she certainly wasn't his. Although he wasn't as promiscuous as her brother, he was certainly no angel.

"No." He brushed a stray hair from her face and tucked it behind her ear. "You're the only woman I feel comfortable enough with, and now that I know how you taste and feel wrapped around me..." He drew in a ragged breath. "It's hard to control what comes out of my mouth when I'm around you. I want to touch every inch of your skin when you're close to me." He squeezed her frame against his body. "Your smell..." His nose ran along her neck. "It all drives me crazy when you're near me."

Wow. Those were not the words she expected him to say. She didn't think he'd be so elaborate or honest considering she knew he was conflicted about their relationship. *Relationship? That wasn't what this was.* She wasn't that naive, no matter what Connor thought. She understood his reservations, even though it broke her heart to think about it.

She caressed his chest, her touch moving up his body to his face. A face she'd fallen in love with over the years without even realizing it until the moment his lips touched the edge of hers. She was desperate for everything with him. Every touch, every word, every moment that kept him near her. Even if only for this weekend.

His words reflected exactly how she felt when she was near him. Like she couldn't get close enough, touch him enough, smell him enough—which sounded crazy. They weren't animals, but when she was around Connor and he touched her, she felt wild and out of control.

When the silence stretched between them, the space between his eyebrows furrowed in worry, as if what he said had scared or weirded her out.

After placing a quick kiss on his lips, she responded with, "I feel the same."

They shared beaming smiles. The craziness between them was understood and, more importantly, accepted. Connor pulled her off the bed with him and toward the toilet. "I don't want to waste a minute of our time together. I want to spend as much time as possible touching you, kissing you." Connor gave a lopsided smirk. "Inside you."

Regan watched him take care of the condom and then turn on the faucet; the tub slowly filled up with water. She traced her hands up and down his back, soothing the marks she'd left there earlier. He turned and lifted her, placing her inside the partially filled tub, and stepped in to join her, pulling her into his lap when he sat. His fingers dug into her hair, tugging her until he was kissing her, his tongue possessing her the way she loved. All-consuming and deep, pushing out thoughts of everything but him. Them.

She shifted until she straddled him. "Are you going to feed me later?"

His eyes darkened.

That was one thing she hadn't done for him. Yet. Although she was certain there were lots of other things Connor could teach her. She planned to squeeze as many in this weekend as possible.

"I meant food, but we can do that too." She bit her bottom lip nervously. "But you'll have to tell me what you like."

"Pet, I'll happily show you anything you want to learn, but I have a feeling you'll be fantastic at anything we do." He pushed her hair over her shoulder and kissed her neck.

"Really? Why do you think that?"

"Because you're so competitive. You want to excel at everything you do."

Regan giggled. "I don't think this is what my parents had in mind when they insisted I strive for excellence in everything I do."

"True, but you won't hear me complaining."

Regan snorted. "I wonder why?"

Connor chuckled. "I only want the best for you."

She expected him to say *And that's me*, but they both knew that wasn't in the cards. Their moment was right now, and they were going to live in it. At least she planned to. Every minute and hour of this weekend they had together.

"I'm going to need sustenance if I'm going to keep going like this until tomorrow."

"You're the younger of us. What is this generation coming to?" Connor tsked.

"I don't know what you're talking about. I'm in the same generation as you. You're only six years older than me. That might seem like a lot to you now, but in ten years, it won't seem like that big a gap." Regan touched her index finger to the side of her lip. "You are going to be an old man by then."

She laughed and her body jerked when Connor tickled her.

"Old man! I won't even be forty in ten years."

"A lot can happen in ten years, Connor. You could lose all this gorgeous hair of yours and be bald. Or maybe you'll start graying or have a big beer belly," she teased.

Regan squealed when Connor pinched her.

"A beer belly? Really? That's what you think will happen to me? I guess I better make sure to stay in shape for all those older ladies who are bound to chase after me."

"Ha-ha! You'll be too busy dodging the young ladies pining after the sexy older man."

His hands ran down her now wet back as the tub filled up. "I like the idea of all the ladies chasing me."

A snorted escaped Regan as she turned off the water. "I bet you do. I didn't think you were as bad as Michael when it came to the ladies, but I guess I was wrong."

Connor captured her face with his hands, and an intense gaze locked on her. "I've only had eyes for you from the moment you kissed me, Regan."

A tremor pulsed through her, settling in her chest, thick and heavy. She longed to tell him she'd only had eyes for him since her sixteenth birthday, but the words lodged in her throat, fear keeping her silent. Fear of his rejection. Fear of yearning for more, only to be disappointed and hurt like before. So only a small smile pulled at the edges of her lips in response before he captured her mouth for another deep kiss that melted her insides. Connor molded their bodies together, water splashing dangerously close to the sides of the tub, threatening to spill onto the tile floor.

"As much as I want to stay here with you in this tub, the condoms are in the other room," he rasped in her ear before running his tongue along the shell of her ear.

Shivers shot through her body, and she gripped his shoulders as he stood. Regan wished in that moment she was still on the Pill so they wouldn't have to stop, but somehow, she sensed Connor still wouldn't take the risk. Nothing was a hundred percent, and having an accidental pregnancy would not end well for either of them.

After wrapping her legs around his waist, she grabbed the towel off the rack as he walked back to the bedroom. She dried off the parts of them she could reach. "What?" Regan asked when he met her with a smirk. "You want to sleep on a wet bed tonight?"

"How thoughtful of you," Connor teased as she unwrapped herself from his body and continued to dry him off until she ended up on her knees.

"I thought so." She rubbed his legs slowly, watching him grow larger with each stroke. She licked her lips and gazed back up at Connor to find his intense stare locked on her, his blue eyes darker than she'd ever seen them. "Looks like I missed a spot. Although..." She dropped the towel. "I'm not sure you want me to dry it off. I'm thinking you want to keep it wet. Am I wrong?" Her tongue ran along the side of him as she held his gaze.

A hand was in her hair and caressing her cheek. "Regan." His voice sounded like he had a mouth full of gravel.

"Might be time for that lesson now, Connor." A confident smirk tugged at her lips, right before taking him in her mouth.

A thrill shot through her from the loud moan that came from Connor. She'd done that to him.

They were mostly dry when they finally reached the bed, and Connor had proved that he was right—she was not only a quick study, but was a skilled learner.

CHAPTER 14

Golden light shimmered through the cracked blinds and made its way along the room until it moved over the covers of the bed. Connor watched Regan sleeping, her hair a tangled mess around her face and his chest. Her soft sounds and the rise of her chest pierced him with a sense of peace he hadn't felt in a long time.

Although his life was somewhat settled with finding a job and getting his parents into their new flat, it was far from calm. Between the long hours and the constant issues from his father that his mother was unable to handle, stress was his best friend. And although he knew he couldn't sustain it for long—it would age him faster than the long hours at work—it was his new norm for the foreseeable future.

Coming to her flat was a bad idea. He knew it the moment the words left his mouth, but right now, it seemed like the best decision he'd made in months. He'd missed her company. Those sweet smiles of hers, her quirky sense of humor that always made him laugh, and the peaceful calm her presence brought from not being able to read her. The silence echoed in his brain like a sweet song only she played.

His fingers itched to touch her, but he didn't want to risk waking her. They stayed up late last night. During dinner, they'd chatted as if no time had passed. As if they were still friends who cared about each other and stayed in touch.

After dinner, they had more lessons in bed because he couldn't seem to get enough of her. A simple look or word from her, and their hands were all over each other again.

Guilt nailed him that he couldn't offer her more than just this stolen weekend. Although she tried to act like it didn't bother her, Connor knew her well enough to understand that, like him, she was making the most of their time together—even though it pained her things would return to how they were before: limited conversations and pretending they didn't know every inch of each other's body.

This was one of the few times he wished her family were strangers to him, and he and Regan had met at a uni party, or any party. Their connection would be one they could explore instead of having to pretend they didn't want to tear each other's clothes off whenever they were in proximity. Maybe it was just him? Connor remembered the way her eyes devoured him whenever they were near. It was something he felt deep in his bones. Whenever those beautiful blues of hers found him, she was all he could see and he had to force himself to act like he didn't care, and she was just another friend.

Connor's relationship with Michael remained strong as ever, for which he was grateful, although spending time together since they both started working was proving to be more challenging. But, surprisingly, he was still invited to parties. They spoke on the phone almost every day, and he was pulled into his and Regan's group chat, although she was mostly silent now whenever he started chatting. Her answers were short and clipped. He couldn't blame her.

Maybe he could mend their relationship so they could at least remain friends, but how? Regan wanted more from him. Deserved more than what they shared behind closed doors. Time. He needed time to fix his life, finances, and coming clean with how he felt about her to Michael and her family. Would she be willing to give him that time?

He didn't want the distance they'd had before, and he sensed she didn't either. Maybe a middle ground was the short-term compromise so they could retain all parts of their relationship. The arrangement wouldn't be exactly what she deserved but was a step toward them being together in the future.

All the hurdles before them could be tackled one at a time instead of trying to overcome them all at once. Those were the words he told himself, even as guilt swarmed him about deceiving his best friend and her family. Moira and Shamus weren't his favorite people, but in a lot of ways, they were like second parents to him. Although he didn't always like the way they treated their children, he cared about them. Respected them. The deception wouldn't be long, he convinced himself. Just long enough for him to get his life together and show her family, including his best friend, that she'd be loved and taken care of by him in a way no other man could.

No longer able to contain himself, his hands brushed her hair from her face so he could see her better, and down her back, enjoying the velvety feel of her skin against his fingertips.

She stretched her body against him. A smile tugged her lips and her brilliant blue gaze found his, sending his heart into a frenzy and spreading a warmth through him that only happened with her.

"Morning, beautiful." He kissed her forehead.

Regan snorted. "I know you're lying. My hair feels like a rat's nest." She tried smoothing it down but without much luck.

Connor tilted her chin toward him. "I made your hair a mess. So, to me, it's beautiful. You're beautiful."

The edges of her eyes softened, and she kissed his lips softly. "I knew there was a reason I liked you."

She pushed against him until she sat on her legs. "After we shower, I want to go for breakfast." The moment she said the words, she realized her mistake. "I mean, order breakfast. Or I can go pick it up," she rambled.

Connor pulled her into his lap, his erection pressed against her.

She gasped.

"I think breakfast is a great idea." A hand caressed her cheek. "But not until we shower, and talk."

The way her eyes lit up in surprise and delight made him grin. That look was one he wanted to keep on her face for as long as possible.

"Come. The sooner you shower, the sooner I can have breakfast, have our talk and then go to breakfast."

"We're having two breakfasts?" Her voice was laced with confusion.

"Just me." His eyebrows danced suggestively.

"OMG. You're so crazy."

"Crazy for you, pet!" He maneuvered them toward the toilet and turned on the water.

"So where did you want to go for breakfast? Hopefully somewhere your friends won't see you and hound you about the devilishly handsome man you're with."

Regan rolled her eyes. "You mean, the old man they'll think is a professor?"

"Ouch. Wait. Professor and student romance is hot!" He kissed her neck and pressed her body against his. They'd gone to bed naked, but strangely, neither of them felt uncomfortable, or if Regan did, she was hiding it well. He'd seen every inch of her naked, so putting on clothes after seemed redundant. Not to mention a waste of time considering they were about to have sex again.

She guffawed, a hand on her hip. "Only you would think so, Connor." Her gaze settled on the toilet floor. "I have no friends other than Eamon. I'm busy with taking extra classes for both degrees."

He tipped her chin to meet his gaze. "I find that hard to believe."

The vulnerability in her eyes shook him unexpectedly. Regan was always popular and was surrounded by other people her age. But then he realized they were just the children of the people in her parents' circle. Not real friends she'd made herself but those cultivated by her parents. It was a lonely existence and why he and Michael became so close, and likely why she had latched onto them whenever she could. And no doubt, Eamon.

"I don't know how to make friends. How pathetic is that?"

He grasped her face with both hands. "You're not pathetic, Regan. Building friendships is a skill like any, and one I know you'd master if you put your mind to it. And that's because you're brilliant!" He booped her nose playfully.

"You're just saying that because you're biased." But a smile lit up her whole face, taking his breath away and reminding him how truly stunning she was. "Let's shower so you can feed me." She put up her hand as he opened his mouth to speak. "Food, Connor." She shook her head at the smirk playing on his mouth.

He shrugged. "It can be nutritious."

"A woman can't survive on penis alone," she shot back.

The press of their bodies highlighted his growing erection against her stomach. "I beg to differ." His teeth nipped her bottom lip. "Hmm. I bet I could survive on you and that lovely vagina of yours."

Regan pushed away from him and got into the tub. "Food first, and then you can have my vagina to your heart's content."

"How about a snack to tide me over until breakfast?" He stepped in behind her and wrapped his arms around her.

She laughed. "By the time you're finished snacking, breakfast will be over."

Connor pouted.

"We have the rest of the day and all tonight together."

"It's not enough time. And that's why we need to talk."

Her body stilled, as if contemplating his words and whether she'd respond. Finally, she grabbed the bottle of shampoo and poured some into her hands. She turned and put the showerhead against her hair until it was soaked, before lathering it with shampoo. Her gaze didn't meet his, and he watched the water and foam make a path down her body. Even though he offered breakfast, he didn't want to leave the flat. They needed food, but he should've suggested they order in again, so he'd have her all to himself.

He lathered his own hair, knowing why he agreed with them going out. If they stayed inside the room, they wouldn't talk. Only when their hands and mouths were filled with something other than each other's skin was conversation possible. And he wanted to talk about their future. Their short-term one, at least, because at this stage in his life, there were too many variables to offer more—even if he wanted to.

What would she say? Will she be offended by my offer or understand? Worry prickled his brain as every negative outcome ran through it, from her slapping him to pouring her beverage—hopefully not hot coffee—on him. His thoughts kept him distracted from attacking Regan for another round before they could make it out the door. He left her in the tub, toweling himself dry, and dressed in the same clothing minus underwear and the shirt missing buttons thanks to Regan. If he'd known she'd be open to him staying the entire weekend, he would've packed clothes. Honestly, he hadn't thought about anything other than seeing her again and getting his hands, mouth, and dick near her again. There was no plan other than them being together as soon as possible.

Now that he'd spent more time with her, he selfishly wanted more. More of her skin, and her smell. That quirky smile and raucous laughter that escaped just for him. He wanted to hear about her day, her classes, and everything that happened in her life.

Jezzus, I'm pathetic!

Michael would tease him mercifully if he saw and heard him. Well, maybe not because his infatuation was with his sister. He winced, thinking about it, but a little less than the first time he was with Regan. *Was that a good thing?* The less he thought about Michael right now, the better. Otherwise, he might lose his nerve and change his mind about talking to Regan.

Before he could think more on it, she came out of the toilet with a towel around her head and her body. The sight of her knocked the wind out of him. Maybe skipping breakfast was a good idea. They could talk while they ate in her flat.

As if reading his mind, she pointed at him and declared, "Don't even think about it. We're going out to eat so my vagina gets a break from our upcoming sex marathon. If you touch me now, we won't make it out of here." She walked into her closet, pulled out clothes, headed back to the toilet, and slammed the door.

Connor grinned when he heard the lock click. *I guess she's serious about getting breakfast.* He'd feed her a full Irish breakfast, and order food to go so once they returned to her flat, there'd be no leaving until tonight, and only when he had no choice because he needed sleep before going to work tomorrow.

The job was new, so taking a day off wasn't an option. Not if he wanted to impress his boss and move up in the company. This job was part of getting his life back and played a key role in his future with Regan. *Future with Regan.* Those were words he didn't think he'd ever utter. What would Michael and her parents think? In the moment, he didn't care.

Regan exited the toilet, dressed in jeans shorts and a silk blouse, her hair pulled back in a ponytail and light makeup on her face. When she smiled at him, his heart rattled around his chest. A mere look or smile, and he was wrapped around her fingers. Had been for most of the time that they'd known each other.

It took time for him to reconcile the little girl he grew up with to the woman she became. A woman who kissed him and then let him take her virginity. Christ, she practically offered it up on a silver platter, and he lapped it up and was going back for more. But he wanted more than just her body. He coveted her laughter, their talks, and the way she smiled and glanced at him as if he were the best man to walk the earth. He always wanted to be that for her. Right now, he couldn't and shouldn't ask for what he was about to, but he wanted her in the worst way and would do anything to keep her in his life if she wanted him.

Saying he didn't care what Michael and her parents thought was a huge lie. He did care, and that was the problem. The stain that was his life right now shouldn't touch her. She was a rising star on her way to the top. A star he should walk away from after tonight. But he wanted her too badly to let that happen.

He kissed her forehead and pulled her against him. "Let's get you fed."

Chilly winter air blasted them when they exited her flat and walked to a nearby restaurant. The university was close to her flat and the restaurant, so there was a chance someone saw them together, but not people who knew them. And even if they did, he and Regan had been friends for years, so being out in public tonight was no big deal. If he kept his hands to himself, which he had no intention of doing. Her hand was in his the moment they left the building, and he had no desire to let it go.

The shade of oak and holly trees followed them along the sidewalk and people passed them, chatting and laughing and going about their weekend. Connor took a deep breath to block them out, their emotions knocking into him like tree branches. The more he explored being open and receiving stronger and deeper emotions, the more he felt from the people around him. Except Regan. Although sometimes it drove him crazy that he couldn't read her like other people, it was a blessing because he could just be with her without knowing what she was feeling. He was free to be with her in that moment and enjoy her company without the barrage of emotions. It was peaceful in a way he hadn't realized he needed.

To know what swirled in her mind, he merely had to look at her face, because her emotions lived there most of the time. Like now, the brilliant smile plastered to her lips spread warmth through his chest. He squeezed her hand and that grin drifted over him, nailing him in the gut, it was so beautiful. She was so beautiful.

"What?"

Connor shook his head, the words lodged in his throat. He tucked her against him, enjoying not only the feel of her warm body, but the freedom to be here with her without wondering about prying eyes. The chances of anyone seeing them here were very slim. They could hold hands, and he could kiss her and be close to her as if they were lovers instead of keeping the respectable distance of a friend.

As they made their way to the restaurant, laughter flowed easily between them, the way it always did. The moment felt like the many they'd shared over the years, but different because of the intimacy they shared last night and this morning. This was what he wanted from her. Their past relationship mixed in with their new one. While they couldn't be open the way he craved, any relationship with her was better than the silence between them the past few months. That silence wrecked him and made him realize how much he wanted her.

Connor took a seat at the back of the café to give them the privacy he wanted for their talk. Once their drinks and food were ordered, he reached out for her hand.

"This is nice." Regan slipped her hand in his.

He responded with a smile.

"So, what did you want to talk about?" Her voice sounded casual; however, her face was etched in apprehension.

Connor kissed her hand softly. "Us."

Surprise jumped across her face before turning into joy. "Really?"

"But, we have to take it slow."

Regan's eyebrows knotted. "What does that mean? We're already sleeping together, so..."

He chuckled. "Not the kind of slow I meant."

"Oh."

"My life is a mess right now, Regan. And you deserve more than what I can offer."

Her hand touched his cheek. "I don't care about that, Connor. I want to be there for you."

Joy rushed through him. He was right. She wanted to support him, be with him, regardless of the mess that was his life.

He covered her hand with his own. "I know you do, Regan, and you can, but imagine what your parents would say if we told them about us right now."

Doubt crept across her face.

"You know I'm right. And what about Michael? We've been best friends almost our whole lives, and while I know he cares about me, he cares more about you. He'd want you with someone who could support you financially." Connor didn't add how her brother would probably want to throttle him for sleeping with his sister. That was another conversation for another time. And another bridge for them to cross.

"I have my own money," she argued.

"Do you? Or does your father hold those purse strings? At least for a few more years." He didn't know the details of her inheritance, but Michael wouldn't have his until he was thirty. Maybe even later if Shamus had his way. Who knew what hidden clauses were waiting for her.

Her eyes avoided him for several moments. "So where does that leave us?"

"I don't know exactly. Only that I want to spend time with you. We've both got a lot going on in our lives right now. Me with my family and our financial problems, and you with working on two degrees. That doesn't leave a lot of time for a normal relationship."

Sharp blue eyes snapped to his face. "Are you asking for a friend with benefits relationship?"

"Heavens no!"

"Then what kind of relationship are you talking about?"

"The kind we keep a secret from friends and family."

She leaned back in her chair, studying him. "Would we be exclusive?"

"Of course." His jaw tightened, thinking of her with other blokes.

"How long would it remain a secret?"

The one question he didn't have an answer to. "I honestly don't know, Regan." He ran a hand through his hair. "I wish I could give you a timeline, but the truth is I can't. I don't know what's going to happen with my parents and financial situation. I am taking steps to get over this slump as quickly as possible, especially with the bookstore, but I don't have a clear answer."

Disappointment and sadness oozed from her eyes and in the stiffness of her body.

"I understand if this isn't what you want, Regan." Even as the words left his mouth, he regretted them. The last thing he wanted was to give her a way to walk away from him. His heart couldn't take it.

"I don't like keeping our relationship a secret, especially with no deadline in sight, but..." She twirled a lock of hair before pushing it behind her neck. "I want you, Connor. I want to explore what we have, wherever that leads. I understand the relationship will be different. I'm in school and you're rebuilding your life. Seeing each other won't be easy, even with the challenge of my family. Just promise me you'll be honest with me, and I'll do the same. If it gets too difficult, we'll agree to walk away but remain friends."

Friends? Could he remain friends after he knew how she tasted and felt to be his? Could he walk away and let another man take his place? The answer was a resounding hell no! Regan was his, and he had no intention of letting her go, even if he sounded like a world-class stalker. He'd do everything in his power to keep her by his side. Even convince her family he was the best thing to ever happen to her life. And would always be. Regan was it for him.

Pain pierced his heart that she didn't feel the same. That she could walk away.

Their relationship would get difficult. He had no doubt about it, but he had no intention of letting it keep them apart. He'd find a way for her to stay by his side no matter what happened in their lives.

"I promise." Guilt nailed him. Although it wasn't a complete lie, it wasn't the whole truth either. "But I'm going to date the shite out of you, Regan. You're not going to want to give me up," he vowed.

Regan laughed, but before she could respond, their breakfast was placed on the table.

Connor picked up his orange juice and raised it before Regan; she followed his lead. "To the future."

"To the future." She clinked her glass against his.

CHAPTER 15

The bookstore was smaller than he imagined. It was off the main road, which was nice, with a tiny parking space to the side. Just a quaint building by itself. A clothing store, art store, and cafe were in separate buildings across the road. Each store had its own frame, giving the appearance they were completely different buildings. The aesthetics worked surprisingly well. As he walked around the outside of the building, he was pleasantly surprised to find a simple wooden fence painted white separating the bookstore from the parking area.

The fencing didn't surround the bookstore but was open to the wooded area behind the whole building that consisted of large shade trees, shrubbery, and wild grass with weeds pushing through. Directly outside the store was a rustic seating area with overhead vines running along the top of a trellis that provided shade and beauty with its blooming flowers. Seated at the tables were people reading books, drinking tea, and eating food that no doubt came from the café across the street considering the bookstore didn't offer food.

He debated whether to alert the manager of his visit or to observe the staff and the bookstore as a customer to get a feel for the place without people acting proper but going about their day as normal.

Inside, the space was much larger than it appeared from outside. Connor wandered around, admiring the beautiful bookshelves lining the back walls, and a couple of smaller tables covered in neatly stacked books scattered in front of them, leaving spaces in between for people to explore without crowding people near the bookshelves.

Surprisingly, there were no areas with toys or anything for kids, not even books, which he found unusual. Most stores had small areas for kids, but he couldn't find anything. Perhaps it was because of the limited space.

The store had endless potential, although he got the impression his uncle didn't want to expand, but concentrated instead on his local customers. Downstairs, he'd noticed a sign with upcoming events, which were focused on writers and a couple of book signings.

"Can I help you find something?" a petite, middle-aged woman asked politely, gray strands creeping between strands of brown.

"Just looking around."

Keen golden eyes assessed him a little deeper before she responded with, "Let me know if you find what you're looking for."

Does she suspect me? Had the manager told the staff about a new owner? Whether she guessed or not, he would soon find out what the staff knew about him. Rumors wouldn't help the transition, but he knew nothing about running a bookstore—or overseeing staff, for that matter—and hoped to gain a sneak peek of what he was getting into. Getting a read into the staff ahead of time would be helpful. The woman before him was suspicious, but not because she suspected he was the new owner.

"I will. Thank you."

The woman smiled before heading toward another customer who waved her over, leaving Connor to wonder whether she was the manager or the only other staff.

The store only had two full-time staff members, including the manager, and a handful of part-time staff who helped with events and during the store's busy seasons. As far as he could tell, the store practically ran itself and could do without his involvement, but he was curious. Not to mention he didn't believe in handing off responsibility anymore, especially after what happened with his father and their family estate. He had no intention of staying behind the scenes and risk losing the bookstore too, even if it ruffled a few feathers.

Don't be judgmental, Connor! He could hear Regan scolding. She'd be right. He knew nothing about these people, and his fear was his and not theirs. He took several deep breaths to still his mind from his jumble of thoughts and the thoughts of the other people around him in the bookstore. A clear mind was needed before meeting with the manager.

He headed to the front of the store to the checkout area. A woman stood behind the very rustic counter, where he expected to see an old cash register but was pleasantly surprised to see a modern system. She wasn't middle-aged, but somewhere between there and his age. Her blonde hair was pulled into a ponytail, and black, wide-rimmed glasses covered her eyes.

"Una?" Connor asked, and waited for the barrage of emotions to wash over him when their eyes met. Thankfully, only curiosity reached him.

"Yes."

"I'm Connor McGrath."

Dark-blue eyes raked over him before settling back on his face. "You're younger than I thought you'd be."

"Thank you?" *Was it a compliment or insult?* He couldn't tell because her emotions remained in check. *Interesting.*

Coming from around the counter, she extended her hand for him to shake. He took it and smiled, hoping he came across as approachable. He didn't always.

"Nice to finally meet you. I've heard a lot about you from your uncle. I was surprised you never came to visit him."

Her disappointment squeezed him.

"Our families were estranged, so I didn't know him that well. I certainly had no idea he spoke about me. An annual birthday card with twenty pounds was the extent of our relationship."

That declaration seemed to surprise her. It certainly surprised him considering he barely knew this woman, but for some reason he didn't want her to think he was some spoiled kid who'd taken advantage of his uncle's generosity.

"Come. I'll show you around. Have you met Deirdre?"

"Sort of."

A sideways inquiring glance found him. "I was checking out the store incognito." Connor grinned.

"Ah. I'm surprised she didn't follow you around the store to make sure you didn't steal anything."

Connor laughed. "I suspected she would've if a customer didn't ask for help."

Una smiled, lighting up her face, and making her look even younger. "I'll introduce you once I finish showing you around."

He nodded and followed her through the store and listened as she gave him all the details of each area of the store, the back storage area, and an overview of how events worked. She happily answered all his questions, including those about his uncle and what his role was while he was alive. Like him, his uncle believed in being hands-on, but didn't micromanage, as Una was clear to point out.

Connor had suppressed a grin at her subtle, or perhaps not so subtle, hint.

When they returned to the front of the store, Deirdre was checking out a customer. She turned toward him, accusations rolling off her in waves when her gaze met his. "I knew you were up to something."

He gave her his most charming smile. "That's because you're a smart lady."

Deirdre grunted. "Flattery won't gain you any points with me, love."

Una chuckled. "No. She'll make you work for her affection." Her statement implied she had the same treatment at one time. "Deirdre was your uncle's first staff when he opened the bookstore and would've been manager if she'd been interested."

"I'm happy with a paycheck and going home at a decent hour and without having to fill my head up with a bunch of numbers and other headache-causing knowledge."

Una rolled her eyes. "The authors love her, and she's great with keeping them grounded whenever they have a book signing."

"Is that your way of keeping them from getting too big for their britches?" Connor asked in a teasing tone.

"Damn straight! You've written a book, not found the cure for cancer."

Connor chuckled, grateful for the ease of tension that had coiled around them earlier. The interaction was easier without heavy emotions. "I'm glad you're here to remind them."

Deirdre crossed her arms and watched him the way he imagined his grandmother would if she were still alive.

"My role here is only to help. Not change anything."

"So, you don't plan to sell the store then?" Deirdre asked, clearly surprised.

"The lawyer mentioned it might be an option given your age and your family's situation," Una murmured, before pink tainted her cheeks. "I'm sorry. It wasn't the lawyer. I looked you up when I found out who Oisin left the store to."

Was she disappointed it wasn't one of them? Those vibes weren't coming from her, but that didn't mean she wasn't thinking about it. "How long have you been the manager?" Now he was curious to know more about her.

"Not long. Only a couple of years, once your uncle's health started to decline and he couldn't run the store anymore." Her voice dipped to a whisper and her eyes filled with sadness.

Connor didn't need his gift to recognize his uncle meant a lot to both women and his death impacted them more than just his presence as their boss. "This bookstore was dropped in my lap, but I have no intention of selling it anytime soon," he said honestly. The income was a godsend, but he avoided the topic, especially with strangers.

After working out a few logistics with Una, Connor left the store, excited about the people and the store and what it meant for getting closer to the future he wanted. Especially the one with Regan.

CHAPTER 16

The noise coming from the ballroom greeted Connor when he exited the lift. The event was in full bloom, and he hoped Regan wasn't too busy to make sure he was let inside. With what he was wearing, he was certain the person posted to greet guests wouldn't let him in, even with his name on the list. Was he on the list? It was hit or miss these days. Almost a year had passed since his parents were exiled from their social circles; he was still invited to most events, but not all. On those occasions, he attended as Michael's guest. However, with his travel schedule these days, having him as a buffer was proving difficult.

Coming with Regan to these events wasn't an option, and not just because she had to be here early. He'd help her with the setup if he could, but their relationship was still a secret, and it was beginning to create tension between them. That, along with the distance and time between them seeing each other, was wreaking havoc on their connection.

Regan's school schedule was as crammed as his between working full-time and overseeing the bookstore. If not for Una and Deirdre, he'd never get any sleep, much less time to see Regan.

As if the thought of her name made her appear, she burst through a cluster of people and sauntered toward him. The mischievous grin tugging at her lips said she'd seen his outfit. He posed for her as she shook her head.

The dress she wore clung to her body, and he forgot himself and let his gaze linger before catching himself. "You look stunning."

"Really, Connor?" She tipped her head, sidestepping his compliment, the way she usually did.

The top part of his outfit was a full tuxedo while his bottom half was a pair of stylish shorts. A rebuke to a comment Moira made at the last event he attended. "You don't approve?"

"You do have sexy legs, but they don't belong at this event." Regan smirked while admiring his bare legs and dress shoes.

"Are you going to let me in?"

"I shouldn't. My mother will have a fit, but..."

"But you will because you adore me and can't say no."

"That and you made a generous donation. At least that's what I'll tell her."

"Hmm. Maybe I should, so you don't get in trouble with your mum."

"You don't need to make a donation, Connor." Her tone implied he couldn't afford to make one.

The dig at his finances stung, even if it wasn't intended as an insult. It was another source of issues between them whenever Connor tried to take her somewhere expensive. She'd find an excuse to avoid going. At first, he'd thought she was having second thoughts about their relationship and being seen in public with him, but when it was every time, the reason became obvious.

"What is tonight's charity?" Connor asked to avoid the subject. They hadn't seen each other in almost a month, and starting a fight wasn't part of his plans. Those plans included getting her alone and very naked.

"Children."

A vague response as usual. It bugged him that she didn't care enough about her family's charities to learn the details, but he understood her interests were elsewhere. He couldn't fault her for that, especially when the charities were forced on her.

"How long do you have to stay tonight?" Connor whispered against her ear. His hand touched her bare back; he longed to run his fingers along her velvety skin. "You smell amazing."

"Connor," she warned, even as goose bumps raced across her arms and her cheeks flushed. "We're in public."

"I know that, sunshine, but that doesn't mean I won't take every advantage to touch you, even if it's not the way I really want to." A teasing smirk pulled at his lips.

"What are you doing to me, Connor McGrath?"

"Not what I want to." He wiggled his eyebrows.

Regan laughed.

A sound he missed. The sound and her presence drowned out the chaotic emotions swirling around him from everyone in the room. Being around her always calmed him in ways deep breathing alone couldn't accomplish.

"I can't leave for another two hours, so make nice with everyone...and fill up on food, because you're going to need your energy," she whispered in his ear before nailing him with a seductive stare.

"Connor."

He glanced behind Regan to find Moira standing almost next to them. *Had she heard the words her daughter said to him?* Even if she did, Moira Doherty would never make a scene in public. He released the breath he was holding the moment he heard her voice. "Moira. Lovely to see you again."

A disappointing gaze raked over his attire before she responded, "Wish I could say the same about you. If you want to attend these events, Connor, make sure to wear the proper attire. Otherwise, you won't make it past the door next time." She hit Regan with a narrowed sideways glance.

Along with the shake of her head, he caught sight of what appeared to be a smile, but it disappeared so quickly he wasn't sure.

"You do enjoy pushing those boundaries with my parents, don't you?" Regan linked a hand in his arm and led him to a group of people.

Connor returned her comment with a sly smirk. He should be on his best behavior to win her parents over to the idea of him being accepted back into their circle, but riling them gave him too much pleasure to stop now.

As Regan introduced him as Connor McGrath to people at the event and not her boyfriend, his annoyance grew. Although it blocked him sensing the people around him, his own emotions expanded until it stretched his skin to uncomfortable. Even being referred to as a family friend or her brother's best friend would be welcomed rather than just his name, as if he were like everyone else in the room and not someone special to her.

"Are you okay?"

Regan's concerned face greeted him, reminding him that even without the introduction he wanted, she cared about him. That's all that should matter to him. They'd been together almost eight months now. The best months of his life, even with their hectic schedule. The world drifted away when they were together. Nothing mattered but them and being together. Not his financial situation, not their families. Nothing but them. But it couldn't remain that way, no matter how much he wanted it to. Regan wanted more and so did he, but more wasn't possible right now. "I'm fine," he assured her with a smile he hoped reached his eyes.

"You're not, but I'll let it slide, because talking here isn't an option." She led him toward her father, who rolled his eyes and locked his jaw with contempt when he caught sight of Connor's attire.

"You should've been barred at the door."

Connor merely smirked at the man he'd known since he was a kid, one who in some ways was more of a father to him than his own father. The father who reeked of disappointing glares and expected great things from you and your life.

"Mum already lectured him, Da. No need for him to have another one."

"How is the new job, Connor?" Shamus asked.

"Good, sir. The salary along with the income from my uncle's bookstore leaves room to invest." Connor watched Shamus's expression for any sign of approval, but none came as he responded. Shamus was often difficult to read; he could only pick up strong emotions from him. Right now, they were neutral. *Was that good or bad?* With Shamus, you never knew.

"Good. Hopefully you'll do better than your father did."

Next to him, Regan's loud gasp couldn't be missed. "Father!"

Shamus lifted a shoulder. "I'm merely stating the obvious."

Irritation rippled through Connor as he sensed the arrogance radiating from him. "Hopefully I won't have people like the Kellys coming after my money."

The shift from arrogance to anger was swift. Connor's words hit the way he intended, implying that he was like the Kellys, who took advantage of people and their businesses.

"Your father made poor decisions that had nothing to do with the Kellys." Red crept over Shamus's skin.

"Keep telling yourself that, Mr. Doherty. For your sake, I hope you don't make those same mistakes. Otherwise, they'll be coming for you."

Regan gasped again, but this time it was from the venom in his tone. This night was not heading in the direction he hoped. Getting on Shamus and Moira's good side was the goal, but that wasn't going to happen after this conversation. Connor cursed himself for losing his cool and gave Regan an apologetic glance. The disappointment in her eyes was a punch to his gut, along with the way she turned and left him alone with her father.

"You're not good enough for her," Shamus said, implying he knew about their relationship.

Did he? Right now, I don't care. "I know," Connor responded without meeting his eyes, and went after Regan, who'd stormed out the door to the patio. *What was it with her and patios?*

When he found her, she was leaning against the railing, looking up at the sky. She didn't turn when his footsteps echoed on the tile floor, and not even when he stood behind her, his body brushing against her back. "I'm sorry." He kissed her neck and wrapped his arms around her, drawing her flush against his frame.

"I know you are, Connor." Her head rested on his chest. "Annoying my parents isn't going to land you on their good side."

He took a deep breath. "Nothing I say or do is going to get me on their good side. Not when it comes to you, Re."

"You don't know that. They just need time."

"Your father just told me you're too good for me. He's not wrong."

"He says that about everyone," Regan tried to reassure him.

He shook his head. "Regan, I'm not sure telling them about us right now is a good idea. I need more time to get my life in order.

Them accepting me will be hard enough, but with my life still in a mess?"

Regan turned to face him. "Your life's not a mess, Connor. You've got a great job, another income source through the bookstore, and you're debt-free."

He snorted. "That won't matter to your father. He considers my family disgraced and not fit to lick your boots." Her father's words he didn't deserve her said as much. They were true, but it still hurt to hear them. *Would Shamus feel the same if my family hadn't fallen from grace?* But they had, so he'd never know.

Regan giggled. "Really, Connor? You're more than fit to lick every part of me," she teased.

He didn't take the bait. "Regan. I know you don't understand, but I'm still not there yet."

"I hate sneaking around and lying to my family."

The tremble in her voice wrecked him.

Tilting her chin, he locked their gazes. "I do, too, Regan, but waiting will make things easier for you. Telling them now will cause trouble with your parents. I don't want that for you."

A deep sigh escaped her. "I know. I'm just eager to shout from the mountains that we're together."

His mouth captured hers in a deep kiss that said what he couldn't say out loud. That he wanted to shout to the world that she was his too. He wanted nothing more than to hold her hand while they walked into these events and keep his hand at her waist so every man in the room knew she was his and to keep their distance. But that wasn't an option. Not now. At one time he thought never, but Regan was slowly changing his mind and showing him having a relationship was possible.

"I love that you want to tell the world, but I'm worried how the world will respond, Regan. I don't want the nastiness that is surrounding my family still to taint you in any way. And it will if they know we're together. Not to mention how your parents and Michael will react."

"They would get over it," she stated quickly.

"Michael might, after he's knocked me on my ass, but your parents?" His thumb ran along her cheek. "They have the power to make your life difficult, Regan. I don't want that for you. Not when I can't step in and make sure you're taken care of the way you deserve."

Her arms went around his neck. "I don't need to be taken care of, Connor. I can take care of myself."

"You're still in school, Regan. School that your parents are paying for. You live in a flat your parents pay for. All your bills are paid for by them."

Her head dropped, acknowledging he was right.

"And you're years away from your inheritance. One with possible strings you don't know about. We're still young."

A smirk and cheeky raised brow reached him.

"All right. You're still young." He chuckled. "Let's take this time to get our lives in order, so when we do tell everyone, there'll be nothing they can do to keep us apart." His arms squeezed her tightly.

"Okay. But the longer we wait, the harder it'll get when they find out how long we've been together."

He kissed her mouth. "By then it won't matter."

"I wish I had your confidence."

"The only thing I'm confident about is how I feel about you, Regan." He tucked a strand of hair behind her ear. "I'm crazy about you." Those feelings ran deeper, but he didn't want to scare her. She was eighteen and he was...older.

"You are?" Surprise flickered in her baby blues.

The fact she doubted his feelings for her showed he was doing a piss-poor job. His hand cupped her chin. "Beyond a shadow of a doubt. I am over the moon crazy for you, Regan Doherty. From the moment you kissed me at your birthday party, I couldn't stop thinking about you, and although I should probably stay away from you for so many reasons, I can't. You're so far under my skin and in my blood, there's no escaping you. And I don't want to." The words *I love you* hovered, almost coming out, but he held onto them with a death grip.

Not knowing what she was thinking caused fear to race through him in a way it rarely did whenever he was around her. Her emotions were usually written all over her face, and they were now, but not being able to sense her caused doubt to tickle beneath his skin to surface and grow like wildfire through him. She loved him. Told him as much at her birthday party. But doubt made him wonder whether that love was what he told her—a simple crush that was bound to change once she became the amazing woman she was meant to be.

A woman who'd realize he didn't belong in her world anymore. A world she couldn't walk away from. Feck! One she wouldn't want to walk away from once she realized everything that was available to her. She'd leave him behind, like Michael would eventually. Like all his parents' friends had...some slowly and others who'd cut them off instantly.

The thought of her moving on with her life without him burrowed a painful hole in his heart like a drill. She'd realize he was dead weight, and she'd leave him.

"Connor?" Her voice pulled him from the dark spiral of his thoughts.

Turning his attention back to her, he gave her lips a quick kiss. "Let's get back inside before we're missed."

Regan's mouth opened as if to say more, but it closed again when she linked her hands into his offered arm.

"Dance with me so we use up more of your time before you can leave. And so I have an excuse to touch you."

"Okay, just no stepping on my feet this time."

Connor placed a hand on his chest. "Me? I am a dance god."

Regan rolled her eyes as they made their way to the dance floor. "Sure you are. My shoes and toes say otherwise."

"That's because you always want to lead instead of letting me lead," he countered.

"Is that the reason you're going with?" She chuckled.

More than anything, he wanted to run his nose along her neck and kiss her jaw, but he settled for touching her nose with his fingertip instead, like how he used to when she was younger. It irritated the shite out of her. He grinned when she glared at him. "Be careful, Re. Everyone's watching and they won't appreciate the bloodshed."

"You're lucky we're in public. You'd be in trouble otherwise. But be warned, Connor. You're going to pay for that later."

"Hmmm. I like the sound of that. We haven't used toys yet or explored your other naughty bits."

Despite the diminished lighting and not being able to see the flush of her cheeks, his words embarrassed her. *Brilliant!*

An annoyed glare cut through him. "Maybe I'll just stay at my parents' tonight," she threatened.

A hoot of laughter shot from him. "Then I'll climb through your window, pretend I'm a robber, and seduce you."

Regan snorted. "Seduce me in the dark?"

"You won't see my irresistible body, but I know you have a weakness for my dirty words."

Her sharp intake and the smack to his shoulder made him roar with laughter, to the point people around them were staring.

After apologetic gazes from Regan, she yanked him off the dance floor and left him by the bar with a mumbled, "You're incorrigible."

Like a bee pollenating flowers, he watched her move about the groups of people in the crowd. She might not know much about the charities these fundraisers were for, but Regan knew people. From the time she could walk, her mother had been grooming her. There was no childhood of running outside, getting dirty, or being a raucous kid. Her mother—and father—kept her on a tight leash. The rare times she let loose were when she was with him and Michael. Although their parents weren't crazy about it, they allowed it if no other kids were around. They'd been preparing her to become the heiress her mother was.

If this were another century, he had no doubt Regan would've been married off for political or business benefits. He was grateful that was one tradition that didn't seem to run in the Doherty family.

As he watched Regan work the room, the emotions of the people around him washed over him in painful waves, from arrogance to fear and insecurities. It overwhelmed him, and he ordered another drink. He didn't like numbing himself to block them out, but right now he needed it because taking deep breaths wasn't working. As his gifts became sharper, he noticed that stronger emotions were challenging for him to block or not let them affect him. Especially negative ones. They crushed and drained him.

It was the reason he loved staying in with Regan. She was his anchor and his peace. Regan had noticed the change in him, that he was no longer eager to be in social settings or around crowds of people like before. Until he learned to better control blocking their swirling emotions, his only options were to either stay inside or let his gift fade into oblivion.

The second was an option he didn't want to entertain as it meant denying a piece of himself. Something he no longer wanted to do. He had done so for too many years. The woman said he needed to develop his gift, and to him that meant becoming a better empath. But the more he embraced and learned about his gift, the more he realized it meant accepting all parts of himself and not hiding who he was. Like his relationship with Regan, he couldn't shout about his gift to the world, but he could be honest with himself and be who he was without verbally telling people. *Not yet*, whispered in his mind. *Will I ever be at that point?*

Telling his parents hadn't ended well—honestly, his father. His mother didn't say much but encouraged him to keep his "vibes" hidden. Memories of the floggings from his father each time he shared a reading from someone he thought would help still haunted him. Having Michael and Regan reject him made his insides churn with bile. They were the two most important people in his life other than his parents. He couldn't lose them.

Those uncomfortable thoughts were shoved aside as Regan strode toward him. A grin crept across his face as he watched her—the gentle sway of her hips, the subtle smile plastered on her beautiful face as she tipped her head at the people she passed. The way she held herself in a room was that of someone beyond her years. But, then again, being in this world tended to force you to grow up quicker than most. You'd think wealthy parents meant you could enjoy your childhood longer, but no. Not with ambitious parents like the Dohertys. Ambition that wasn't limited to Michael. They pushed Regan just as hard to fit into their mold.

A mold that didn't include him in her life. Her father had said so with his words. A knowing ache nailed him as her father's words rattled around in his brain.

You don't deserve her.

CHAPTER 17

A knock on his office door interrupted Connor's attention from his computer. When he started working with the firm, he was fortunate to get an office instead of a cubicle. Being behind a closed door meant he could shut out the noise of emotions from the people in the office. Noise that made it difficult to focus on work. Some days he wished he could find the woman who insisted he should embrace and grow his gift and ask her what the hell she was thinking. This gift wasn't meant for normal life.

"Come in," Connor greeted while bracing himself for the barrage of emotions from whomever was behind the door.

To his surprise, Shamus strode in and took up all the space in his small office, the way his presence usually did. Annoyance roiled from him in waves, making Connor wonder whether it was for him or another reason. *It's me!*

"Shamus. What can I do you for?" He relaxed in his chair while taking a deep internal breath. With this man, he'd need every single one.

"You need to stop seeing Regan."

Connor raised an eyebrow in surprise. He suspected Shamus knew he was interested in Regan, but his words meant he knew they were together. Or was he guessing? Somehow, he doubted Shamus left anything to chance when it came to his daughter.

"If you don't want me attending your parties, Shamus, you should tell your children not to invite me."

His annoyance turned to anger. "Don't try to deny it. I know everything." The thickening line along his jaw tightened. "I know you're sleeping together."

The words "We're doing more than sleeping together" flashed in his mind, but they stayed behind his lips. He wasn't stupid enough to say them to Shamus. Not if he valued his job—or his life.

"I care about her." Not a lie. *Would he believe me?*

Shamus snorted. "You saw an opportunity and took advantage of a young girl's crush."

"That's not what happened! And for you to think that says you don't know me, Mr. Doherty." A layer of hurt lay beneath his tone. The truth behind their relationship wasn't meant for his ears, but Regan's father thinking he took advantage of her? Bile rose in his stomach.

"She just turned eighteen. Merely a child. You watched her grow up. She was like a little sister to you," he bit back.

"I never saw Regan as a sister. We were…are friends. That friendship is what bloomed into a relationship, Shamus. I've always cared about her. Now it's different." Her nineteenth birthday was around the corner, but that wouldn't matter to Shamus.

The red spreading across his face told Connor he wasn't pacified. "I could have you fired!"

Dread assaulted him, settling like a stone in his stomach. He couldn't afford to lose this job. The money from the bookstore helped, but it wasn't enough to dig himself out of the hole.

Victory raced over his face with the confidence Connor had seen most of his childhood. The man got what he wanted and to hell with everyone else. The thought of losing Regan spread an ache in his heart he knew wouldn't easily go away. "No," he said with conviction.

Surprise flickered in his eyes before it was quickly replaced with fury. It rolled off him and over Connor in waves that stole his breath with its intensity. His hands gripped the armrests, while his eyes closed for a moment to recover.

"I'll give you half a million dollars."

Connor's eyes snapped open and settled on Shamus. The solemn expression etched on his face said he was serious. Was he that repulsed at Regan being with him that he'd pay for him to leave her? He wasn't financially stable as the other men in Shamus' circle right now, but he was a better choice for her than most of those men. He wouldn't treat her like an object or pawn.

"You can't buy me out of Regan's life, Shamus."

To Connor's surprise, he remained calm as he walked over to the window, his back turned so his face—and, amazingly, his emotions—was hidden. Like his daughter, he was a blank slate.

"There's six years between you. That's years of life and experiences. She's still financially dependent on us and you're not financially stable enough to take care of her, and I don't expect that to change anytime soon given the weak stock you came from. Regan needs a strong and wealthy man who won't rely on her inheritance."

The silence stretched for what seemed like forever before Shamus spoke again. "Regan is strong-willed and might walk away from her family and her responsibilities if you asked her. But what kind of life could you offer her? She deserves better—will have better with her family. When she comes to realize that, she'll resent you."

Those words tore through him as swiftly and painfully as the emotions that struck him when Shamus finally turned around.

Regan was in his bones in ways no one ever would be. He knew that as surely as he knew Shamus was right. Although she was mature beyond her years, she was just eighteen and they were at different stages of their lives in so many ways that couldn't be rectified easily. But the thought of giving her up? It was too painful to think about. Regardless of whether it was the right thing to do or not.

"My relationship with your daughter is between us. No one else." The wrongness of those words sounded as hollow as they felt saying them.

"I'll do everything in my power to protect my daughter, Connor. Know that. You've always been a friend of this family, but I won't let you ruin my daughter's life. Think about Michael. Are you willing to lose his friendship, knowing you're seeing his sister behind his back?"

The last comment gave Connor pause. They had discussed telling her family, but he'd planned to tell Michael ahead of time out of respect that he hadn't come to him before he and Regan became involved. To find out from his father in such a way? Their friendship might end. Michael was his only true friend. A rift with her parents was bad enough, but with Michael too?

"Is this about protecting Regan or controlling her?" Connor shot back as that emotion crept between the tight lock Shamus had on his emotions.

Shamus stopped at the open doorway. "Break it off or suffer the consequences. You won't survive them, Connor. You think things are bad now? I will decimate your life in ways you can't begin to imagine. Think of your parents. What will happen to them if you can't financially support them? Your little bookstore won't be safe either. Nothing of yours and what's left of your family will be." The venom rolling from him and his words nailed Connor in the heart and spread over his body like wildfire with no sign of being tamed.

Connor slid off his chair when the door closed and crawled under his desk, taking a deep, calming breath. But the bile from Shamus's words and emotions pressed against him like an elephant sitting on his chest. Immovable and heavier than anything he'd ever experienced before.

Tear stung his eyes as he remembered the day the Kellys took away his family's business and home. Shamus could be just as ruthless, and Connor knew he meant every word. Without his job and the bookstore, he had nothing.

Shamus was forcing him to choose between the woman he loved, a stable life for him and his family, and his friendship with Michael.

He wished he was in the room above the bookstore that was his new home so he could lock himself away from everything and everyone, but especially the blaze scorching through him right now. There was no escape. He was trapped in his office and in his body. The worst part—not every emotion raking through him was from Shamus. He could escape the world around him, but himself? That was another story.

CHAPTER 18

Regan stared at Connor, certain she misunderstood the words leaving his lips. "What?" She needed to hear his words again.

"I think we should take a break. From us," Connor clarified; however, his eyes were everywhere but on her face.

"Are you breaking up with me?" Her heartbeat stuttered in her chest. Things between them had been strained with their busy schedules, but Regan never imagined they'd come to this point. "Why?"

The look on his face said it all. The reasons they shouldn't be together were endless.

"I thought we'd moved past this?"

Connor sighed as he tucked a strand of hair behind her ear. "The reasons are too many to ignore, Regan. I care about you. So much. But you've got your whole life ahead of you and I'll only drag you down."

Tears burned the back of her eyes while her chest felt like someone had hit her with a wrecking ball. The words he "cared about her" were fingernails on the chalkboard. Once again, she'd ripped her heart out and gave it to him, and he "cared about her." The ways he'd held her when they were together and his sweet words that he cared more than he should had fooled her into thinking he felt the same, or eventually would. She should've known better.

"You won't drag me down," she argued, but sensed it was in vain from the resolute expression on his face and distance in his eyes that normally devoured her.

"It'll be years before I recover financially, Regan. I can't expect you to wait around while I get my shite together."

"I'll get my inheritance..."

"No! No woman of mine is going to use their money to help me. That money belongs to you. To your family."

"I thought you were part of my family, Connor." She gulped down the giant lump pressing against her throat.

He shot up, his back toward her, stiff and straight as a rod. When he arrived at her flat, she knew something was off with him, but she hadn't pushed, certain he'd share with a little space. She figured it was something with his parents or the bookstore or maybe work. Other than her, those were the only other things going on in his life. She was wrong.

Dinner was long, drawn-out moments of silence that were usually filled with chatter about their days, from funny events to something or someone who annoyed them. Tonight, only the sounds of clinking silverware and munching kept them company.

When he finally turned to face her, his face held an expression she'd never seen before.

"I lied to you, Regan."

"What do you mean?"

"I didn't want a relationship."

A jolt of shock hit her like lightning. "What?" He was lying. He had to be.

He shoved his hands in his pockets. "After everything that happened with my family, I needed a distraction. I was hurt, angry, and so lost. You were so caring, and I—"

"No. I don't believe you!"

"Now that everything between us is escalating, I knew I couldn't keep lying to you. Lying to myself. I can't have a relationship with you, Regan. Not the way you want. I don't feel the same way. I've been trying to find a way to tell you."

Disbelief and pain pierced her as his words worked over her like a broken, endless Ferris wheel.

I was lost.

You were caring.

I don't feel the same way.

Each word was a spike to her already fragile heart. His reasons explained why he wanted to wait to share their relationship with others. Why he was hesitant to tell her family and his best friend. He was waiting for a way out. A way to tell her he was just using her for comfort? Her body? Her love? All of the above?

Every conversation they shared flowed through her brain like a movie, reminding her everything about their relationship was one-sided. He'd tried to warn her the first night she told him she loved him, but she hadn't listened. She'd thrown herself at him. Given him her body, and every piece of her heart and soul with each moment they shared. She'd offered herself up on a silver platter and he'd lapped it up. Now he didn't need her anymore. The stable job and bookstore provided him with an income and security for him and his family.

Although it wasn't the kind of wealth they had before, it was a step in the right direction. No matter his words that he needed to be more financially stable for them. For her. Merely placating words until he could tell her the truth—he didn't want her. Not the way she wanted him.

The truth of those words sent a tremble through her, starting at her lip and traveling through her like a piece of ice, cooling her veins with reality. Connor didn't love her. Didn't want her.

The vacant, empty look on his face cemented that thought.

Gone were the eyes that looked at her as if she were the most beautiful woman in the world. As if she meant everything to him. The way he did to her.

No more dazzling smiles that lit him up from inside when he saw her after a long time apart. No urgent romp against the door or on the nearest surface because they couldn't wait to reach the bedroom. No more eating together in or out of bed. No walks holding hands and laughing at private jokes only they knew the meaning behind. No coffee dates filled with stolen kisses and starry gazes. All of it was nothing but a means to an end for him. A soft place for him to land and find comfort until he was strong enough on his own. Without her.

"I'm sorry, Regan. I truly am. I never should've started this with you, but—"

"Don't. I can't take any more lies, Connor." Her voice cracked as she lifted a hand. "No more words you don't mean." Regan shot off the couch, strode toward the front door of her flat, and yanked open the door. "Please leave."

"Regan."

The ache in his voice gave her pause.

"You've made your feelings clear, Connor."

"I was hoping we could talk about eventually getting to a place we could be friends again."

Bitter laughter shot from her lips. "Friends? So my parents or Michael won't know what happened between us? That you used me? Lied to me that you wanted me for more than just sex?"

"We were friends before, Regan. That friendship meant something to me."

"Before you lied to me, Connor. You could've been honest from the start and given me the choice to be with you in the ways you needed, but you didn't. You made me believe you cared about me."

"I do care about you," Connor insisted, closing the distance between them.

Regan stepped back, keeping the space she needed. "Just not enough to love me."

The words were a statement, not a question, because she knew the answer. The strong tone of her voice didn't match her insides, which crumbled with each minute that passed. She needed him gone. The last thing she wanted was to break down with him in her space.

"Goodbye, Connor."

The seconds ticked by as she waited for him to walk out the door she held.

The thin line of his lips opened and closed; he graced her with a mournful glance before leaving.

She closed the door quietly behind him, despite wanting to slam it loud enough for him to hear. But if her mother taught her anything, it was grace and silence over making a scene. A lady never acted out of anger but tact.

Once she was certain Connor was no longer in earshot, she slid to the floor and wept, her body shaking with the force of it, as her chest burned as strongly as her eyes.

"Stupid. Stupid. Eejit," sputtered from her lips between sobs.

Never did she imagine Connor would use her the way he did, but people had a way of disappointing you. She knew that better than anyone each time her parents let her down with their unrealistic expectations and pressures of being the perfect daughter.

Connor was supposed to be her safe space. The person she could confide in and be herself without fear of judgment. Now it would just be Michael, or no one, considering he spent more time away working than he did at home. But maybe it was better that way because she'd have to explain why she and Connor weren't talking. Thankfully, with his crazy work schedule and her hectic school calendar, they'd be too busy to see each other. She could avoid the questions about Connor and avoid the man himself. At least there'd be no reason to slip his name on the invite. If Michael wasn't at their fundraisers, he wouldn't be either.

No more hidden glances or stolen moments in dark corners. No more lying to her parents and to herself that her feelings for Connor weren't one-sided. He'd stay on his side of Ireland, and she'd stay on hers.

CHAPTER 19

Regan's heart stopped dead in its tracks before it stuttered to a racing start when she saw Connor seated next to Michael and her parents in the crowd of people at her graduation. Months had passed since they'd seen each other last and three years since Connor broke her heart. No doubt he was here because of Michael, who still hadn't uncovered why she and Connor barely spoke anymore. On the rare occasion they were at the same event, they played it off to their busy lives. When Michael had questioned her, she told him she wasn't a kid anymore and Connor was his best friend, not hers.

The surprised and disappointed look on his face had weighed her with a lot of guilt at the lie, but it was easier than telling him the truth: his best friend had used her and broken her heart. Like her, Michael didn't have a lot of close friends and no matter how much she hated Connor for what he did, she couldn't bring herself to deprive her brother of his best friend.

The sound of her name being called pulled Regan back to the noise of the convention center crammed with people. She rose and strolled across the stage and shook hands, accepting her degrees, and turned so her parents could take a picture. They'd been furious when they learned about her second degree, while her brother was proud and ruffled her hair like a good big brother and told her well done and told her parents it was something for them to brag to their friends about. How many of their kids received two degrees in the same four-year period? That fact pacified their parents.

Eamon waved at her, and she winked when she passed him. She was grateful for his friendship after her relationship with Connor tanked. He was there for her in ways her brother couldn't be.

His friendship was the only one she'd miss when she returned home and back into the controlling fold of her parents. She was looking forward to learning more about the charities and being on the boards; she wasn't looking forward to the control that would come with it through her parents. She only hoped she'd have some freedom with the decisions. She had three more years before she received her inheritance. Three long years before turned twenty-five and have the financial freedom she craved. Although she'd still have the responsibility of her family's charities, relying on her parents for financial support would come to an end.

The first thing she planned to do was what Michael did: buy her own place and get from under her parents' house. If she could afford it on the salary she received, she'd do it in a heartbeat. Her father paid her just enough for a little bit of freedom, but not enough to break away.

The time would pass as quickly as her four years at uni. She was certain of it. She waved gracefully at her parents and Michael, who smirked before taking his seat, but refused to see whether Connor was still there.

The ceremony ended, and she chatted with friends she'd made at school and Eamon, who'd found his way over.

"Eamon. How lovely to see you again," her mother cooed.

Regan resisted the urge to roll her eyes. Her mother had tried on numerous occasions to set them up, despite her insistence they were just friends.

"Join us for dinner," her father stated, giving him no choice.

"Da, I'm sure he has plans with his own family." Michael offered him a way out.

Connor stood on the edge of their circle, hovering.

She tried to ignore him, but his glare scorched her skin. *Why the hell is he still here? Is he coming to dinner with us?*

"I'd love to join you," Eamon said with an easy smile, his arm going around her shoulder casually.

"Wonderful!"

The level of enthusiasm in Moira's voice made her cringe.

Shamus patted Eamon on the back as they headed toward the exit. The only people not excited about Eamon joining them were her, Michael, and Connor. His face appeared neutral, but she knew otherwise.

The car ride to the restaurant was torture, with her parents asking Eamon personal questions. Ones they couldn't ask on the rare occasion he attended events with her. In the closed space, there was no dragging him away and no escaping their questions. Thankfully they didn't ask about their relationship.

Connor and Michael took a different vehicle, which she was grateful for. The thought of being crammed in the car with her parents, Connor, and Eamon wasn't appealing.

When they reached the restaurant, her mother insisted she and Eamon sit next to each other. His arm was resting on the back of her chair when her brother and Connor arrived. He visibly stiffened before quickly catching himself and sitting across from them and next to Michael.

"How are things at the bookstore?" Moira asked.

"Fine." His response was flat as he fixed the napkin, laying it across his lap.

"And he just got a promotion. Much better company to work for. His boss at that other company kept passing him over for promotions," Michael declared. "The man had the nerve to let Connor go when he was bringing in the most money and client. Prick!"

"Michael!" Moira scolded.

A cheeky smirk tugged her brother's lips while her thoughts raced. Michael's revelation about Connor shouldn't surprise her since they didn't share anything about their lives anymore. Barely spoke until forced to because of proximity.

"Seeing anyone, Connor?" Shamus asked, diverting the conversation.

Don't look up. Don't look up. She kept her eyes on the silverware, straightening them even as her heartbeat turned into a slow blip while she waited for him to respond.

"That's none of your business, Shamus." His tone was full of venom.

It was none of hers either. Not anymore. Besides, she didn't want to know. Not knowing was better than thinking about Connor with another woman. Men for her had been few and far between, consisting of botched one-night stands she regretted the next morning and a feeble attempt to move on from Connor.

Dating required time she didn't have to spare in school and, truthfully, her heart wasn't in it. And a small part of her had hoped Connor would realize his mistake and come back to her. Stupid, foolish her.

"What are your plans after university?" Shamus asked Eamon.

"I head overseas to work for one of my family's companies."

Regan coughed to hide her laugh at the crestfallen expression on her mother's face. "How long will you be gone?"

"At least two years, maybe longer. But I will be returning to Ireland regularly."

Moira straightened in the chair, and sunny delight spilled from her mouth with, "How lovely! You and Regan can keep in touch and catch up."

Regan resisted the urge to roll her eyes, knowing she'd get a stern glare from both parents. "We're friends, Mother. Of course we'll keep in touch."

Across the table from her, Connor visibly relaxed, causing her treacherous heart to jump with excitement.

"I thought we were more than friends," Eamon whispered in her ear.

That's when she realized what he was up to. Although she never mentioned her relationship with Connor, Eamon was smart and must've figured it out considering he was the one who helped scrape her off the floor and get back to some semblance of her old self. He was trying to make Connor jealous. *Was it working?*

The bland expression etched on his face said otherwise, but her parents and Michael were here. "We're the best of friends." She smiled up at him brightly and laughed when he booped her nose.

"That's what I thought," he said with a chuckle before returning his attention to her parents, who grinned from ear to ear.

A slight groan escaped as she realized they would hound her about Eamon. As much as she'd miss him, she was grateful he wouldn't be in Ireland and be forced to endure her parents' matchmaking. Eamon had a specific type, and it wasn't her. Their connection was unique, but not one based on attraction. They considered each other siblings. A bond much stronger than a simple male-female attraction that could fade or turn into something that wouldn't last. *We are besties for life*, Regan thought with a smile. A situation that would disappoint her parents, but at this moment she didn't care. Nothing they could do or say would change their relationship, and she couldn't be happier.

Friends were hard to come by in their world, and losing Connor—and, in some ways, Michael—she would've been lonely if it hadn't been for Eamon. Her circle was about to get smaller and lonelier again, but she'd do what she did for the last four years while at school: bury herself in work. She had a lot to learn, and her parents were not easy teachers.

"What charities are we focused on next year, Mum?" Regan asked, eager to steer the conversation in another direction that didn't include her love life, especially with her ex sitting across the table.

"The usual ones, but with the option for you to choose one and give you an opportunity to assess them and see if they'll be a good fit for our foundation." Moira adjusted her plate so it was centered.

A snort came from Connor.

For the first time since they sat at the same table, her eyes shot to his. *Was he mocking my mother? Or me?*

Michael jabbed him in the ribs.

"Do you have a problem with me choosing charities for my family's foundation, Connor?" Her tone dripped with distain.

Embarrassment crawled across his face before it shifted to indifference. "I think your family has a lot to learn about compassion and what charity really means before they can offer it to others."

"Are you trying to imply my family doesn't have compassion?" Regan retorted before going into a spiel about the various charities her family funded and how much they helped their community.

"I'm sure you think you're helping, but what does a little rich girl know about helping less fortunate people?"

Regan and her mother gasped. Connor had never spoken to her that way before. If anything, he'd always defended her.

"Oi. Ease up, mate." Her brother's expression was as shocked as everyone else. "What's gotten into you two? You used to be peas in a pod and now you barely speak to one another and can barely tolerate each other when in the same room."

Regan shrugged, pushing down the burn of tears stinging the back of her eyes. She wouldn't give him the satisfaction of seeing her cry. "We've outgrown each other. That's easy when someone turns into a twat."

"Regan Doherty!" Her mother quickly glanced around to make sure people at the tables near them hadn't heard her.

"That's rich coming from you, Regan. You're the one who's turned into a spoiled rich girl who thinks she can save poor people while knowing nothing about them."

"I know about you," she shot back, cringing inwardly at the wounded expression on Connor's face.

"Enough!" her father said firmly, but quiet enough not to be considered too loud to draw attention. If it wouldn't have caused a scene, she was certain he would have asked Connor to leave.

"We do not argue in public places. Whatever is going on between you two needs to be taken outside, or better yet, not spoken about at all. If you want to ruin your friendship more than it already is, that's your business, but I won't let it disrupt family events."

She and Connor glared at each other before looking away. Her father's words sunk in. They were in public and had a guest—Eamon—who was staring at them with the same shocked expression as her mother.

He'd never heard her raise her voice before, much less insult someone unless it was someone on the telly. His arms went around her shoulders in comfort as he whispered, "Are you all right?"

Regan leaned into him and nodded. Connor's already hard jawline flexed as his eyes bore into her and then Eamon as his brother whispered in his ear. Moments later, he relaxed.

The rest of the dinner was uneventful, with the conversation leaning more toward her moving from her flat on the campus back into her parents' home.

She longed to broach the topic of her eventually buying her own home, but she had a couple more years before that would be possible. In the meantime, she'd bide her time and save whatever money she made from her salary from the foundation. No rent and most of her expenses paid for the next few years—she planned to not only save but start investing too.

Connor called her a spoiled rich girl. *Was that how he see me now? Was that how he always saw me?* She took a sip of the wine in front of her, smiling at a comment Eamon made. The burn of it on her throat was a balm to her bleeding heart. As much as she tried to move on from Connor, seeing him was always a painful reminder that she still loved him. A feeling she hated and wished she could move past.

"When do you leave for Australia, Eamon?" Regan asked, no longer wanting her thoughts to be filled with Connor.

"In a week."

"Excellent. Plenty of time for us to spend together before you leave."

"You should also visit me while I'm there. Australia is beautiful. I could show you around."

She ignored the knowing look between her parents and the raised eyebrow from her brother. Regan's gaze avoided her past obsession completely.

"I think that's a brilliant idea. I've never been there. I'd love to see all the sights."

Moira clapped her hands. "Wonderful. Then it's settled."

Regan and Eamon laughed at her mother's enthusiasm. It was then her gaze moved to Connor, whose eyes held a sadness, before they narrowed and became the indifferent stare he always watched her with now.

An indifference, as if he hadn't been her first love, and everything she ever wanted for her future. As if they hadn't laid in bed together, sharing their hopes and dreams. As if he hadn't been one of her best friends in the whole world. As if she meant nothing to him.

She wished at that moment she could be as indifferent to him, but the ache ripping her heart apart declared he was lodged in there and wasn't going to leave anytime soon.

Every time she saw him, it became painfully clear her heartbreak hadn't healed the way she thought. The way she'd worked so hard to move on from Connor so that looking at him didn't make her heart race or being in the same room with him wasn't an agonizing reminder of everything she'd lost. When he shattered her heart into a million pieces. Each time she thought she'd patched her broken heart, seeing him removed the glue that held it together.

Regan wished she and Eamon were more than friends, that she liked him enough to start a relationship and mend her heart. No other man filled that gap, no matter how many dates she went on and how many seemingly nice men she met. None of them touched her heart the way Connor did.

Soon he'd meet someone special, get married, and have children with them and not her. A lump lodged in her throat; she reached for her glass of wine and gulped it down, ignoring the stern glare from her mother.

"Are you all right?" Eamon whispered, squeezing her shoulder.

Regan tipped her head, afraid speaking would pull out the tears that were stinging behind her eyes and threatening to spill.

A sudden calming warmth reached her, rippling through her from the top of her head, making its way down to the tips of her toes. She chalked it up to Eamon's hands around her, and she leaned into him, kissing his cheek. The best thing about her friendship with Eamon was his ability to know when she needed comfort, the way Connor used to. Although she was grateful his absence would remove her parents' matchmaking, she was going to miss her friend.

The burn of someone's gaze made her look around the people sitting at the table. Connor's blue eyes blazed as they moved from her and then Eamon, who appeared oblivious.

What the hell was that about?

CHAPTER 20

Connor shifted his attention away from Eamon and Regan and focused on the people in the pub, their laughter, the music, and let it flow around and through him, taking parts of the joy to soothe him and push back the earlier tension between him and Shamus.

He wanted to fist-bump his friend when Michael mentioned his old boss letting him go, hoping it would pull some guilt from Shamus, but he sensed nothing but his usual arrogance. Would that arrogance remain if Connor told his family he was the cause of being fired? He never told Michael about that incident or the one where a developer tried to buy the building his uncle left him. Buy was too kind a word. More like muscle him out of it. The company finally relented when they realized their tactics weren't going to work with him. Or maybe it was because he broke up with Regan and Shamus called him off.

As heart wrenching as it was to break her heart the way he did, Shamus pushed it to the point where there was no other choice if he didn't want his parents to end up on the street. If there was enough room for them above the bookstore, he would've held onto Regan longer, but there was barely room for him.

In the end, Shamus got what he wanted, he only wished he hadn't hurt her the way he did, but if there wasn't a firm wedge between them, he would crack and beg her to come back the way he wanted to every time they were in the same room. It was the reason he antagonized her instead of trying to mend at least their friendship.

He stroked the fire by using energy first and amped it up with words if necessary. The pull to her was strong, whether it was to shift closer to her, or speak to her. Connor knew distance between them was necessary until Shamus no longer had control over her and him financially. The moment he broke things off with Regan, he formed a plan. He increased the money he was investing and took risks he wouldn't usually take. Each time he lost more money than he made, he saw the look on Regan's face at his cruel words and he pushed harder.

It was only when he started using his gifts that everything turned around. Using his intuition when it came to investing made the zeros on his bank account balance multiply. While it made him happy and life for his parents easier, there was still an emptiness in his life left because of Regan.

Seeing Eamon with his arms around Regan gutted him. Especially when she thought her sudden calm was from Eamon and not him sending her soothing energy. It wasn't something he did often because to him it was manipulating their emotions and crossing an ethical line. He preferred to keep his own energy boundaries free from the emotions of others—a skill he still struggled with.

Knowing that Eamon cared about her should ease the ache in his heart left since she didn't have their friendship, but it didn't. He was grateful she had someone like Eamon in her life, especially with Michael still traveling so much for work and their shattered friendship, but it still hurt she leaned on someone other than him.

Eamon leaving for Australia for years didn't make him feel better either. She'd need a friend since she was about to start working with her parents. The stress would be a heavy weight for her. One Michael understood himself but was powerless to help much himself since he was in the thick of it too.

The past three years had been long and hard without her in his life. Was it the same for her? He'd like to think so, even with Eamon in her life.

Friendship didn't come easy for either of them and not having each other and only Michael in passing was challenging. The companionship he found with Una and Deirdre at the bookstore helped, along with the people he aided by reading their energies and directing them to the books they needed. Deirdre claimed his uncle had the same talent for helping customers.

The revelation gave him a connection to his uncle he didn't have before, making him realize they likely shared the same gift. A gift his father didn't inherit and why he took his anger out on him. In some ways it helped him to understand his father, but still didn't ease the heartache of knowing he hated him for something beyond his control and that instead of loving and accepting him because he was his child, he turned that resentment into hatred that exploded into physical abuse. Abuse not even his mother protected him from.

While he missed Regan, their breakup pushed him to face memories and pain from his past he might not have if they had stayed together and he had used his relationship with her to avoid the truth.

After lunch he headed to his parents for his routine check-in to see what they needed and how they were doing. He was in the process of finding them a small house with the garden his mother wanted. Despite her husband's wishes, she got a part-time job at a florist, and her transformation was beautiful to watch and feel.

Connor tried everything to help his father, but the more he tried, the worse his father got: angry, drunk, and vicious until he stopped trying and only interacted with his father when necessary.

He shut off the car and sat in the parking lot for several minutes, looking out at the building where his parents were. In a couple of months, he'd be moving them to a home, a small place he was able to purchase for cash further out of the city. It meant a longer commute for him and his mother if she wanted to keep her part-time position, but it had the garden she wanted.

His mother opened the door when he knocked.

"How is he today?" Connor asked, but he suspected the answer.

A small smile tugged at his mother's mouth but didn't reach her eyes. "Same."

When it came to his father, same could mean worse. Connor braced himself with zero expectations, which was safest. "I have good news."

"You got another promotion?" His mother's face lit up.

He chuckled. "No. Better."

"What news?" His father stood in the entryway to their seating area. He'd lost even more weight than the last time he visited, his already thin frame fragile.

Connor forced a smile, pushing back the shock of the changes to his body. According to his mother, the little he ate she crammed with as many nutrients as she could to compensate for how much he drank. She was fighting a losing battle.

"I found you guys a lovely cottage in Dalkey. Nothing fancy, but it comes with a garden and has lots of beautiful places to walk around.

"A garden? How wonderful!"

Rory snorted at his wife's comment. "Maybe now you can quit that foolish job and take care of me like a real wife."

Connor clenched his fist at his side to keep from grabbing his father and shaking him until his bones rattled, especially from the hurt expression on his mother's face.

"A cottage? Really, Connor. With all the money you make you couldn't splurge for something better?"

"You haven't seen the place yet. I'll take you there to see it. I have the keys and you can move in whenever you want." He left off the part about the lease for their flat ending in a couple of months.

"That sounds lovely. Doesn't it, Rory?"

Rory sniffed. "And just how did you pay for this cottage? You won't increase our funds, but you can buy a new place?"

"I can afford the cottage because I didn't increase your funds. All your needs have been met and more."

"So you say." He shuffled to the front door to grab his coat and put on shoes. "Let's go then."

Maeve clapped her hands in excitement before grabbing her own coat.

As they drove to the cottage, his mother chatted about the different kinds of plants and flowers she would grow and asked about the size of the yard. Connor happily answered her questions, caught up in her open joy and enthusiasm.

"You can continue working if you like, Mum."

"Thank you, son, but I'll be fine staying at the cottage and tending to the gardens and going for walks when things get too much." She meant her husband but didn't have to say the words out loud for Connor to understand her.

His father grunted when he pulled up to the cottage while his mother gasped and cried. "It's just like the house from The Holiday."

Connor hadn't considered it when he purchased the place, just wanted something with a yard big enough for his mother to grow a garden, and a home big enough for them to feel less cramped than their flat.

While the cottage didn't have as large as a yard in the front as the cottage in the movie, it did have a cute fence leading up to the home.

His mother's smiles were endless as they strolled through the home before she headed outside to see the gardens. There wasn't much there now, but soon enough his mother would turn it into a blooming oasis.

The rage rolling off his father the longer they roamed the cottage was crippling to the point Connor had to gripped kitchen counter. "Da, please."

"You're just like my brother. Weak."

Connor gaze snapped to his father.

"He couldn't handle strong emotions either. That's why the gift should've been mine." He sat on the large couch in the seating area. "My life would've been different. Better."

A shudder ran through Connor, imagining his father with being able to read and alter the emotions of the people around him. The Kellys would be tame compared to him.

"I tried to mold you to be stronger using your gifts but you were weak. Even beating you didn't help." The raw disappointment behind his words gutted Connor. As a child he remembered the beatings, he didn't remember the reasons behind them. He always thought it was because he had the gift when his father didn't, but that was only one part of it.

"Your mother wouldn't allow me to use you that way. Said you were too young, but when you grew older, I could see you were more like her and not me. Soft and kind. Like Oisin." He adjusted his thin frame, so he leaned against the cushions. "Your grandfather could mold people to his will by manipulating their emotions. Did you know that?"

The revelation stunned Connor. He remembered his grandfather as a loving and kind man.

"That's how he was so successful in business."

"He was a good investor and businessman," he countered, remembering the summers he spent learning from him.

"More than anything he wanted Oisin and I to work together, but Oisin was weak. He couldn't handle the negative emotions. Had a nervous breakdown before disappearing. Leaving our family disgraced," Rory said with disgust, as if the financial ruin he left them in was nothing.

"Our family could've been financial giants. Expanded what the rest of the family had created."

It was then Connor realized his father wanted power and prestige, and like Shamus, the control. Everything that came with wealth.

"You have so much power in the palm of your hands and you waste it on places like this," he waved his hand around while shaking his head. "You're wasting your life on mediocrity." The venom in his tone made Connor catch his breath. "What good are you if an emotion like anger can topple you," he said snidely.

Connor glanced out the window to see his mother looking closely at a tree, even from inside her joyful vibe emanated. He focused on it before taking a seat next to his father.

"Let me enlighten you, old man," his father's nostrils flared. "You wasted your life chasing the wrong things. I found this out the hard way, and when I changed, the numbers in my bank account changed too. It isn't others I needed to change, but myself. I had to remember who I am. Strong negative emotions might affect me now, but I'm getting more powerful than you can imagine because I focus on something better than control and manipulation." Connor placed a hand on his shoulder because he wanted his father to feel the full effect of the emotions he was about to share with him.

The moment his father felt it, his face distorted. "That is the joy your wife is feeling from seeing her new home and garden. Merely a glimpse. Imagine if you felt a smidgen of this emotion every day? How much better is that than rage and hate you chose to feel in your lifetime. Who has wasted their life now, father?"

Connor didn't wait for a response, but stood and headed outside where his mother stood, but the misery radiating from his father was enough for him.

CHAPTER 21

Eight Years Later

Heavy rain hammered against Connor's raincoat as he stood next to his mother, holding a giant umbrella that did nothing to keep them dry against the rain coming at them from every angle. As he watched them lower the casket, numbness spread through his chest, making him wish there was a stronger emotion. The man in the hole was his father, but if he were honest, Rory didn't qualify as one. For this reason, he spent most of his time at the Dohertys' and not just because their kids were his best friends.

As much as Shamus and Moira could be invasive and controlling, they cared. They loved Michael and Regan, even though sometimes it didn't appear that way. Connor knew the difference between a parent who cared and one who despised you and didn't try to hide it. His mother loved him in her own way. He never felt anything close to love from his father.

The sounds of her sobs, the feel of her body shaking against him, and the barrage of emotions that hit him pulled him from his thoughts. Only a handful of people gathered around the hole as they lined up to drop flowers onto the casket. Moira and Regan were among them, along with a few other people from their old circle of friends. No doubt there to appear supporting and civil.

Where was that civility when they were kicked out of their home? Maybe guilt brought them out. Whatever the reason, Connor couldn't bring himself to respond to their words of condolences. He blocked out their emotions, not wanting to feel them or anything right now.

Regan and her mother approached them, Moira taking his mother's hands in her own.

"You call me if you need anything, Maeve."

His mother nodded, although Connor was certain there would be no calls.

In the days leading up to his father's death, the man he knew had withered away to nothing, his body appearing to be eaten away by his misery and jealousy. The more successful Connor became in his job and the bookstore, the more bitter he became until Connor stopped sharing his good news. He never told his father about how much money he made, but there was always more than enough money in their account. At first, he'd happily spent the money, even splurging at times. But as the amount in the account increased over the years, he became belligerent and demanded more money, wasting it on gambling and bad investments.

The emotions of the crowd were quiet because he blocked them. As he developed his gift, he found it easier to obstruct the vibes of people he didn't know than people he knew. Except for Regan. For the life of him, he couldn't figure out what it was about her.

Right now, it didn't matter. What mattered was that she was there. Standing next to her mother and dressed completely in black, she still managed to take his breath away when their gazes met.

Connor stood frozen as she hugged his mother and then wrapped her arms around him. Their mothers held umbrellas as if sensing their need to embrace with both hands.

He hugged her back with everything inside him—all the pain, hurt, guilt, and regret he felt in the moment. Tears poured down his face, thankfully hidden by the rain.

"I'm so sorry, Connor," she whispered, so quietly he barely heard it.

"Thank you for coming today." His voice was raw and broken. He was grateful to have her here, because Michael was halfway around the world traveling for business and couldn't make it back in time for the funeral.

"I wouldn't have missed it for anything." Her hand touched his face.

He didn't deserve her condolence. He'd hurt her in ways that broke not only their relationship but their friendship.

A sad smile tugged at the corners of his mouth. Then she stepped out of his embrace and was the moment was gone.

"I'm so sorry for your loss," Moira shared as she embraced him.

Connor could only nod, overwhelmed by the sudden rush of emotions overflowing from inside him. Pain at losing his father. Hurt that their relationship was never more than suffering and animosity. His father was gone. Forever. And with his death, a gaping hole of remorse made its way in, like a virus spreading through his blood.

The rain eased to a trickle before stopping. He folded up the umbrella as the people who attended the funeral departed. There was no wake because his mother was scared no one would turn up and she didn't want to face the humiliation.

Regan and Moira headed to their car.

Turn around. Let me see your face one more time. A sight that would sustain him until the next time he saw her.

But she climbed into the car and didn't look back, no matter how badly he wanted her to. The distance he'd put between them felt like a chasm too great to breach and he had no one to blame but himself. He'd pushed the woman he loved away and the reasons that were valid years ago hadn't been valid for a long time.

As Connor helped his mother into the car, he vowed to make things better. He couldn't lose any more people in his life, especially those who meant as much to him as Regan did. He and Michael were still close, but them?

The number of people in his life who he trusted and loved was a tiny circle that became smaller when he lost Regan. That changed from this moment on.

Later that evening at his flat, he sat next to the fireplace, a Scotch in hand, when the doorbell rang. He'd offered to stay with his mother, but she insisted she wanted time alone to grieve. Before reluctantly leaving, he dosed her with love and comfort and made her promise to call him. No matter the time, if she needed him.

Once he was home, he was grateful for the time alone. Time, he realized, he needed for himself to dwell on his next steps. His father's affairs were taken care of by Connor as he'd been taking care of his parents for years now.

When he opened the door, he was surprised to find Regan in the doorway.

"I don't want to keep you at a distance anymore, Connor. I miss you. I miss our friendship," she said. Her gorgeous blue eyes that he loved losing himself in held a vulnerability he hadn't seen in years, along with hope.

Shock radiated through him before it settled into relief. "I feel the same. I was coming to see you this week and talk to you."

And say I wanted you back. Those words lodged in his throat. Her clarifying she missed their friendship was what stopped him from pouring his heart open and spilling what was inside. She trusted him enough to restart their friendship, and that was adequate for him. For now.

He'd broken her trust in the worst way and gaining it back wouldn't be easy. He didn't deserve it to be easy. Regan was everything to him. Even if the only relationship he ever had with her was friendship, he'd be grateful and watch from the sidelines of her life, thankful to be a part of it.

Connor opened his arms for her, and she stepped inside his flat and into his embrace. They stood, holding each other, for what seemed like a lifetime. He quietly inhaled her scent instead of letting his fingertips run along her arm just so he could touch her. She smelled the same. Vanilla and something else that was uniquely her. *I missed that smell. Missed her.*

"I missed you, too, and I'm so sorry for hurting you the way I did. I know you won't believe me, but I never stopped caring about you."

"You were so closed-off and distant. That hurt more than you know," was mumbled against his chest.

Not seeing her eyes was killing him. He couldn't read her emotions, but one look in her eyes and he'd know what was in her mind. But before they took that step, he sensed they both needed to get the words out before they lost their nerve.

"I had to keep my distance. If I didn't, you would've ended up in my bed again and that wasn't an option." He didn't share it was because of her father's threats and consequences when he refused to end thing with her.

"What happens now?" Regan whispered.

Connor tilted her chin until their gazes met. "I don't expect things to return the way they were before." His hand slid into her hair, as if no time had passed between them. "I just want to find a new way for us to be in each other's lives without us hurting or ignoring each other. Our friendship is too precious for me to lose it again."

Tears pooled in her eyes. "I feel the same. With Michael away for business so much, not having you in my life has been painful and lonely."

The grief in her words cut him deeply. She needed him, and he wasn't there for her. One thing about their relationship: he was always there for her when she needed him. He'd failed her as a friend.

"Never again. You'll never lose me again."

I'm yours forever! Those were the words he wanted to share, along with kissing her like he used to. Until they were breathless and clinging to each other. But he kept those thoughts to himself. The last thing he wanted to do was to scare her away when she'd just opened the door to having a relationship, even if it was just being friends.

They started as friends the first time around. Maybe this time when their friendship grew into a relationship—and it would...a fact he knew in the deepest parts of his heart—he could make it last for as long as he'd intended when they dated. Forever.

CHAPTER 22

The soft glow from the fireplace in Connor's flat cast shadows across his face, showing off the hint of a beard sprouting. At the funeral, she could see it even with the heavy rain but figured he was busy, and shaving hadn't been a priority. Not that she could blame him. She'd fall apart if one of her parents died.

The relationship with his father was not a good one. That was obvious when they were kids. Connor's father always seemed annoyed with his son, for no apparent reason. Maybe the reasons were only ones they knew, but their relationship—or lack of one—had caused Connor pain. Pain Connor was unable to hide. Even the strained relationship with Shamus was better than the one he had with his father.

"How's your mother doing?" Regan asked, wanting to break the silence, even though silence between them had never been awkward.

"As best as can be expected. I'm thinking of taking her on a trip to distract her and just to get her out of the house. Up to my father's death, she barely left the house. A change of scenery will be good for her, I think."

"I agree, but I wouldn't push her too much, too soon. She'll need time to grieve."

"Agreed. I'll know when she's ready."

What did he mean by that? How could he possibly know when his mother was done grieving? She pushed aside the thoughts and took a deep drink from her wine glass.

She focused instead on why she came over tonight. The truth was, although she'd told Connor she'd missed his friendship and didn't want to continue as they were, those weren't the words she'd planned to say. Her intentions were to offer Connor a bit of comfort and see if he needed someone to talk to. Being alone was good at times like this, but she also knew he'd been more distant and agitated than usual. When she heard about his father's death, she understood the reason.

Part of her wanted to stay away and let him wallow in his grief, but the ache and depth of sorrow in his eyes at the funeral broke her. Connor was hurting and that caused her to hurt too. Hurt in a way she'd been pushing aside for years out of self-preservation after he broke her heart and then acted as if they were nothing to each other. Not even friends. It had taken a lot of time, throwing herself into her work and dating to distract her from how heartbroken she'd felt.

In the beginning, Michael had tried to pry it out of them about what happened between them, but she'd stayed as steadfast in her silence as Connor obviously had. It wasn't something they could tell him. Not without hurting him and their friendship.

What puzzled her was his words that he never stopped caring for her. *Then why did you break my heart?* She burned with the need to ask those words but was terrified that his answer might hurt her worse. Clawing her way back from the heartache wasn't an easy journey, and the last thing she wanted or needed was to open old wounds. Wounds that had scabbed over, because they never really healed. How did you heal from your first love? A love that you saw all the time, reminding you of what you lost and could never have again. Or with anyone else. The pain was one that remained and that she'd learned to live with.

Was his father's death the reason for the change? For him saying that she'd never lose him again? Death had that effect on people. Maybe he was experiencing the same thing. When she spilled that she wanted their friendship back, he'd said he was coming to talk to her. Was he beginning to feel the pain of their lost relationship? Did it take his father's death for him to want a chance? Then what? Things couldn't go back to the way they were. They weren't the same people, and they were in different places in their lives now. She was no longer the naive and hopelessly in love girl with stars in her eyes, thinking that nothing could keep them apart.

Connor ending their relationship had broken something inside her. In some ways, it made her stronger than she realized and willing to stand up for herself with her parents. In the beginning, it had been out of anger and pain, but it gave her confidence in herself that she could make decisions without her parents and that what she thought and wanted mattered.

In other ways, with relationships, she compared every man she tried to date with Connor, and they came up lacking every time. She eventually decided to just serial date rather than let things go further. She convinced herself it was to make sure she found someone who was worthy. Casual sex wasn't appealing to her when she was in university, and certainly not after.

Restoring her friendship with Connor wasn't something she was looking forward to. Being civil was easy when he was distant, but what about when he was his old self again? Charming, caring, and considerate? Listening to her and really seeing her for who she was, and knowing her completely? She wasn't certain she could handle it. If her heart could handle it. Keeping him at a safe distance to prevent him from burrowing his way back into her thoughts, life, and heart? The challenge was one she wasn't sure she could survive. They needed that distance and occasional animosity. Okay, *she* needed it.

Letting Connor back into her life was something she'd have to do carefully and in ways that kept him at arm's length and her heart safe.

"Let's have lunch tomorrow." Connor's baritone voice interrupted her thoughts.

The sincerity and excitement in his eyes tugged at her. "I have meetings."

She had no idea whether that was true or not, but lunch with him tomorrow was too soon. Emotional preparation was needed so she didn't melt at the first sign of any show of affection or kind words. *Geez! I need better people in my life if those are my first thoughts.* And perhaps a boyfriend. Would he believe a fake boyfriend? The excited expression of her parents shut down those thoughts. Her parents were already pushing her to get married. More after she turned twenty-five, constantly reminding her she wasn't getting any younger, especially if she wanted kids. Her reply about adopting one of the millions of kids in foster care didn't go over well.

"No, you don't."

Regan clucked her tongue. "You don't know that."

A smug smirk curled his lips. "You didn't check your phone."

"I have meetings every day," she defended.

"All day?"

"Most of the day. I usually have lunch delivered and work at my desk." That wasn't a complete lie. She tried to get out of the office for lunch, so she didn't end up eating lunch at her desk.

"Fine. I'll come to your office and have lunch with you."

She snorted. "That won't send my parents into a tither."

A pensive expression passed over his face before he continued. "Then let's make it dinner."

She was tempted to say she had a date, but no doubt he'd find a way to make her do something with him. Lunch or dinner in public was a safer bet. The last thing she wanted was being alone with Connor. Tonight was one thing, considering his father's funeral and their apologies and renewed friendship were still in the early stage, but when a bit of time passed and they were spending more time together?

Alone?

A shudder ran through her, laced with fear and anxiety.

"Cold?" He pulled a blanket from the back of the couch and spread it over her legs.

She nodded even though she wasn't cold. The heat from the fireplace was radiating more than enough warmth.

His hand brushed her jean-covered leg after placing the blanket, but it might as well have been her bare leg for the way her body reacted. *This is bad news.* Thankfully he appeared not to notice the shift in her body, but the way his gaze scorched her made her pulse jump and her heartbeat start racing in a way it hadn't in years.

Restoring her friendship with Connor was the worst idea she'd ever had. One that was certain to come back and bite her in the arse. And not in a good way.

CHAPTER 23

Regan rang Connor's doorbell and clenched her hand into a fist to taper her nerves that were making their way from her stomach to the rest of her body. Agreeing to meet at Connor's flat was a huge mistake. Two weeks had passed since his father's funeral and she was running out of excuses.

Connor's actions left her wondering about him in ways she didn't allow herself to think about in a very long time. Too afraid to unbox any feelings for him beyond the relationship they had. Opening her heart to him again was a pain she wasn't willing to explore.

As the years passed, he continued to keep her at arm's length. A realization that had stung in the beginning, but one she replaced with intellectual, and sometimes petty, banter. It worked for them. Anything closer was dangerous for her heart.

Connor's intimate touches had blown everything up with their existing relationship, along with this invitation to dinner, leaving her to wish she had agreed to lunch instead.

Regan wasn't sure how she felt about the change in him toward her but didn't have time to think about it when the door opened.

He checked his watch. "You're right on time."

Regan plunked the bags with wine and the dessert she'd picked up on the way in his hands and brushed past him. "Of course I am.

I'm never late." She circled his flat, her mind racing. *Why the hell did I say it that way?*

She expected a snide remark from him, but no words came. *Nothing! Strange.* She continued perusing his flat after she hung up her coat by the door.

It was quaint, and not what she expected from him. She thought his place would be more modern like Michael, but it had an old-world charm and character with original wood beams and stone flooring. The only modern parts were the appliances and the giant TV. The décor was minimalistic with only a few personal pieces and tons of books, which she expected no less from Connor. He was always a voracious reader.

Connor was in the kitchen, unpacking her bags. "Can I pour you a glass or is drinking not allowed?" A hint of sarcasm in his tone.

There's the Connor I know. "I'll have a glass." She was certain she needed more than one to help her relax for the rest of the evening.

He rummaged in the drawer for a bottle opener while she sat on a barstool at the kitchen counter. He popped the cork and poured her a glass in surprisingly nice wine glasses.

"They were a gift," he offered, as if reading her mind.

"Not from me." She took a sip, noticing for the first time the wine rack built into the kitchen cabinets with a fully stocked amount of wine. Hopefully she didn't insult him by bringing a bottle over.

He grinned. "No. They were from your mother."

"My mother?" *My mother had bought Connor a gift?* She assumed it stopped after he became an adult.

"She sends me a gift every year for Christmas and my birthday."

Ah. Now she understood. "Are you sure it's from my mother and not her personal secretary? You know, the one who makes sure all my father's employees get a gift of some sort."

He gave her a look she hadn't seen on his face before. She couldn't decide whether it was annoyance or hurt.

"Yes. The gifts are too personal to be from anyone else." Connor then turned his attention back to the food on the stove.

"So, what's for dinner?" she asked, changing the subject.

"Beef bourguignon with garlic mash potatoes, green beans, and Yorkshire pudding," Connor replied, not turning but keeping his attention on the stove.

"Really?" she asked, genuinely surprised. When Connor mentioned he could cook, she never imagined anything so fancy. *Wait a minute.* It was then she noticed his shaking shoulders.

"Very funny, Connor. What are you really cooking?"

"Spaghetti with my famous Bolognese sauce."

Not convinced, she stood and walked around the counter to see for herself. The pots were covered so she couldn't say for sure. She reached out to remove the lid, but he pushed her hand away and led her back behind the counter.

"No chef reveals their secrets."

She snorted. "You're no chef."

"You'll change your mind when you taste my food," he assured her. "Why don't you make yourself useful and set the table—or rather, the counter. Everything you need is in the drawers underneath the counter."

Shifting her gaze and position, Regan noticed the set of drawers built into the frame under the counter. Opening them, she found a selection of fancy placemats, napkins, and silverware. She pulled out what appealed to her and set a place for her and Connor.

She glanced over at the dining table that was too huge for just the two of them. "Were these from my mum too? Did you consider she's trying to make sure you and your guests aren't eating on paper plates, or ones with a footy team on them?"

Connor smiled. "The thought had crossed my mind. One set was a housewarming gift. I think it was her way of making sure she had something nice to eat on were she ever invited to dinner at my place."

His back was to her, but occasionally he'd shift so she saw the side of his face. Such a nice face. He hadn't shaved, and his face was covered in a stubble that made him more appealing. The kind of stubble you wanted to feel grazed against your face as he kissed you, or between your inner thighs. A feeling she remembered well. *Regan, stop it!*

She blushed at her own thoughts, knowing those thoughts were a waste of time to indulge in. Still, she couldn't deny he was delicious to look at, whether from the back or the front. Like her brother, he'd kept his muscular physique. A stunningly gorgeous man who caused havoc on her insides whenever he zeroed his gaze on her, even though she'd written him off. Her body and heart hadn't gotten the memo, which was why she never watched him for too long when he was anywhere near her.

Connor grabbed the plate in front of her, piled it with food, and returned it to her. "Voilà!"

On her plate was a large helping of Spaghetti Bolognese and a mountain of freshly grated cheese. She loved cheese. "Are we sharing this or are you just trying to get me fat?"

He grunted. "You're too paranoid about your body to allow yourself to get fat, which is a shame. I've always had a thing for chubby women."

She threw her napkin at him. "Stop lying. I've seen the women you date."

The napkin was returned, neatly folded next to her. He made a plate for himself and took the seat next to her.

They ate in silence, which was rare for them. There was always a topic to argue about, but she realized the silence was nice. She sensed he appreciated it also.

She held off talking about her latest charity project until they opened another bottle of wine.

He paused in the middle of taking a drink of his wine. "Still fooling yourself, Regan? I thought we'd move past that?"

"We do good work," she declared. "People's lives are better."

He touched her hand. "I'm not saying you don't, Regan. I know you put a lot of time and effort into raising money for your charities, but there's more to charity work than that. My comments are not an attack on your efforts. I just know you'll make a bigger impact if you see the faces of the people your charities help and maybe even have it impact you, too. There's no greater feeling than sharing the experience in person with those people. It'll be good for your soul."

Warmth radiated from his hands, and it spread from her hand and across her body. "My soul? Since when did you become so spiritual?"

Connor removed his hand. "I've been exploring a lot about myself for years, what I want from my life and who I want to share my life with." His gaze settled on her.

Was he talking about me? Excitement and dread shot through her at the same time, creating havoc.

"Meditating really opened my eyes to see things in my life I wasn't happy about and wanted to change. Things about who I'd become, the kind of person I wanted to be, and the mark I wanted to leave on the world."

Regan took a long drink from her glass of wine. The night was proving to be heavier than she expected. Heavier than she was ready for. His words hit her hard. Words she'd been dealing with herself recently and why all the charity work didn't seem to fill the void in her life like it had before, nor the men she'd tried to fill it with. Those men were starting to feel like she was dating the same man but with a different face.

Maybe Connor was onto something, but she wasn't ready to say the words out loud. "I'm happy it's working for you." She scooted away from him.

"Don't be afraid of the emotions that surface, Regan, and what you discover about yourself. Maybe you'll even remember the life you once wanted to create for yourself."

Those words took her by surprise.

"What do you know about the life I wanted to create?" As the words left her mouth, she remembered how he knew. They shared everything years ago, especially in those intimate moments. She swallowed the sorrow of the memories and all the things she'd lost. Everything she thought she'd have with him.

"I just want you to be happy, Regan."

She was about to shout at him that she was happy, but he'd know she was lying. He knew her too well for her to lie.

She managed to smile even as her heart thundered in her ears and fear crushed her chest. Did she want to feel the emotions? To what? Remember everything she lost? Feel what she couldn't have? Become a different person? What would that mean for her life now? Unhappiness was creeping into her life in ways it hadn't before, and nothing she'd done in the past changed things.

Maybe it was life's way of saying changes were needed. Something different was needed.

But the minute shift of his interaction with her sent her spiraling in a direction she wasn't sure she wanted or would know what to do if things changed between them. She still guarded her fragile heart around him. She'd worked hard to make it that way. What would happen if his feelings for her changed? Was she misreading his intentions?

"I can see and hear those words turning in your mind. Stop overthinking. Just take it one day at a time and deal with what comes when it comes."

The advice sounded simple enough, but it wouldn't sink in past her ears as much as she wished it would. "That wouldn't make me very good at my job now, would it?"

Regan pushed the chair away from the counter, downed the rest of her wine, and kissed him on the cheek—surprising herself. "Good night, Connor."

"I'll walk you out."

"No need. I've got it."

He stood. "I know you do, but I'll do it anyway."

The heat of his gaze on the back of her neck followed her to the front door and while she put on her coat. She opened the door and turned to face him. "Thanks for dinner and the advice," she said politely, although part of her wished he'd kept the advice to himself as his words would haunt her and send her thoughts spiraling out of control.

The palm of his hand found her face and then cupped her chin. "I see you, Regan. The real you hiding behind the façade you show everyone. She's stunning and vibrant. I just want you to embrace her fully, so you aren't afraid of anyone else seeing her."

Regan's skin turned hot and then cold in the next moment, and she squeezed her knees together to keep her legs from wobbling. His blue eyes bore into her, making her believe his words to the core of her soul. *Holy shite!*

CHAPTER 24

The bustle of the small crowd in the bookstore brought a smile to Regan's face. Having lunch with Connor wasn't at the top of her list of things to do today, but when he suggested the café across from his bookstore, she jumped at the chance.

Guilt swirled in her stomach when she realized this was the first time she'd been here since they broke up. Being around Connor was the last thing she wanted when they were no longer together. She was happy to see it continue to thrive under his management, although that shouldn't surprise her. Connor was a whiz when it came to business and investing. Always had been. That was another reason their breakup was heartbreaking. In her heart, she knew he would be a success, and money wouldn't make or break their relationship. That wasn't enough for him. She wasn't enough for him to wait, which made his reasons even more painful.

Regan shook the thoughts aside. Delving into the past and why he didn't want her anymore didn't matter right now. They had agreed to work on their friendship, not dig up the past. As she strolled about the store, she found him chatting with a woman with two small kids hanging onto her legs. Connor signaled the woman behind the counter, and she came over and distracted the kids. She moved closer so she could observe him.

"I'm looking for a book on childcare," the woman said quietly.

Connor studied her for a moment before pulling a book off the shelf. "Isn't this the book you're really looking for?"

Regan couldn't see the book, but the woman's eyes teared up as she nodded, took the book from his hands, and held it close to her small frame.

His hand rested on her shoulder, giving it a slight squeeze. "It's going to be all right. You're a wonderful mother and your children will remember that more than anything else."

The woman glanced up at him as if he were an angel and brushed tears away from her eyes. "Thank you."

"You're most welcome. Come back anytime if you need help or have questions."

She nodded and ambled over to her kids.

What just happened? How did Connor know the woman needed a different book from the one she asked for? From her expression and their interaction, it wasn't a simple change in book. Just like he said he'd know when his mother was no longer grieving, Connor always seemed to know what she and Michael needed from him when it came to support. She'd always chalked it up to their longtime friendship and being in tune with each other better than anyone. Was it something more?

Before she could dwell on it, his eyes were on her. His expression lit up, and his face softened when he saw her. Like it always did, her traitorous heart skipped, and a goofy grin pulled at her mouth before she could stop it.

"You're right on time," he said, without glancing at his watch.

"How do you know for sure?"

"I've been checking my watch every five minutes." His hand brushed a strand of hair away from her face.

The confession melted her even more, and she swallowed a happy moan before it could escape. The man was sexy trouble on a stick. Dangerous to her eyeballs and her heart. "You've obviously got nothing better to do if you're waiting around for me." She smirked, using humor to calm her nerves.

He graced her with a dazzling smile instead of a witty comeback like she'd hoped. The banter she could handle. It was what their relationship had morphed into over the years. But this sweetness? That's what made her lose her heart to him the first time around.

"Feed me. I've only got a short time before I must get back to work."

"Doesn't being the boss have its perks?"

Regan snorted. "Not with my parents. They're the bosses. I just fill in when they're not there."

"I don't believe that." He opened the front door, placing his palm on her back to guide her through.

They walked a few yards to the café next door and placed their order before heading to the back of the bookstore with the scenic outdoor seating area.

The cool air embraced them as they sat and ate, chatting about the latest charity event, while Connor shared who the next guest author was at the bookstore, insisting she attend this time. He avoided saying how she used to love them. Those words would take them back in time and bring back memories she wanted to forget, because with the memories came the pain she didn't want to remember. Not when she was trying to move forward.

"How did you know what book that woman wanted?" Regan asked as nonchalantly as she could muster. She watched his expression carefully.

Surprise lit his face, before a teasing smirk tugged at his lips. "Customers usually tell me what books they want."

"Not this one. You offered her a different book. She cried when you did," she said tentatively.

Connor leaned back in his chair and studied her for what seemed like forever before responding with, "I just had a feeling she needed more than the book she was asking for." He added, "I can't explain it. I just knew," before she could speak.

She longed to ask him more questions, but there wasn't enough time and what she really wanted to talk to him about what the woman he met while in the Cayman Islands. She was certain Michael told Connor all about her while the only thing she could pry out of him was that she was an exceptional accountant and wonderful woman. Words her brother rarely said about anyone.

But what made her the most curious about this woman was the way her brother's eye lit up when he spoke about her, as well as the hint of sadness that he didn't want to leave her.

"So, what do you know about this woman in Cayman?"

Connor eyes lit up and a wide grin spread split his lips telling her whatever he was going to share about this woman was good.

CHAPTER 25

Connor's gaze drifted as casually as he could manage without bringing attention to the fact he was looking for Regan.

Rachel, the woman Michael recently hired, stood next to him, attempting the same with Michael. She was also the woman he met while buying a new company in the Cayman Islands over a year ago. The same one he'd confessed to meeting in his dream, which was crazy to imagine.

The anxious vibe rolling off her was palpable, even with the emotions of everyone else in the room. These days, it was easier for him to filter which emotions he allowed to affect him, so he was merely observing them rather than allowing them to affect him. Public interactions were easier because of it. Something he was grateful for as he could attend more parties where Regan would be so she was more comfortable in his presence.

They had moved past snide remarks to playful jabs, although she never let it become too personal or intimate, no matter how much he pushed her. Gaining her trust back was a difficult road, but he was happy to wait as long as she needed.

He contained his excitement and racing heart as she burst through a crowd of people, stunning in a dress that hugged her curves. Her hair was styled so it lay in curls on one side of her face. When her eyes settled on him, he lost his breath the way he always did when he first saw her. That never changed in all the years he'd known her.

She hugged Rachel and acknowledged him with a joke about the time he wore shorts to one of their events. A time when they were still together. A glimmer on her wrist caught his attention and he realized she wore the strawberry bracelet he'd given her for her eighteenth birthday. She stopped wearing it when he broke her heart and he hadn't asked her about it, scared of hearing her say she threw it away or, if he knew Regan, gave it away.

The glitter of it on her wrist gave him hope that she was one step closer to forgiving him. One step closer to hearing that he hadn't stopped loving her and hearing the truth behind why he'd broken her heart all those years ago. Only a couple months had passed since they renewed their friendship, but with each day they spent together he was hopeful.

Fear welled inside him. That meant telling her about what her father did. And eventually about his gift. *Would she choose him when she learned the truth or push him away?*

Before he had time to dwell more, Michael found them—or rather, found Rachel. The heated way his eyes raked over her from head to toe made him chuckle. He was doing a shite job of hiding his feelings for her, as she was with him from the longing he saw in her eyes. His gift wasn't needed to see those two only had eyes for each other.

From the way Michael first talked about her, he could tell she was someone special to him. The changes in him attested to that fact, along with the way they gazed at each other.

Regan's teasing comment confirmed his suspicions. They were dating or would be starting soon. Her statement about how intensely Rachel watched Michael walk across the room got him thinking. *Did I watch Regan that way?*

Connor resisted the urge to read Rachel. It sometimes felt like an invasion when he pushed instead of letting it flow over him. The chat they had on the way inside told him she was a good person. The way her eyes devoured Michael spoke volumes about the way she felt about him. Her whole aura lit up when she mentioned him and again when she saw him across the room.

Seeing people's auras was a new and unexpected gift that had manifested itself as he explored and expanded reading people and they had to be in a high emotional state at the time. He tried absorbing the energy in the room if it was negative to remove the tension of the situation, but it nearly crippled him. Not something he wanted to delve into. Auras were easier, even when they were negative. He could observe them without feeling the emotions behind them. What he did excel at was changing the energy of people in the room, calming them or giving them comfort. A talent he cultivated at the bookstore.

A pang of jealousy stabbed him, making him wish he and Regan were at the same place. They were one step closer than before, but still too far for his liking. He wanted to hold her hand when they were together or just touch her. Anywhere. It didn't matter as long as he could. So many times, he'd caught himself before brushing a strand of hair away from her face or tucking it behind her ear. Rushing her wouldn't help. When they came together again, he wanted her forever. If that meant just being around her and seeing her face, hearing her voice, or just sitting near her? He was grateful for anything he got. For now.

Navigating her family was going to be an issue, but right now he wasn't worried about it, knowing they—Shamus and Moira especially—had their hands full with Michael and Rachel. He fully planned to use it to his advantage and take their distraction as time to rebuild his relationship with Regan. Build back the betrayal and heartbreak he'd cause all those years ago.

"Dance with me?" Connor asked when Michael and Rachel were eaten up by the people in the room. The ballroom was packed with people, so it would be easy for them to hide in the crowd without anyone noticing them. And by anyone he meant her parents.

Regan glanced down at his hand and then over the crowd before placing her hand in his and letting him lead her to the dance floor.

Her gasp warmed his ear when he placed his hand on her bare back. He'd never been happier for her to be backless. He'd keep her on the dance floor all night, especially because the only music playing would be soft instrumental.

His fingers longed to graze the soft skin of her back, but instead only his thumb caressed her slowly as he turned them around the wood floor.

Only in this setting could he hold her this close without raising eyebrows and drawing attention, and he was grateful they hosted several parties that gave him this opportunity. With her pressed this close to him, he felt her tremble at his touch, certain her heart was racing as rapidly as his was, being so close and touching her. It was the first time in years he held her this close or even danced with her.

His self-control would've evaporated if they'd been this close after their breakup; he would have caved and begged her to forgive him. There was no way in hell of that happening considering they both avoided each other like the plague—him to get his life together and her time to live her life instead of being tied down with someone her father disapproved of.

Connor shoved thoughts of the past aside. Regan was in his arms, and he was touching her. This moment was meant to be savored, and he intended to do just that and repeat it several times tonight before the party ended.

The song ended and before Connor could talk her into another dance, she blurted, "I need air," and headed toward the large French doors at the back of the room.

He trailed after her, not knowing whether he should give her space. He decided to chase after her, grabbing a glass of champagne from a passing waiter.

Regan was leaning against a railing when he found her, looking out at the dim and scattered lights in the distance. The night was cool, but not chilly, but Connor still removed his jacket and placed it on her shoulders after setting the glass on the railing edge.

A small smile tugged at the corner of her mouth. "Thank you. Always the gentleman."

Not so much with the way his fingers caressed her bare back moments ago. He couldn't resist touching her. Never could whenever she was close to him. The strawberry bracelet on her wrist winked at him.

"You started wearing it again." He touched the bracelet and then started to caress the skin beneath it.

Their eyes locked as she nodded; he felt the slight shiver that ran through her.

"I'm glad." What he really wanted to know was whether she'd forgiven him in her heart and not just with her words. *Was that why the bracelet was on her wrist?* Fear kept him from asking. Knowing the truth might break him, and he wasn't ready to hear what the truth might be. It'd mean letting her go for good as anything other than a friend. He wasn't ready for that. Never would be.

"What are we doing?" Regan whispered, almost as if she were saying it to herself.

Connor closed the space between them. "Enjoying each other's company."

"Is that what we're doing?"

"Did you want it to be more?" He held his breath.

A mixture of emotions crossed her face, making him wish he could read her vibe the way he easily read everyone else. She was conflicted, that much he knew. Was it because she was scared or because she didn't want to hurt his feelings when she rejected him? Had she moved on from how she felt about him?

Sometimes the answer was an easy one, based on the way she responded when he touched her. But other times, the wall she put up was as high and thick as ever. He didn't just want her to remove that wall between them. He wanted to blow it to smithereens. He wanted a second chance at her heart. One that wouldn't end the same way.

"I don't think that's a good idea, Connor."

"Why not?" He'd broken her heart and she was scared.

"Because I'm not the same person anymore."

Her words sliced his heart. She didn't feel the same way about him. "I'm not the same person either, Regan."

He lifted her hand to his chest. "But I still feel the same way about you." His other hand lifted her chin as he lowered his face to hers.

Before their lips touched, she yanked her hands away and pushed against him.

"You keep saying that, Connor, and it scares me. You left me. Broke my heart. Pushed me away when things got hard and without really saying why." She lifted her hand when he started to speak. "It doesn't matter anymore, Connor. We just got our friendship back and that's all we can be." Her voice warbled. "I can't give you anything more."

The resolve of her words shattered him. He'd pushed too much, too soon. She wasn't ready to renew their relationship. The years between then and now didn't matter to her. What happened was still raw for her, and he had no one to blame but himself. He'd let everything he shouldn't have come between them. He was the reason for these walls she was reluctant to bring down.

He longed to comfort her with his touch but resisted. "You're right. I'm sorry for pushing. Too much has happened between us for things to go back the way they were."

She visibly relaxed. "Thank you for understanding, Connor. That means a lot."

"The last thing I want is to make you uncomfortable around me, Regan. I value our friendship too much to let that happen."

"Regan?" Shamus stood by the French doors. His steely eyes moved between them. "You're needed inside." His gaze narrowed with disapproval when he settled on Connor. "You're taking my daughter away from her duties."

"I just needed air, Da. Connor wasn't taking me away from anything. I'll be right there."

Shamus glanced at him again before finally leaving.

"Your father doesn't like me."

Regan shrugged.

It wasn't a secret. Her father liked very few people, and he wasn't one of them—for many reasons.

He escorted her back inside and spent the rest of the night watching Michael and Rachel interact, ecstatic for his friend being reunited with the person he cared deeply for, and observing Regan with the room of businessmen who, in his mind, were vultures. It was evident in the way their beady eyes raked over Regan's body, like she was a prize for them to win. He clenched his fists more times than he remembered, wanting to pull her away, but knowing also that she could handle them. She was strong and had been around men like them all her life. She didn't need him to rescue her. No matter how much he wanted to.

He had bigger issues to worry about. For one, figuring out how to regain Regan's trust while navigating his relationship with her parents. This time around, things would be different. He'd be honest with Michael about his feelings for her. As for her parents? They were another matter completely.

CHAPTER 26

The ding of the doorbell from the front of the store echoed throughout the empty bookstore. The store was closed, so there could only be one person outside—Regan. He'd invited her for dinner tonight to talk about his next bookstore event. She was a whiz at organizing events and reaching the right people.

He glanced at his watch. Fifteen more minutes before the curry was delivered.

"It's open."

The Closed sign was on the door, but he purposefully left it open for Regan as they were meeting shortly after the store closed. Burglaries weren't an issue in this area, and every shop owner looked out for one another.

"Lock the door behind you," he bellowed. He was unpacking a new shipment and wanted to get it logged into the system before tomorrow. The task was therapeutic and didn't require the same amount of brainpower as trading, which was why he enjoyed it.

"I'm back here."

He was shifting one box onto the floor when he heard the clicking of Regan's high heels. She came straight from work most days when they had dinner together. Working long hours was the norm for her, no matter how much he urged her to unwind. Next time he'd suggest an event other than dinner to get her out of her work clothes and her comfort zone.

Since the night of the party, when they almost kissed, she was more relaxed around him, but still wary. As if he'd devour her if she wasn't on her guard. She wasn't wrong, thinking he wanted to devour her, but surprising her wasn't the plan. Alert and aware was how he wanted her when they were together. Eyes wide open so he could read every emotion and not have to wonder.

"Connor. What the hell!" she exclaimed from the doorway.

He glanced around, wondering what she was talking about before he realized he'd taken his shirt off, so it didn't get sweaty.

"Nothing you haven't already seen, sunshine," he smirked before winking.

She rolled her eyes. "If we're going to be friends, you can't go around half naked."

"You used to like me going shirtless," he shot back.

"That was when I was young and naive."

"You weren't that young," he countered, reminding her of the times when they spent most weekends at her old flat naked.

"But I was definitely naive," she murmured, her eyes shifting away from him.

The lingering sadness in her eyes didn't escape him as he reached for his shirt thrown haphazardly over a box in the storeroom.

"I ordered curry for us," Connor said, showing his back as he buttoned up his shirt.

"How did you know that's what I wanted for dinner? Maybe I wanted Chinese."

"Did you?" he challenged, a sly grin tugging his mouth.

She crossed her arms. "No, but that's not the point. You didn't ask."

Connor studied the slight pout of her lips and the defensiveness of her stance. Making decisions was important to her because it was taken away in so many other areas of her life, even as an adult.

"I'll let you choose next time."

"What makes you think there will be a next time?" Her eyes lit with mischief.

"Because we're not done." *We'll never be done.*

Surprise and fear filled her eyes before she shrugged it off and plopped herself onto the nearest surface, which turned out to be a box of books halfway unpacked, so she fell in.

"Aahh!"

Regan's feet were in the air, one of her high heels hanging from her toe, and her arms were on either side of the box, trying unsuccessfully to pull herself out. Her pantsuit jacket was twisted around her as she tried to push herself out of the box.

Connor roared with laughter until he was holding his side.

"Connor! It's not funny!"

He laughed louder.

"Help me up." She waved an arm at him.

"You'd think it was funny if you saw the look on your face when you fell." Arms locked, he pulled her carefully out of the box, her frame falling against his.

The heat from her body and the heavenly smell of vanilla and her own scent engulfed him. His hands grazed along her arms, sending a whirlwind of tingles down his spine and to his cock.

She pushed against him and proceeded to adjust her jacket, giving him a perfect view of the swell of her breasts spilling out above her bra.

She had exquisite breasts. At least from what he remembered, although they appeared a little bigger than when she was in university. No doubt because her small figure had filled out with age.

Filled out in the best way possible. In ways that made his mouth water and forced him to look away before he started fantasizing and remembering how her body felt beneath and around him. Sweet memories that still haunted him at night and more frequently now that they spent more time together.

When they weren't talking, it was easier to find an excuse not to stare at her like she was the most beautiful woman he'd met. To him, she was. From school to now, she'd shifted from a girl into a stunning woman who continued to captivate him.

Being around her since they called a truce was painful in different ways. Instead of the aching longing he'd experienced before, now it was agony being near her and having to keep his hands and eyes to himself. Especially if other people were around.

When they were alone, he stared at her endlessly without worrying about someone catching him. It was the reason he wanted so much time alone with her.

If she caught him staring, she looked away or kept eye contact if they were talking. When she wasn't looking, he memorized every curve on her face and neck. The way her eyes crinkled when she laughed, or her mouth pursed when he annoyed her. Everything about her fascinated him.

As difficult as it was being around her without touching her, he'd rather have her company and spend time with her than for their relationship to return to the awkward, avoidant one they had before.

Two weeks had passed since the party and the moment they almost kissed. That moment lived in his head rent free, with him cursing himself for not pressing his lips to hers before she pulled away. If he had, at least he'd have a new memory of kissing her instead of the ones that were tainted by their painful breakup.

"Food's here." Regan waved her hands in front of his face. "Where did you go?"

A small, sad smile curled his lip. "Nowhere."

He headed to the front door and returned with their dinner. After laying out the boxes on a table in the storeroom, they dug into the food.

"No wine?" she teased.

"I couldn't risk you taking advantage of me."

Regan scoffed. "Not a chance."

"Too bad. You're missing out." His eyebrows wiggled.

She shook her head. "Hardly."

They laughed and chatted like old friends until the food was done.

"Did you want help with the books?" Regan glanced around at the boxes.

"It's getting late. I don't want to keep you up."

"You're not. I'm done for the night and don't have any early meetings."

"Show up late for work?" He tsked. "What will your mother say?"

She laughed. "Nothing. She doesn't get in until ten most mornings."

Connor stood and cleared away the table, throwing the boxes in a nearby bin.

He returned to working on the box he'd started before she arrived and talked her through the steps while he handed her books and pointed where to place them.

At one point, she was on the ladder, and before Connor could warn her to be careful, her heels slipped off the step.

He rushed forward and caught her before she hit the ground. He eased her feet down carefully, his hands tracing the lines of her body until she stood pressed against him. When she didn't move away, his hand trailed up her back to her neck before one hand was buried in her hair and the other one held her waist.

Her soft gasp of breath reverberated through him like a welcome sign.

The blue of her eyes were blown open as he lowered his head and captured her mouth, pressing her body closer to his until her breasts flattened against his chest.

Her mouth was as warm and soft as he remembered, and he groaned when she opened for him, their tongues mingling. His fingers dug into her waist and tugged her hair as he deepened the kiss until she clung to him, moaning.

He lifted his head and nibbled a trail along her jaw and the spot on her neck he knew drove her crazy.

"Connor," she whispered, breathless.

Her hands mangled his shirt as his lips devoured her neck and collarbone before returning to her mouth. He stepped between her legs, moving them against one of the bookshelves and pressing his erection against her core, loving the soft sounds she made.

"God, I missed you." He captured her face in his hands. "I missed you so much." His forehead pressed against hers.

"I missed you, Connor." Her hand touched his face, and he leaned into it, reveling in the warmth and feel of her skin.

Regan's ringtone radiated against the wall of the small space, interrupting their moment.

She uncoiled herself, reached for her phone, and flinched when she saw the name on the screen. "Hi, Mum."

She paused. "Out with a friend." She adjusted her clothing with the hand not holding the phone. "No one you know."

Connor flinched, feeling like he did when they dated and her parents called. Like a dirty secret she didn't want anyone to know about.

"Everything is ready for our meeting tomorrow." She ran a hand through her hair, trying to fix the mess he made and return to normal.

He hated that she was wiping away the signs of their kiss from her body. He wanted her wrinkled clothes and messy hair to remain the same, so she'd remember him and not make him disappear. Her lips were still swollen, and he was grateful for that much.

Although he understood why she couldn't tell her mother she was with him, it still didn't stop the painful ache in his chest. Would she try to erase the kiss they just shared?

To hell with that. He wanted their kiss branded in her mind like her first kiss had been branded on his mind so many years ago.

He wanted her to remember how good they were together...their laughter, easy conversation, and the heat between them.

Each encounter was a step closer to reuniting. And in a deeper way than they'd been before. She was going to be his again. And this time he wasn't letting her go.

CHAPTER 27

Regan sat in stunned silence after her assistant said Connor was waiting to see her. This moment approached faster than she wanted. They kissed weeks ago, and she'd been avoiding him. Ignoring his calls and pretending she wasn't at home when he stopped by. She'd hope to put him off for longer. No such luck.

She stood and smoothed the fabric of her skirt.

Telling her assistant she was unavailable was an option, but she couldn't avoid Connor forever. No matter how badly she wanted to. Speaking with him at her office was safe.

Their kiss had shaken her more than she expected and, if she were honest, more than she wanted it to. It wasn't just a kiss. No matter how much she wanted it to be. A simple kiss was easily brushed off and explained away, but there was nothing simple about Connor's kiss. There was nothing easy about her relationship with him either. A relationship she was beginning to wish she hadn't restarted, no matter how much she missed him.

Being around him was dangerous territory. She knew that and yet she still forged forward, regardless of the minefield waiting for her. A minefield filled with old memories, heartache, and sweetness and naivety she couldn't just brush away even with all the time that had passed and words of forgiveness between them.

The longing in Connor's eyes was dangerous for her heart. Being naive again wasn't an option. She wasn't that girl anymore. Wouldn't allow herself to be pulled into his alluring gravity filled with sweet words, caring gestures, and heated glances. She barely survived him the first time. If he broke her heart again? It would wreck her.

"Show him to conference room one." That room was surrounded by glass walls, removing any temptation from Connor being alone with her. Hopefully her mother stayed in her office during his visit.

Her assistant responded, and Regan waited a few minutes before heading to the conference room herself.

Taking a deep breath for courage, she opened the door.

He stood with his back to the door, glancing outside the window at the view of downtown Dublin. This room had one of the best views, other than her mother's office.

"What can I do for you, Connor?"

His stunning smile caught her off guard. She'd expected animosity, hurt, something. Definitely not being left breathless by his gorgeous smile.

"Have you eaten? I thought I'd take you to lunch."

He closed the distance between them until he was close enough for her to see his concern. She was known for working through lunch.

"I've already eaten." It was a lie, but lunch with him was the worst idea. She was trying to avoid being alone with him.

Her treacherous stomach growled at that moment.

Connor raised an eyebrow.

A blush rushed across her face.

"Lying doesn't become you, Regan," he teased.

"I'm busy," she retorted.

"Then why not say so," he challenged.

She lifted a shoulder noncommittedly.

"You're avoiding me."

"I've been busy," she countered.

"I don't doubt that, but you've also been avoiding me." His hand brushed a strand of hair away from her eyes, touching her cheek before withdrawing. "We kissed and you ran. We need to talk about it."

"There's nothing to talk about."

"If you weren't avoiding me, I'd agree with you. But you are, so a talk is required."

"We've already talked. I told you we can only be friends, but you kissed me, so obviously you didn't get the memo."

A smirk pulled at the corners of his mouth. "You kissed me back and rubbed yourself all over my erection."

Heat rushed to her face as she blurted, "You were the one doing the rubbing."

He laughed. "I was, and you weren't complaining at the time."

She crossed her arms.

His hands rested on her arms. "Do you regret kissing me?"

No. The open and vulnerable expression in his eyes tugged at her. "Us kissing is not a good idea."

"Why?"

"We just renewed our friendship, Connor. Besides, us being a couple didn't work the first time around, what makes you think things will be any different?"

"As you said the other night—we're different. We're not those people from all those years ago. I still care about you, Regan. All I'm asking for is a chance."

Silence stretched between them before Connor added, "I'm not trying to push you for a relationship, Regan. I just want to start over. To see what we could be if we took a chance."

Tears burned at the back of her eyes.

"We can go as slow as you need to. I'm not in a rush. I'm happy to be your friend if you need time to adjust to a relationship with me again." His voice was calming and assuring.

"I don't know, Connor." *I'm still recovering from the first time.* She hadn't realized it until she'd looked into his eyes after their kiss and what she saw there terrified her.

Over the years, she'd gotten accustomed to his distant, cold demeanor. That Connor made it easy to move on with her life. Not to mention burying herself in work. Keeping him at arm's length was easy when all she felt was pain and disdain.

Connor being his sweet and caring self was difficult to resist, especially when her body still reacted the way it did when he touched her. What scared her was she didn't know whether she could trust him again. She'd given so much of herself to him. Lost herself to him so completely that when they broke up, he took pieces of her she still hadn't regained. *Can I put myself through that again?*

"What about Michael? My parents?"

"I plan to tell Michael this time how I feel about you. That I want a relationship with you." He raked a hand through his hair. "Your parents are another matter. Until you know this relationship is what you really want, telling them should wait."

A distant sting pulled at her inside. The same one she felt years ago when she wanted to let the world know about their relationship.

As if reading her mind, Connor asked, "Are you ready to tell them about us now?"

She shook her head. He was right. Until she decided she wanted a relationship with him, telling her parents would only create more trouble than it was worth. The pensive expression on Connor's face drew at a place in her heart she had locked away all those years ago. A place only he'd held the keys to.

"You promised to feed me," she told him, unwrapping her arms.

The smile that lit Connor's face set her heart into a gallop. His smile always had a way of dismantling her insides and turning them to mush.

"I'm at your service, milady. I will give you anything your heart desires." Connor offered his arm.

She ignored his arm and strolled toward the conference room door, yanking it open. "Come along, Romeo." Him offering her heart's desire was exactly what terrified her the most, because her heart's desire was him.

CHAPTER 28

Regan stared at the text message on her phone that was addressed to her and Connor. A reminder about dinner at Michael's tonight. Her heart made an excited leap in her chest. The message sent to them both gave the impression they were a couple. Did Rachel suspect? Did Michael? Had Connor told Michael about them? *There's nothing to tell.*

True to his word, Connor had kept a respectable distance since showing up unexpected at her workplace. When they ate together, he kept the conversation uncomplicated, with no more talk about relationships or her family. She visited him at the bookstore when she could, and he stopped by her office to take her out to lunch or dinner.

He kept his hands to himself, along with his lips. Regan thought she'd be happy without the pressure of knowing he wanted more than friendship, but the truth was she missed that side of him. Missed his blatant attempts to touch her for any reason, whether it was his hand on her back, or holding her hand while they walked, or when they sat across from each other, talking. She missed him sneaking kisses to her neck or forehead each time he found an opening, along with his teasing innuendos and playful remarks about kissing or touching her.

Although she was grateful for him respecting her boundaries, she was also aware, if their relationship was going to shift from friendship to kissing and other intimate activities, she was going to be tasked with taking that step. Her nerves were on edge with the thought of making the first move. Not technically the first move, but a move nonetheless.

Maybe she could drop subtle hints to him and save herself the humiliation. How did she go about doing that? She hadn't needed to flirt or tease someone for so long. Most of the men she'd gone out with made their intentions clear, so there was no need for her to hint at anything.

She jumped in the shower, knowing Connor would be here in an hour to take her to her brother's flat for dinner with Rachel. This was their first dinner together with just the four of them. Had Connor told Michael about them? *What's there to tell?*

Nothing, because they were only friends.

Regan cringed at the word *friend*. The word didn't fit their relationship, which was much more complex. Or maybe, as usual, she was overthinking it. Connor made his intentions clear. She was the unsure one. Their relationship had hit a comfort level better than it'd been in the past, but she kept the wall up between them. She wanted closeness without the consequences if their relationship went sideways again. She wanted guarantees before risking her heart, but this was her and Connor. Like any relationship, there was no reward without risk. Was she willing to risk her heart again?

The hot water washed over her as she stood in the shower long after her hair was washed and her body scrubbed. Connor continued to claim he felt the same way he did all those years ago. Did he forget the words he said to her that shattered her heart? That he'd used her compassion and her body for his own comfort? Those words still stung when she thought about them. *Was I right all those years ago? Did he lie to me? That he loved me as much as I loved him? Or did he finally realize what he lost and wanted me back? But why now? Why after all these years?*

She turned off the shower, grabbed the nearest towel, and wrapped it around her before wiping moisture from the mirror to see her reflection. The woman in the mirror was the same one she saw every day. Smart, confident most days, and competent as hell. But when it came to Connor? She was a blubbering mess. The same way she'd been all those years ago.

She'd declared adamantly to Connor that she was no longer the same woman he knew, and that was true. The way she felt about him hadn't changed the way she'd thought. The way she'd hoped.

No matter how much she thought she'd excavated him from her heart, she was wrong. So very wrong. The only thing that kept him out of there for so long was her hatred for the mess he'd left her in. Hatred of the way he'd hurt and broken her in a way no one, not even her parents, had. He was only one of the two people in the world she trusted deeply, and he broke her trust, shattered her heart, and—worst of all—detonated their friendship. She had hated him for that more than anything. When his friendship was gone, she felt lost and scrambled for months without him. She hadn't realized how much she had relied on him.

Losing herself in work had helped, but it was a slow process that caused her many sleepless nights, caught between crying and yelling angrily at a pillow who couldn't defend itself. In that moment, she realized why giving Connor another chance was so difficult. She needed to know the truth. Why he used her the way he did when she would've gladly offered him the comfort and friendship he needed, and why he'd crushed her with his breakup.

She was afraid to ask him sooner. That maybe the truth would hurt more than she could handle. She'd known Connor all her life and would never think him capable of hurting her the way he did. It made her wonder whether she really knew him at all, or whether she'd been living with an idealistic view of him, and the real him was the man who hurt her.

Believing the best of Connor was proving difficult, along with opening her heart again. She wanted to believe the boy she grew up with, who doted on her, was the same man who she'd seen recently—the one she remembered with rose-colored glasses—and that the distant stranger over the years was the lie. The man he was with her now was the Connor she remembered and fell in love with. A man she could easily fall in love with again if she gave him the chance he asked for. The chance, if she was honest with herself, that she wanted to give not just him but herself as well.

No other man had compared to Connor. All other men had come up short and extremely lacking in all areas. As she dressed, she knew there was only one way for them to move forward.

Moments later, the doorbell rang. Connor was here to pick her up. They decided to drive to Michael's together.

"Hello, sunshine," Connor said when she opened the door and kissed her on the forehead.

The gesture surprised her, considering he'd kept his distance the last few weeks.

"Hello yourself."

"Are you ready to go, or did you want to have a drink before we headed out?" He glanced around her flat.

She checked her watch. They had time, because Michael's flat was a short drive from her place. "Let's have a drink. And a chat."

"That sounds ominous." He shrugged out of his coat and hung it on the rack by the door.

"That depends."

"On what?" He was facing her again and studying her nervously.

"On your answer to my question."

"Only one?" He winked.

"We'll start with one." She sat on the couch and patted the seat next to her.

Connor strolled to the spot cautiously, as if he suspected there was a trap waiting for him.

"What's your question?" He rested his arm along the back once he was seated.

Regan took a deep breath to muster courage she didn't feel. "You've been saying you still feel the same way about me as you did years ago. That you never stopped caring about me."

"Yeah?"

"But when you broke up with me, you told me you didn't feel the same way I did. That you didn't love me. Was that the truth or a lie?"

Connor's expression ran through a series of emotions before ending on contemplative, as if deciding what to say.

"I need to know the truth, Connor. If you want a fresh start with me, I deserve the truth."

He raked a hand through his hair, mussing the controlled style he came with. "You're right. You deserve the truth." He clasped her hands in his. "I never stopped loving you."

Agony ripped at her heart at his words. "Then why would you lie to me?"

"You were going to throw your life away on me. I could see it in your eyes. I know you, Regan. You would've walked away from your life for me. Can't you see? I couldn't let you do that. You deserved so much more than the life I could offer you then."

She yanked her hand away. "That wasn't your decision to make."

"I couldn't let you ruin your life for me."

"But why did you end our friendship too? I was hurt and angry, but you pulled away and acted like even our friendship meant nothing to you." Her voice croaked. "That I meant nothing to you."

Connor pulled her into his lap and held her face in his hands. "You mean everything to me. Being cold and distant was the only way I could be. Otherwise, I would've crumbled and begged you to forgive me when nothing had changed."

"I needed you, Connor."

His hand slipped into her hair. "I know. I'm so sorry, Regan. I know I still don't deserve you after everything I did to hurt you, but I can't stay away from you. Not anymore."

"What's different now?"

"Like you said. We're different people. In a place in our lives where our being together is possible now. No matter what."

"I don't know if I can forgive you." Even as the words left her mouth, she knew they were a lie. In some ways, she'd already forgiven him. Trusting him was another matter.

"I know regaining your trust will take time, Regan. I broke that between us. You can't imagine how sorry I am for that. How breaking that trust and your heart broke me too. I hated myself, and how I destroyed us. But I promise you from the bottom of my heart, I won't betray your trust again."

His forehead rested against her as he held her, waiting for her to either make her decision to give them another chance or move from her position.

Her fingers dug into his hair and pulled tightly. "Don't hurt me again, Connor."

"Never again. At least not on purpose," he promised, kissing her forehead.

She pressed her lips against his and wrapped her arms and legs around him, holding onto him as tightly as he was holding her. Tears trickled down her face when she broke the kiss and rested her head in his neck as he rubbed her back and whispered reassuring words in her ears. They both breathed a deep sigh before their eyes locked.

"So, we're doing this?" His tone was full of hope.

Regan nodded, pressing her lips to his before covering his face in kisses, making him laugh.

"Good. Now let's get going before we're late." He stood, pulling her with him as he guided her toward the door, helping her with her coat before putting his own on.

"I have a feeling they're going to share some big news with us tonight." Regan grabbed her keys from the hook on the wall.

"Bigger than telling your parents they're dating?"

Regan grinned. "I forgot about that. You missed a show."

"So I heard." He opened the car door for her before walking around to the driver's side. "But don't worry. I'll have front row seats when I tell them about us." He winked before starting the car and pulled onto the road toward Michael's flat.

CHAPTER 29

The silence in the car was agonizing, but there were no words for what just happened at Michael's flat. His best friend and Rachel were engaged. Of all the news he expected to hear tonight, that was not it.

Their announcement was worth being there, for the look on Shamus's face. A smirk lit his face. Shamus wasn't supposed to be there, and in Connor's opinion, he got what his interfering ass deserved: a mountain of shock without the awe.

The excitement he reveled in at Shamus' discomfort evaporated when he realized any plans to tell Regan's parents about their relationship was not a good idea. Not now and not anytime soon. The drama stirred by the engagement was evidence of that, along with any plans to tell Michael about his feelings for his sister. The last thing Michael needed was more stress, and considering he had no idea how his best friend would react to the news? Their relationship remaining a secret for a little while was the best idea for everyone.

Besides, telling Shamus would end in a worse disaster than before he found out about his son being engaged to a woman he despised. Well, maybe despise was a bit much, but Shamus certainly didn't think Rachel was worthy of being his son's wife and a part of his family.

Connor raked a hand through his hair.

That was the bad part about all this, making him feel like they were back to square one and in the same situation as they were years ago. Telling her parents right now wasn't an option. Their reaction to the news was going to be bad, but now, with everything going on? Who knew how they'd react? The last thing he wanted was to add pressure to Regan's relationship with her parents.

She had enough pressure between working with her mother and her father's expectations. *What now?* The last thing he wanted was to pretend they weren't together. He'd done enough pretending these past few years. He wanted to take her on real dates and not pretend to be out to dinner with a friend. Hold her hand whenever they were in the same room and kiss her whenever he wanted without worrying about her family's reaction.

Keeping secrets was what destroyed their relationship the first time, and he'd be damned if he'd let that happen this time around.

He took the turn for her flat.

"I don't want to go home, Connor. Not right now."

He started to ask where she wanted him to take her, but he decided to choose for her. He obviously wasn't the only one with too many thoughts in their head. As much as he wanted to take her to his place, it was a terrible idea. If he took her home, he wouldn't want her to leave.

Instead, he turned his car toward a spot he went to when he needed to think or be alone. The time he spent there over the years was significant, especially when he and Regan had a blowup or ignored each other to the point where it was brutal. A place he could collect his thoughts while not having to worry about anyone else's emotions overwhelming his already cluttered thoughts.

He placed the car in park and shifted so he faced her. "What's on your mind, Regan?"

Sadness-filled eyes stared back at him. "You know what tonight means, don't you?"

He longed to pull her into his lap, but the space in the car would be cramped and she needed comfort right now, not have her knee jammed between his seats. So he cupped her face and pressed a soft kiss on her lips. "I do."

"I'm so sorry, Connor." Tears pooled in her eyes.

"Why are you sorry?"

"I know you want to tell everyone about our relationship. I did, too. But now..." Her words trailed off. "This is just like before. I can't go through that again, Connor."

"I know, sunshine. And I'm sorry too." He dropped his hands and opened the car door. "Let's go for a walk."

The cool night air washed over them as they exited the car and headed to the water. Lights flickered in the distance from buildings filled with people going about their evenings. Connor wished they were one of them. Just another couple sitting down to dinner or curling up on the couch to watch a bit of telly before heading to bed. Normal shite that most couples did. But they'd never have a normal relationship. When it was just the two of them, yes—but as soon as their circle expanded?

Connor linked their hands and pulled her as close to him as possible while they strolled along the beach, their shoes sinking in the sand. The sounds of the ocean rolled over him, calming nerves he didn't realize were on edge.

His mind filled with the memory of Shamus' reaction to the engagement. The fury in his eyes and radiating from his body was palpable and drowned out everyone else's emotions to the point he couldn't read them. *Would he react that way to our relationship?*Regan was a grown woman, but Michael was his own man and that made no difference to Shamus, who was a stickler for appearances. Although their situation was nothing like Michael and Rachel's and they weren't in the same place in their lives as they were years ago, that wouldn't matter to Shamus.

Fear and doubt about himself along with Shamus' threats had coerced him into breaking up with Regan. And although at the time it was the only choice, he was no longer that scared man who wasn't financially stable who felt unworthy of love. Of her love. She was everything to him, and nothing would keep them apart again.

Nothing?

He hadn't told Regan about his gift. Something she observed; although she hadn't pushed him about it, she would ask him eventually. She was smart and now that they spent more time together, she was bound to notice. He'd come too far with growing his gift to pull back now.

Regan was not his parents, but could he trust her? Michael didn't know either. Both of them deserved the truth. As he opened his mouth to tell her, he stopped himself. This was just one more obstacle in their way. Between Michael's engagement and their own relationship issues they'd have with her parents, the last thing Regan needed was one more burden.

That's what the knowledge of his gift would be to her. A burden. One for her to overthink about and be wary of every time she was around him. It wouldn't matter that she was unreadable to him. It'd be in the back of her mind. And what about Michael? His plate was full of his own troubles right now.

The thought of Shamus finding out and seeing it as a tool for him to use, especially if he found out about his relationship with Regan, made bile rise in his throat. His already complex relationship with Shamus would implode.

He couldn't risk losing Regan again. His plans were forming brilliantly for them to be together. Not yet. Soon. He'd tell her soon.

"What are we going to do?" Regan asked, pulling him back to the beach and their other problem.

"We continue with our relationship, and when things calm down with Michael and Rachel, we'll tell them."

"That could take forever." The strain in her voice broke his heart.

He pulled her into his arms. "It won't. They love each other very much and once your parents see that, they'll back off and let them live their lives."

"We're talking about Moira and Shamus Doherty."

He laughed. "I know, but I also know they aren't getting any younger and they want the legacy of their family to continue, even if it's not exactly the way they hoped. At least it's not Ciara." He shivered at the thought.

Regan chuckled at his reaction. "She's not that bad."

He gave her a look that asked *Are you crazy?*

"All right, she's not ideal for Michael, but she's just a product of her parents and the life we live."

"You're not like her."

"Maybe not, but I'm not exactly brave either."

His finger lifted her chin. "You're the bravest woman I know. You didn't take crap from me when I broke your heart. You could've crumbled or tried to get revenge. You didn't."

"That makes me stupid."

Connor shook his head. "No. You continued with your life and became the amazing woman I knew you'd be."

"It wasn't that easy, Connor."

"I know, love. And I'm sorry for that. But never say you're not brave, 'cause you are. Brave enough for us to make it through this."

Doubt flickered in her eyes.

"This is nothing like last time. You're not a kid who is financially dependent on their parents, and I'm not a destitute man whose family just lost their fortune. We're not kids anymore, Regan. We are adults who are masters of their lives."

She snorted. "Have you met my parents? My father has already delayed my inheritance for the third time."

Michael had mentioned it to him, since the same thing happened to him, but Connor wasn't worried because he'd take care of her. "Yes. But I also know I'm not letting you go this time. No matter the circumstances, nothing and no one is going to keep me from being with you. Do you feel the same?"

Connor held his breath as he waited for her response.

Those stunning eyes of hers tore into him with an intensity he loved because it showed him her thoughts.

Regan nodded while her arms went around his neck and his went to her hips.

"Then it doesn't matter when we tell your family about our relationship. Once we're good, nothing else matters. Agreed?"

"Yes." She pulled his face toward her and kissed him.

He crushed her to him and kissed her back with every emotion pulsing throughout his body and in his heart.

Although he sensed the doubt between them, interlaced was an assurance that this time around they would hold onto each other and not let the people in their life or the circumstances keep them from being together. No matter the challenges tomorrow brought, they would face it together this time.

As their kiss continued, it morphed into heat. Connor's fingers dug into her back, pressing his erection against her. He groaned when she grinded against him. "I wish I'd taken you to my flat."

"Why didn't you?"

"Because you wouldn't've have made it home tonight."

A radiant smile lit her face. "That sure of yourself, eh?"

"You know how dangerous I am with my hand and my mouth." He playfully smirked and tugged his lips.

"Hmm. I don't know. You're much older now. Maybe you've lost some of your stamina."

"I've only gotten better with age."

Regan shrugged. "So you say."

"You don't believe me?"

"I guess I'll just have to take your word for it."

Connor ran his hands along her side before his fingertips brushed against her blouse, teasing her already taut nipple before pinching it.

Regan gasped.

He licked the shell of her ear before whispering, "You only saw the surface of what I'm capable of, Regan." His hand traveled underneath her skirt until he reached her core and caressed it with this thumb, chuckling as she shivered and her body softened.

"When you're in my bed again, it's going to be so much better than last time. But only when your heart is mine again. And only when you trust me again," he clarified.

He removed his hand, grabbed her hand, and guided them back to his car.

"You are an evil man, Connor."

He grinned wickedly. "You have no idea."

CHAPTER 30

To say the atmosphere around the table was strained would be an understatement. Shamus' and Connor's gazes were locked. As usual, the conversation drifted to Michael and Rachel, and Shamus still expressed his disappointment, even with everything that happened with Michael.

"I still don't understand what you're doing here, Connor. Michael ran off to the Cayman Islands to chase Rachel, so there's no need for you to attend our family brunches."

"I invited him," Regan stated firmly, placing her napkin on her lap to keep from throwing it at her father.

He was the reason Rachel had left in the first place, and Michael had stayed to clean up the mess he made of the business getting involved with the Kellys. Not only that, but Michael also threatened to stay on the island until they accepted Rachel as their future daughter-in-law.

Since then, her parents set their sights on her, trying to pull her back under their control. One she'd only clawed herself away from a few years ago. When she arrived at brunch, her mother said this was a special brunch. Those words were the reason she invited Connor. She needed the buffer, and now that the Michael and Rachel situation was mostly resolved, she wanted to tell her parents about her and Connor.

The time wasn't ideal, but as more time passed, she realized there was never going to be a good time to tell her parents that she was in love with Connor. The boy she grew up with who was their son's best friend, and who they verbally regurgitated would never amount to anything. Much like his father.

Connor had proved them wrong, but she sensed her father was still waiting for him to screw up so he could say *I told you so*.

"Let's keep the peace today, shall we? Our special guest will soon be here."

"Who's this special guest you've been on about, Mum?" The last time her mother was this excited, Eamon was the special guest. But to her parents' disappointment, he'd been called back to Australia and the last time they spoke, he didn't know when he'd return to Ireland.

"You'll see soon enough."

As if on cue, Eamon strolled in, dressed like he was about to go into a business meeting rather than having brunch with friends. His usual laidback smile was absent from his face. Instead of rushing over to hug her, he headed to her parents and shook their hands.

Has this suddenly become a business meeting? From her mother's earlier excitement, she would say no; however, that Eamon circumvented her to greet her parents made her nervous.

"Lovely to see you again, Regan," he said more formally than any conversation they'd ever had and sat on the other side of her. His expression reflected her own nervousness.

Eamon glanced at Connor as if just realizing he was also seated at the table. "I'm sorry, lad—I don't remember your name."

Connor's jawline jumped as he said through gritted teeth, "The name's Connor, and I'm older than you, mate, and hardly your lad."

"Ah, right. Michael's friend."

"Connor is a longtime family friend," Regan added. She tried to catch Eamon's attention with her gaze and ask what the hell was going on, but he avoided looking at her directly for too long and looked nervous as hell. *Something's wrong.*

Fear gurgled in her stomach like acid. She grabbed her glass and took a drink of her mimosa, sensing she was going to need it for whatever the hell her parents had planned.

"I know you're wondering why Eamon was invited." Her father steepled his fingers. "We've come to an arrangement that will benefit both our families."

Regan longed to blurt out that her father hadn't learned his lesson from the last merger he tried to conjure, but she remained silent, waiting like everyone else around the table to hear the news. Well, only her and Connor, because everyone else seemed to know what was going on.

"You and Eamon are set to be married."

"What?!" both she and Connor shouted at the same time.

"The arrangement is a marriage agreement. One that will benefit both our families," her father stated, as if he were talking about the weather.

"Over my dead body," Connor declared.

"That could be arranged," Shamus shot back.

"I'm not marrying you, Eamon. This is madness and you know it." She glared at him as if he were a stranger. "What the hell happened to you? I know you don't want to marry me anymore than I want to marry you."

Eamon remained silent, his gaze shifted to Shamus.

She searched through all their memories over the years, and nothing indicated he wanted anything more than friendship much less want to marry her. Something else was going on. "You never even asked me out or tried to make a move in all the time we were together."

"I wanted us to get to know each other so you'd be open to the prospect of our marriage."

"This is crazy!" She looked to her parents for a clue or understanding. They'd never mentioned anything to her over the years. Her voice cracked as she asked, "How long has this been in the works?"

Shamus glanced at Connor before his gaze returned to her. "Since your eighteenth birthday. Why do you think I've been putting off your inheritance age? You'd never agree to this arrangement if you had the money."

"And you think I'll agree to it now? I have my own money, Father."

Shamus laughed. "You think that's enough to live on for the rest of your life?"

"I can take care of her now, Shamus. I won't let you keep us apart this time," Connor interjected.

"What do you mean by that, Connor?" Regan's face scrunched in confusion.

Shame and regret passed over his face. "I was going to tell you. Your relationship with your father was already strained. I didn't want to make things worse."

"What is he talking about, Da?" Regan asked, the napkin in her lap wrung tightly to keep the anger bubbling beneath the surface from spilling out.

"I'm the reason Connor broke up with you all those years ago."

"What?" Regan shot to her feet. "Why?"

"I'd just signed the agreement with Eamon's family. I saw the way you acted when in the same room. You thought you were being careful and clever. You weren't," Shamus said snidely. "I had you followed to make sure."

The room started to spin around her. *My father was the reason Connor broke my heart?* Her anger turned to rage as she remembered the times her father found her crying. He'd known the reason. And Connor...he'd kept this a secret from her. Her hands shook, not knowing where to direct her wrath first.

"You let my father separate us? Did he give you money?"

"I refused it," Connor said quietly, his eyes sad.

"What did he offer you that made you walk away?"

"He threatened me. My family."

"Shamus!" Moira cried, disappointment burning in her eyes as she glared at her husband.

"I did what I had to for this family."

"You don't care about this family!" Regan yelled. "The only thing you care about is your reputation and the business."

"This business is part of our family. Without it, we are nothing," he retorted.

"You mean you're nothing," she shot back.

"Don't you take that tone with me, young lady. What do you think pays for this luxury you live in, grew up with?"

"That's all you ever care about." She turned to Eamon. "I don't know what my father promised you, but I won't marry you."

"It's not that simple, Regan," her mother said tentatively. "Your inheritance is tied to marriage. Without marriage, you'll never receive your inheritance." She lowered her face. "The way mine was."

"What? You had to marry Father to get your inheritance?"

"Yes. But luckily, I loved your father, so the choice was an easy one."

"What happens if I don't marry Eamon?"

"You lose everything. All the money, your seat on the charities. Everything."

"What?" All the hard work she'd put into building up those charities would be gone. No one would care about them or the people who needed those resources the way she did. She cringed, thinking about someone like Ciara taking them over. They would return to what they were before.

The warmth of Connor's hand touching her pulled her from her thoughts.

"I can take care of you now, Regan. You can walk away."

"You think I'd go anywhere with you now?" Pain etched her face. "You promised not to hurt me again...that I could trust you...all while holding this secret?"

"Regan. I didn't want to hurt you with the truth about your father."

Bitter laughter slipped from her throat. "Hurt me! You broke me. Made me believe I meant nothing to you. For years, Connor. You ripped my heart out, knowing you could've told me the truth, but you didn't. That makes you just as bad, if not worse than my father."

"That's not the only secret he's hiding, Regan." Shamus looked at Connor with contempt. "You haven't told her about your gift. Have you?"

"What gift?" Regan and her mother asked in unison.

Connor's jawline jumped as he glared at Shamus. "How the hell do you know about that?"

Shamus snorted. "Your father and I were friends for years. The man couldn't hold his tongue to save his life. Especially when he was liquored up. He told me all about your gift. That stupid man was jealous of you. Jealous you could read people's emotions while he couldn't. You'd think he'd make good use of it, but he didn't, did he?"

Connor remained silent.

"Since the moment he told me, I started noticing things about you I hadn't before. I knew then you manipulated Regan's feelings for you. You preyed on my daughter. For that reason alone, I couldn't let you be together. She deserved someone better than you. Someone who wasn't tainted and wouldn't taint my family."

Betrayal ripped through her. That's what she'd been noticing about Connor when he was at the bookstore. It was the only time he seemed to be different. How many times had he used her emotions against her, or for his own purpose? Tears burned her eyes. "You promised me things would be different this time, Connor. But I guess that's what you do best. Lie."

Connor stood and took tentative steps toward her, as if he were afraid, she would bolt if he moved too quickly. "I was going to tell you, Regan. I swear!"

Her laughter was mirthless. "How convenient, but a little too late, Connor. I never want to see your face or speak to you again." She backed away from him and rushed out of the room.

CHAPTER 31

Connor watched Regan race out of the room. *I'm a feckin' fool!* Not only did he withhold the truth from her, but he also kept secrets. It didn't matter he had reasons for waiting so long to tell her. *Will she forgive me?*

There were too many already, but that didn't matter. He swore not to let her go again, and if that meant groveling for her forgiveness and waiting years to earn back her trust? Then that's what he'd do. Regan was his heart. His everything. And he wouldn't let anyone, not even him, keep them apart.

"Regan," he called, ready to go after her, when Shamus and Eamon stepped in front of him.

"Unless you want to lose an arm, you'll step out of my way," Connor warned.

"Regan is no longer your responsibility," Eamon said coolly, as if Regan hadn't said she'd never marry him.

Connor's laughter was bitter. "She was never my responsibility." His gaze settled on Shamus. "The joke's on you, Shamus. Regan was the only person I could never read. I never knew how she felt about me. All I knew was how I felt about her. I love her. I've always loved her."

Surprise flickered in his eyes before it vanished. "She was never meant to be yours."

"That's always been your problem, Shamus. You want to control everything and everyone, but control is an illusion. If you force Regan to marry him," he pointed with his chin at Eamon, "you will lose both your children. And then what will happen to your legacy? You will be the last one to claim it."

Shamus' jawline clenched. "Get out!"

Connor's gaze narrowed on Eamon. "She trusted you as a friend, and you betrayed her. If she won't forgive the man she loves, do you think she'll forgive you for deceiving her? I had my reasons. What are yours?"

"Regan loves her parents and believes in family. That's all the reason I need." Despite his confident words, guilt flickered in Eamon's eyes, making Connor wonder whether Shamus was pulling his strings.

Connor laughed. "All that time you spent with her, and you learned nothing about her. You're more of an idiot than I am, mate." His attention turned to Moira. "A lovely brunch as always, Moira. My apologies for causing a scene."

Moira's shocked expression that'd been on her face while watching a regular family brunch morph into a dramatic fiasco softened. Usually, she was the voice of reason, but the secrets revealed kept her silent. Her head tipped.

With the heaviness of everyone's glare on his back, Connor left the room, his heart weighted with the hurt he'd caused Regan by waiting too long to share his secrets with her. If she never spoke to him again, he had no one to blame but himself.

He slid into his car and pulled out of her parents' driveway, toward the bookstore. His flat held too many memories of them together, and although the store did too, the people there would give him the distraction he needed. Helping others would soothe his aching heart and drown out his own swirling emotions with theirs.

In the moment, he wished more than ever he could read Regan's emotions. At least then he'd know whether there was any lingering love for him beneath the surface of hurt, betrayal, and rage churning in her eyes before she stormed out.

You're a right Eejit! All that time and effort it took to gain back her trust, and he'd thrown it away because of his own fear. Fear he thought he'd conquered when he confronted his father. But he was wrong. If his own family couldn't accept him, what chance did he have of other people in his life accepting him?

Regan isn't your father!

Although that might be true, that didn't stop doubts flooding his mind each time he opened his mouth to tell her about his gift. He'd told Michael, but that was only to save his relationship with Rachel, whose gift was revealed in an explosive moment. One that was in front of Shamus.

Even Michael struggled with swallowing the truth about Rachel's abilities. She was the woman he loved. He'd lost her because of it but chased her back to her home to repair the damage he inflicted on her and their relationship. But that was only after cleaning up the mess Declan's family almost caused.

Connor still couldn't believe Regan's parents had signed an agreement for their daughter to be in an arranged marriage. All this time, he thought her parents wouldn't stoop to such levels as to bargain their daughter's life away for the family and probably business too. He was horribly wrong.

What was Regan feeling right now? Not only did she find out her parents betrayed her, but that the man she loved had lied to her when he promised not to. Everyone in her life who was supposed to love and support her had failed her. Himself included.

He parked the car and stared at the bookstore. People sat at the outside tables, enjoying the weather and beautiful scenery surrounding them, smiling and happy. He'd never been jealous of them until now, remembering the times he and Regan had sat out there sharing lunch, tidbits about their day, and imparting funny stories. All those moments were gone, and he might never get them back.

Pulling his phone from his pocket, he typed a message to Regan because she wouldn't answer his call. *I'm so sorry, love. I was going to tell you. I have no excuse but please know it was because of my fears and not you. Never you!* The message remained unread. He hoped she didn't block his number.

Getting out of the car, he slid his phone back in his pocket and headed inside the bookstore. His only happy place other than being with Regan. Una, who was behind the counter, waved her hello as he walked around the store, looking for people to help.

If Regan refused to forgive him and give them another chance, this bookstore would become his life because helping people would be the only joy left in his life.

CHAPTER 32

Connor dialed Michael's number, dread pressing against him like an elephant sitting on his chest.

"Connor. What's the crack?"

"Tell him I said hello," Rachel said groggily in the background.

"Hi to Rachel from me."

"Do you have any idea what time it is, mate?"

"Shite. I completely forgot about the time difference. What time is it there?"

"Too early to be calling, but I figured it must be important."

"I have something to tell you, and I figured it was better if there was distance between us."

"Why's that?" Michael asked, an edge to his tone.

"I've been seeing your sister for the past few months."

There was a long silence before "I told you so" came from Rachel.

"Why didn't you tell me sooner?"

"You had enough on your plate with your da and your relationship with Rachel, the merger with the Kellys, and then when all hell broke loose..."

"Understandable."

Connor took a deep breath, wishing he could gauge Michael's emotions over the phone.

"There's more." Here was the moment when he could lose Michael's friendship forever. "We dated when she was in uni for almost a year."

"What?! What the hell, Connor?"

"That explains my dream," Rachel said.

"What dream?" Michael asked.

"I'll tell you later. Finish your conversation," she urged.

"You dated my sister for almost a year, and you didn't tell me about it? Why the hell not?"

"It's complicated."

"She's my sister and you're my best friend. I deserved to know. I always knew Regan had a crush on you, but I didn't think you'd take advantage of her crush," Michael yelled.

"She was the one who kissed me first and then tried to..." The last thing Michael needed to hear was a story about his sister offering him her virginity.

"You're an adult. She was just a child!" Michael yelled.

Connor moved the phone away from his ear to save his ears. "She was eighteen, Michael. And trust me. It wasn't easy for me."

"Not so hard—you dated for a year. Did my father know? Of course he didn't. He would've ruined you."

"Actually, he did know. He's the reason I broke things off with Regan. He almost ruined me."

"Is that why your relationship changed suddenly?"

"Yes."

"Jezzus! I thought it was because my parents were starting to rub off on Regan and pushing her to distance herself from you since she was getting older and with what happened to your family. I should've known better."

"I hurt her because I didn't tell her he was the reason." Shamus wasn't the only reason, but it made it easier to force Regan to make the decision.

"No doubt my father's idea." Michael's tone was laced with annoyance. "How's he handling you dating again?"

What do I say? That I screwed up again? Yes. He needed someone to talk to about it. He needed his best friend, even if the woman he loved was his sister.

"I messed up again."

"You men!" Rachel said in the background.

"Are you going to listen to the entire conversation?"

"I'm a package deal!" she shouted.

He and Michael chuckled.

"The best package ever."

Connor heard what sounded like kissing. "If you two start making out over the phone, I'm hanging up."

"It was just a kiss, Connor," Rachel tried to assure him.

"We are naked."

"Michael!"

Connor made a gagging sound. "I really didn't need that image in my head."

Laughing came through the phone.

"So how did you screw up?" Michael asked.

"I didn't tell her about my gift or that Shamus was the reason I broke things off after promising her I wouldn't lie to her again."

The silence stretched for so long, Connor wasn't sure Michael was still on the line.

"What's your gift?" Rachel broke the silence first.

"The easiest explanation is I'm an empath. Except, for some reason, I can't read Regan."

"I thought empaths could sense everyone's emotions?"

"Me, too. However, I've never been able to read her vibes or see her aura like others. I can only tell what she's thinking or feeling the old-fashioned way—her eyes or body language."

"You see auras?" Rachel said excitedly. "That's so cool. I wish I could see auras. I just pick up on dreams and emotions from the people in those dreams if they're strong enough."

"That's pretty amazing, too." Rachel was the second person he met with a gift but, maybe like him, they kept it a secret due to people's negative reactions.

"Look at you two, becoming gift besties," Michael interrupted. "How about we get back to why you hurt my sister. Again." The agitation in his voice echoed through the phone.

"I didn't want to ruin her already tense relationship with Shamus by telling her. And as for my gift..." He paused to take a breath. The next words were painful. Even after all these years and even now that his father was no longer alive to mock him.

"As for my gift—my parents didn't react well when they learned about it. Badly, in fact. I was terrified you both would react the same way and end our friendship. I couldn't risk that. You and Regan are the only two people who are more like family than my own family. The only ones I care about and who care about me. To lose that?" His voice cracked so much he stopped speaking.

Michael's voice was heavy with emotion. "Don't you know us well enough by now, Connor? You could never lose us." There was rustling in the background, as if he were moving around. "Well, except for when you piss one of us off. But to learn about your gift? Never. You're like a brother to me, and if you didn't date my sister, she'd consider you a sibling too," he ended with a teasing tone.

"You mean that?" Doubt asked that question, because he knew from Michael's words and the emotion in his tone that he meant it.

They were family and nothing would change that. "I had a special trip planned and I was going to tell her then."

"Why didn't you lead with that?" Michael asked. "Makes you less of a fool. Did you tell Regan that?"

"No. Everything happened so fast...I am a stupid idiot," he whispered. "I let the woman I love get away."

"Fear is a powerful motivator, especially when that fear is rooted in family trauma."

"Like parents who neglect you and who treat you like a plague because they're jealous of you?" *And beat the snot out of you.*

"Or want you to live your life for them."

A long silence stretched between them until Connor heard Rachel speaking so quietly, he knew her words were for Michael only.

"Good talk, mate."

"I couldn't agree more." Connor wiped tears from his eyes, grateful he decided to call his friend at home and not in his office at the bookstore.

"We have news!" Rachel said in her bubbly voice.

"Yes. I was going to call you this week to ask you a very important question."

"What question?" Connor's curiosity was piqued. A change in topic, especially happy news from Rachel's tone, was a welcome change from their earlier emotional chat.

"Will you be my best man?"

"Of course I will, mate! When's the wedding?" He was thrilled that they were going ahead with their wedding, especially with the drama in the wake of Rachel's departure back to the island.

"In a couple of weeks," Rachel said excitedly.

"We know it's short notice, but we wanted to remove the possibility of family interference." Michael added, "It's nothing extravagant. Just a simple wedding with a handful of guests. You and Regan and Mum and Dad, if they decide to come."

The mention of weddings reminded Connor of what happened at his parents' house last weekend. "Have you spoken to them or Regan recently?"

"No. Why? Did something other than what you told him at brunch occur?"

"You could say that." Connor raked a hand through his hair. "They're trying to force Regan to marry Eamon."

"What? Bloody hell! I'm going to kill Da. What is he thinking?"

"You might need to get in line, mate." Connor relayed the whole story to them. A series of slurs came through the phone from them both.

"This is a disaster."

"That's an understatement." Michael added, "I need to come back and sort this out."

"No. You need to focus on your wedding," Connor insisted. "I'll deal with things here." He wished he felt as confident as his words that came out. No ideas formed about how to handle the situation with Regan and her parents, but he'd find a way so Michael wouldn't have to worry about it. An actual plan could wait until tomorrow.

"I'll call Regan and my parents to tell them about the wedding. I planned to call them tomorrow anyway."

"In the meantime, I'm going to work on getting your sister to forgive me for being the biggest idiot."

"Good luck, Con."

"Thanks." He was going to need it.

The crinkle of the paper clutched in his fingers was the only proof he had that although he had withheld his secret, he planned to tell her the truth and soon, even if it wasn't in the time she wanted or deserved.

He'd give her the space she needed to overthink like he knew she would and be angry with him. He wouldn't take that away from her. She needed to process it. Just like he needed time to believe that, like Michael, Regan would accept him as he was—faults, gifts, and all.

CHAPTER 33

Regan opened the front door of her flat to find Connor in the doorway. The light cast shadows on his face and showed off the different highlights of the brown and red in his hair. Her first instinct was to slam the door in his face, but the haunted look in his eyes stopped her.

"You're not answering your phone."

"For good reasons."

He cupped the back of his neck. "You're not wrong."

They stood in the doorway, staring at each other in agonizing silence before she spoke. "What do you want, Connor?"

"To apologize."

She shifted her weight from one leg to the other. "Fine. You've apologized. Now you can leave."

"Will you please let me explain?"

A hand went to her hip. "What is there to explain? You lied. Again. When you promised you wouldn't."

He shoved his hand in his pocket. "I know. And I'm an idiot for not telling you sooner. But I had every intention of telling you."

"When? On our golden wedding anniversary?"

A mischievous smirk tugged at the corner of his mouth. "Still want to marry me, eh?"

Regan scoffed. "I was merely making a statement." She tried to close the door in his face, but he slipped his shoe in, stopping it.

"I know I hurt you and you needed space, Regan. But I told you I'm not letting you go again. I messed up by not telling you sooner about your father and my gift, but I was going to tell you this week."

"That's convenient."

"It's the truth. We just got back together and the last thing I wanted to do was unload all this information on you. On us. I was just starting to earn back your trust. I didn't want to scare you away." He was leaving out the deeper reason why he didn't tell her sooner, but sharing that with her would come once he got inside her flat. Letting all her neighbors hear his darkest secrets was not part of his plan.

Regan sighed before opening the door. "You can come in, but the entire truth about everything better come out of your mouth tonight, Connor." She pointed at him. "If not, consider us done. For good this time. We'll remain civil acquaintances but no more."

"Got it." He released the breath he didn't realize he was holding as he followed her inside the flat. He hung up his coat, strode to the couch, and sat down next to her.

She shifted away from him.

He wanted to hold her hand while he confessed, to touch her in any way. But the stiff posture of her back and the firm lines around her mouth spoke volumes. That wasn't going to happen, no matter how badly he wanted it to. She needed space and time, and he had to respect that. The fact she let him inside was a win. His calls had gone ignored and he didn't want to show up at her workplace again. Not with her mother there. Not to mention, their topic of conversation was not work friendly. The last thing he wanted to do was create more chaos for her by bringing their argument to her work.

She crossed her arms as she waited for him to speak. The torment in her eyes was the only indication she was hurting but hopeful.

"When I was eight, I realized I could sense what people were feeling and, in a way, thinking. I found out from my father, it was a gift that ran in the family. One that skipped him." Connor left off it was the reason he hated him so much.

"My mother forced me to hide it from everyone while my father..." He remembered the times his father had beaten him. What they thought or felt about him. Those feelings shifted from love to something hurtful. "He beat me into being stronger and using my gift for his use."

Regan gasped.

"By the time we became friends, my gift had caused me nothing but pain and shame from my family and whenever I shared what I sensed from the people around me..." Things ended badly. He was barred from kid's parties at school and lost the few friends he had as a kid.

Connor raked a hand through his hair.

"I was scared to show you and Michael my true self because I was terrified you and Michael would leave the way everyone else had. I'd lose your friendship, and it meant everything to me back then. And now."

"We're not your parents or other people, Connor."

He rubbed his hands on his jeans. "Knowing that doesn't stop the fear, Regan. I couldn't risk losing the woman I love. My best friend. You two were all I had in the world."

"That day at the bookstore...you sensed what that woman needed."

"Yes. It's how I help people. The bookstore allows me to help without anyone suspecting I'm anything more than an insightful book enthusiast."

"How can I trust you to be honest with me again?"

He took her hands and relaxed when she didn't yank them back.

"You know me, Regan. I let your father separate us because I knew you deserved better than me back then and because of his threats. I almost lost the bookstore because of him. And I lost my job when I refused to break up with you when he first asked me. But now that you're back in my life, I won't lose you again. I wasn't lying when I said I planned to tell you this week. I was going to surprise you with a trip to the country." He released her hands to get something from his pants pocket. He handed her tickets that confirmed they were purchased before the disaster at her parents' house.

Regan stared at the tickets, tears pooling in her eyes.

"I was going to tell you everything." His arm went around her shoulder, pulling her against his frame. He lifted her face to his. "Everything, pet. I didn't want any more secrets between us. I wanted us to have a real fresh start. I wanted you to know everything about me. All of who I am."

Regan started sobbing when he pulled her against him and kissed her forehead. He didn't need to sense her emotions to know she needed comfort, and he did just that as she soaked his shirt with her tears.

He held her and ran his hands down her back to soothe her as the tears subsided.

When she finally looked up at him, he was gutted by the hurt still brimming in her eyes.

"I am truly sorry, but I promise never to lie to you ever again."

She yanked the collar of his shirt. "You better not, or I'll cut your bullocks off and put them in the drawer in my nightstand."

After the horror of her words subsided, a smirk tugged at his lips. "You love them too much for that."

Regan burst out laughing, and he joined her.

CHAPTER 34

Humidity and heat slammed into Regan as she stepped out of the car. *Whose idea was it to get married on an island? Outside? That's right. My crazy brother and future sister-in-law, that's who.*

Perspiration formed on various spots on her body as she strolled through the parking lot of the wedding venue. The ceremony was set to happen at sunset, so she was hopeful it would cool down by then. Thankfully, she chose a dress with thin straps and without many layers because Michael said it was a small wedding.

A short, plump woman in attire that screamed she wasn't part of the wedding but worked at the venue greeted her at the entrance. "Welcome to Pedro Castle. Walk straight ahead to the seating area. Please sign this photo of the bride and groom as a memento of the guests who attended their happy occasion."

Regan took the pen and signed the creamed-colored paper section around a photo of her brother and Rachel. They stared into each other's eyes lovingly, reminding her of what she lost with Connor.

After their talk, she suspected he assumed they would kiss and make up. Hell no! She understood his reasons for why he kept secrets from her and even sympathized with him, but that didn't erase what he did. How could she build a life with someone who didn't trust her enough to share such an important part of himself? Who he was at his core? She'd opened herself to him completely once again and that hadn't been enough for him to do the same.

She couldn't trust that he wouldn't do the same thing again when it got difficult for them, and let his fear keep distance between them.

She wanted someone to share themselves with her as completely as she shared herself with them. She deserved someone like that.

Forgiving him for keeping her father's betrayal from her was easy. She knew firsthand how brutal her father could be when it came to what he wanted. The ruin he rained down on Connor was just the tip of the iceberg. It would've set him back years. As much as it hurt that he walked away from her, and the words he used to push her away, she could forgive him for that.

Not telling her about his gift was another matter.

A beautiful array of decorated chairs and a large archway, with a backdrop of the ocean and the cliffs, stole Regan's breath. The colorful flowers and plants surrounding the area were a combination of greens and whites, with splashes of mixed colors layered in from the plants in decorated pots at alternating rows. Simple, elegant, and a pinch of exotic was the word for it. Just like the bride.

A handful of people occupied the carefully laid out seating. The only one she recognized was Rachel's mother. She was almost too embarrassed to say hello, given the excitement when they met at her parents' brunch. Rachel's father had put everyone in their place when they tried to insult his daughter and his island. Although the scenery was enjoyable, her father's and Ciara's behavior were not.

"Lovely to see you again, Mrs. Miller," she greeted politely.

"Glad you could make it, Regan." Karol smiled but glanced behind her, as if expecting to see her parents. Thankfully, she didn't ask if they were coming.

"I wouldn't miss it for the world."

"I hope you're not upset about not being included in the wedding party?" Karol asked.

A friendly smile tugged at the edges of her mouth. "Not at all. I know they wanted a small ceremony." Part of her was a little sad, but then she remembered it wasn't about her. At least she was here to support her brother, whereas their parents were nowhere to be seen. "Enjoy the ceremony." She sat in the aisle across from them in the front row, not only for the spectacular view, but she wanted to see her brother getting his happy ending up close.

On one hand, she was ecstatic for Michael and Rachel, but a small part of her was jealous. They were able to work through their problems, even if it meant him walking away from the life he built in Ireland. Rachel was his life now and where she lived was where he wanted to be. His words were swoon worthy...if they weren't coming from her brother's lips.

Connor was in the wedding party, and she wasn't looking forward to seeing him, even though she missed him terribly.

When she left Ireland, her parents were still arguing whether they'd attend the wedding or not. If they didn't, she knew it would break Michael's heart. Although their father was grateful for the sacrifice Michael made, he wasn't thrilled about him leaving Ireland to be with Rachel. In his words: "She's your fiancée. She belongs where you are."

"You're right, Da. Where Rachel is, that's where I want to be. Even if that's in Cayman." Those were his last words to his parents before he jumped on a plane to chase after her.

From what she heard from her mother, because neither of them were there when the drama unfolded, Rachel had an episode, quit her consulting job with the company, and headed back to Cayman, breaking her engagement with Michael.

Regan was dealing with the fallout with her parents from Michael leaving, along with her relationship with Connor falling apart. Then there was her forced marriage. She felt bad about not reaching out to Rachel; however, she knew her best friends Skylar and Arlene, along with her family, were here on the island, so she had support. Support Regan envied.

Connor and Michael were her supporters and lately, it felt as if they were both slipping away. Well, one of them she had pushed away. But the relationships in her life were falling apart, and there was no one in the background to fill those gaps. For once in her life, she wished she'd taken the time to make real friends instead of losing herself in work and hiding behind the fear that everyone wanted her friendship because of her family's connections or to use her in some way.

Her close friends consisted of her brother's best friend, who was essentially an ex, and Michael's fiancée. How pathetic was she? The people in the past who had tried to cultivate a friendship with her were ignored or pushed aside because she doubted their intentions. And, if she were honest, she wasn't sure they'd like her for who she was if they got to know her. Even Eamon had disappointed her and proved that point.

She barely knew herself. How did she expect anyone else to get close enough to see the real her—whoever that was? Connor saw the parts of her she knew about herself as well as the parts she wanted to cultivate but was too scared. The man loved her for who she was when they were just friends and accepted her as she was when they were together, both now and in the past.

Music drifted through the air as if by magic, considering no band or speaker was in sight. Michael walked up to the archway in preparation for Rachel, giving her a head nod. A bright smile lit his face and spread to his eyes when his gaze settled on her. She'd missed the rehearsal dinner due to work obligations and trying to convince their parents to come with her. Her mother had joined in the argument, but her father remained unconvinced.

Moments later, Connor and someone who Regan assumed was one of Rachel's friends, strolled past her, arms locked.

Her heart ached as her eyes followed him. He didn't glance at her, which made her ache even more. Had he taken her words to heart and moved on despite saying he'd never leave her again? *Get it together! It's your brother's wedding, and Connor is the best man. This isn't about you.*

Next down the aisle was a couple whose faces were etched with so much discomfort Regan wondered how they ended up together. The animosity rolling from the woman who Regan believed was Skylar was palpable; the man, she learned from Michael was a new friend of his, Matteo, had a *how am I here right now?* expression on his face before it morphed into an arrogant smirk when his companion gave him a side-eye that could cut diamonds. *What the hell?*

So much for a drama-free wedding. Her parents hadn't made an appearance, which was just as well. Apparently, there were enough theatrics to go around already.

The wedding song started, and Rachel and her father marched down the aisle. Her dress was stunning and clung to her frame like it was painted on. There was no veil on her head, no doubt because of the cool breeze that started moments earlier, and the warm weather. Her eyes were glued to Michael as each step took her to him.

When she glanced at Michael, his gaze was locked on Rachel. From where she sat, she could see the tears pooling in her brother's eyes with the happiness that exuded from him. Her chest tightened as she watched them, tears burning at the back of her eyes.

She wished she could say it was because of them, and in a small way it was, but mostly it was because she wanted what they had for herself. In that moment, she knew: Connor was her person. If she were honest, she knew when she was eighteen, and when he confessed he loved her only cemented it. When he broke her heart, she thought she'd lost it, but finding out he'd never stopped loving her had broken her heart all over again.

So much stood between them...and not just the secrets he withheld. Her parents, this ridiculous forced engagement, and their own fears. Fears that kept the distance between them. A distance that was just as detrimental to their relationship as her parents' interference was.

Their fears would keep them disconnected from themselves and each other. Her fear of being a puppet for her parents and living her life for them, no matter how hard she tried not to. His fear of not feeling worthy of her or their love, no matter what words came from her mouth. Words and the best intentions wouldn't stop their fears from tearing them apart. If she were honest, that's why she was avoiding Connor. Forgiving him was just one step.

Michael and Rachel faced each other as they said their vows.

Regan didn't hear a word because her eyes were on Connor, who stared straight at her, his eyes filled with love and a brokenness that tore at her insides. They showed what he couldn't say out loud in that moment: *I love you. I miss you. I want you.*

Look away, screamed in her head. But she couldn't, because she felt the same way, even with all the fears, doubts, and obstacles that stood between them. Those obstructions didn't seem to matter whenever she looked into his eyes or was in his arms. The world faded away, along with every sensible thought telling her that their relationship was doomed and walking away so they didn't hurt each other more was the right thing to do.

But as Connor mouthed the words *I love you*, Regan's resolve crumbled. They were as far as possible from Ireland as a person could be. Her parents were nowhere in sight; neither were the obstacles keeping them apart. When they returned home, she would deal with everything, but while she was here on the island, she would do what her heart wanted more than anything else.

To be with Connor.

CHAPTER 35

Connor shoved the food on his plate around. He'd lost his appetite after seeing Shamus stroll through the door, eyeing the restaurant and everyone in the room like they were beneath him. *Arrogant bastard.*

He and Moira greeted the couple, apologizing for missing the ceremony. Shamus's exact words: "I had no interest in sitting outside and sweating my arse off to watch my son get married."

Michael had remained silent, but the hurt behind his eyes made Connor fume. Bloody man couldn't even put his son's needs before his own, for what? A couple of hours of discomfort at most? Cutting words burned the back of his throat, but, like Michael, he remained silent, not wanting to cause any more drama than what happened at the rehearsal dinner.

Connor glanced at said perpetrators, who seemed to be on their best behavior. No doubt because of the tongue-lashing Arlene, one of Rachel's bridesmaids and best friend, had given them at last night's dinner and then again after the ceremony.

Arlene was a spitfire and whatever drama overflowed between Skylar and Matteo appeared to be stamped out. No fake smiles graced their lips, but at least they weren't giving each other death glares.

Given that Skylar and Rachel were best friends, and Matteo and Michael as he learned from Arlene were in a serious bromance, he hoped the drama between them remained peaceful.

Connor's gaze moved about the room until he found Regan, sitting next to her parents, a solemn expression etched on her face. At least they didn't bring her fiancé with them. His hand clenched the fork until it bent. *Shite!* He used both hands to straighten it and leaned it against his plate.

They shared a moment as Michael and Rachel said their vows. One not full of her anger, disappointment, or hurt. That moment was filled with everything he wished was theirs. A wedding. A life where they didn't sacrifice their happiness to please others or let their fears keep them from being together.

When she stood and walked toward the toilet, he followed her and waited outside for her to come out. The alcove provided privacy from the dining room so her parents and the rest of the guests couldn't see them.

"Connor?" Surprise lit her eyes when she saw him.

He pushed her against the wall and crushed his mouth to hers. A soft moan escaped them as their tongues danced together and their hands pulled at clothing. There was nothing he wanted more than to drag her out of here, but he knew that wasn't an option. Not with her parents here. He shoved his room card in her hands. "I'm in room 501. If you don't show, I'll understand, but I hope to hell you do."

He kissed her quickly before wiping his mouth to make sure there was no residual lipstick and headed back to the table. As badly as he wanted to look back, he didn't—afraid of what he'd see in her eyes, because that was the only part of her he could ever read.

Shamus gave him a death stare when he sat back down, especially when he saw Regan's disheveled clothing she missed pulling straight and their swollen lips.

Eat shite, old man!

Connor was done fearing him. The man had kept him from the woman he loved for years, caused him to hurt her not once, but twice. He was not in the same position as he was the first time. In fact, they were both in better financial positions than they were years ago.

Even though Shamus thought he was still not financially stable, Connor knew better. He almost lost his business, if it wasn't for Michael's sacrifice. The incident still hadn't humbled him considering the arrogance rolling off him in waves, along with the disdain for Rachel's family; even though there was a glimmer of respect, it was buried deep.

He'd expected Michael to sacrifice Rachel for the sake of his family, but Michael was smart and chose the woman he loved, even if it meant walking away from his family's expectations.

As strong as Regan was, could she walk away from her family? *Would I? For him? Do I want to after he hurt me again?* Hope was his only ally.

The family charities were everything to her. She worked hard for them to make the impact they did. That alone would keep her tied to her family, and her father knew it, too. With everything that happened with Michael, Moira was the only one who had slowly changed toward him and even Regan. She had loosened the reins more in the past few years and it was obvious she was not crazy about the marriage arrangement Shamus made for Regan.

Despite her faults, and the mistakes she made with her kids in the past, Moira loved her family. Fiercely. Shamus loved his kids but to a fault where he felt he knew what was best for them and they weren't adults who could make their own decisions.

Plates of desserts were brought out, and Regan's eyes lit up when a giant piece of strawberry cake was placed in front of her while everyone else got the local coconut cake or chocolate.

Her eyes found him, and she gave him a brilliant smile and mouthed *Thank you*.

He tipped his head, ignoring the scowl Shamus fired in his direction.

Shamus shoved his chair away from the table. Moira grabbed his hand, a pleading looking in her eyes. He pulled his hand away and headed toward him.

Oh shite! Was he going to make a scene?

Connor glanced at Rachel and Michael, but they were oblivious, feeding each other cake and laughing as they stared into each other's eyes.

"A word, Connor."

He stood and smiled at Regan, as if to say *don't worry*, and followed Shamus to a door leading outside.

"What the hell are you doing, Connor?" he bellowed the moment the door closed behind them.

"I could ask you the same thing, Shamus. Marry your daughter off to another man when you know she loves me?"

Shamus snorted. "Love? What she feels for you is childish."

"You could argue that when she was eighteen. What about now, Shamus? I still love your daughter, and I know she still loves me."

"You can't provide for her. Not then. Not now."

"And that bloody idiot you chose can?" He longed to tell Shamus he had more money in just one of his investment accounts than Eamon had in all his accounts, but Connor doubted he'd believe him.

"Yes."

"She doesn't need me or any man to support her. She has her inheritance."

"An inheritance she can only get if she's married. I'm doing this for her."

Connor's laughter was bitter. "This isn't for her. It's for you, so you can continue to control her, especially now that you can no longer control Michael."

Shamus' jawline jumped and his eyes narrowed to slits. "I know what's best for my children!"

"Do you? Because before Michael found Rachel, he wasn't happy. Not the way he is with her. Trust me, I know." And he did. The love between them was something he envied, even with what he shared with Regan.

"He was successful!"

"Success isn't everything, Shamus. Not if your life is empty."

Shamus snorted.

"I am successful, Shamus, despite what you think, but it means nothing to me without your daughter. I love her, and I can take care of her in any capacity she needs from me. But she is strong enough to financially stand on her own. What she needs from me is my support and my love. To be the man who doesn't let anyone, or anything, stand between us, not even her family."

"I thought you couldn't read her?"

"I don't need to feel Regan's emotions to know what she needs from me. I've known her for most of her life, and I've just listened to her when she speaks. She's told you and Moira over the years. The trouble is you never listened. Your daughter is an incredible woman who's capable of anything, if you'd open your eyes and put your damn ego aside and really see her. And listen to what she wants. If you don't, you're going to lose her the way you lost Michael."

"He's right," Moira said from the doorway. Regan stood next to her.

Did she hear everything? For once, he couldn't tell from her expression, mainly because his own emotions were swirling from his encounter with her father.

"He doesn't know what's best for her. I do." He strode past his wife to Regan, taking her by the shoulders. "Marrying Eamon is the right thing to do. You get the security from your inheritance."

"If I can get my inheritance from marrying someone, why can't it be Connor?"

The question took them both by surprise.

He'd happily marry her under any circumstances and was about to say as much when Shamus answered.

"No. Look at his family. His father destroyed their wealth."

Connor was about to remind him he'd nearly done the same himself.

"Mine was a temporary setback, not complete decimation."

"So, what you're saying is I can only get my inheritance if I marry someone you approve of," Regan stated calmly.

"It's for the best."

She remained silent, staring at her parents for several minutes before she held out her hand to him. "Let's say goodnight to Rachel and Michael, and then you can take me back to the hotel. I'm done here."

Shamus moved to stand between them. "You're making a mistake!"

Connor put his hand on his shoulder. "This is what I feel for your daughter." All the love he shared with Regan over the years washed over Shamus in multiple waves until his breath became erratic. Connor took Regan's hand and headed back to the reception, leaving a stunned Moira and a comatose Shamus outside.

"You're leaving?" Michael asked them.

"And you're leaving together?" Rachel's voice was high with excitement.

"Anything to do with the conversation I saw you having with my father?" The question was directed at him.

Connor lifted a shoulder.

"I'm still jet-lagged," Regan offered. "I need sleep."

"Yeah, you do," Rachel teased with a sly wink and smirk.

"Rach, that's my sister and best friend you're talking about. I don't need that image in my head."

"Grow up, Michael. They're adults now."

"I don't care if they're old and gray. Hearing about their sex life is disgusting."

Rachel shrugged.

Skylar and Arlene were behind them, arms opened.

"Remember what I told you," Skylar whispered in his ear.

"Don't listen to anything she says," Arlene joked. "It was nice meeting you both. I hope to see you again. If not here, then maybe in Ireland."

Regan nodded, accepting their hugs.

Matteo waved from his seat, despite eyeing him with a wary glance between him and Skylar. Connor almost wanted to stick around so he could find out what the story was between those two. The only thing he'd overheard was they were high school sweethearts before they fell apart—badly.

Regan intertwined her fingers in his as they walked out the main exit and away from her parents, but the anger pulsing off Shamus was palpable enough it followed him out the building and to the parking lot.

CHAPTER 36

Regan tried not to burst into tears when Connor closed the car door after she got in. She'd cry later once she figured out what she planned to do about her parents. She focused instead on the words she overheard Connor say. If only she was as confident as he believed she was. Confidence her own parents didn't have in her, if they felt she needed marriage to be responsible enough for her inheritance but had to accept the man they chose for her. A man she cared about but didn't love. Loving her future husband didn't seem to matter to her father. She wasn't sure about her mother anymore.

Their lack of faith in her sliced through her like a hot knife, brutal and unforgiving. Once again, no matter how much she proved how capable she was, it didn't matter. It wasn't enough. She wasn't enough.

Connor grasped her hand and kissed her knuckles. "You okay?" His question implied he knew she wasn't.

A weak smile pulled at her lips, but he wasn't fooled.

"Give them time," he said, but neither of them believed those words.

Her mother might come around, but her father? He was still angry about Michael running off to be with Rachel, leaving Ireland and, in a sense, his family behind. But what her father didn't understand was that Rachel was his family now, and sacrificing her, their future together, wasn't an option.

What would happen when she refused to marry Eamon, which she would do? She knew with every ounce of her being she couldn't marry a man she didn't love. If Connor hadn't confessed he never stopped loving her, she might've considered it. Gaining her independence meant financial freedom from her parents in ways she couldn't claim now.

But life with Eamon would be hollow and loveless. Their relationship had never been more than friendship and that wouldn't change with marriage. That kind of relationship held no appeal for her.

Not when the man she wanted more than anything else loved her the way Connor did. Being with him meant turning her back on her life, and in some ways her parents. Would she have a job when she turned down Eamon? Shamus was brutal when he wanted to bend people to his will, and that rarely excluded his children.

Ocean views and brilliant star-filled skies passed by in the windows of the car. Regan wound down her window so she could smell the sea air. A blast of humid, hot air crashed into her before it thinned into something cooler. She closed her eyes, trying to find the smell she was looking for beneath everything that assaulted her senses.

Moonlight flicked inside and outside the car as they headed back to the hotel, which was on the other side of the island. Rachel hadn't wanted the wedding in a fancy hotel ballroom, even though it was on the beach.

Not that Regan blamed her. The location she chose was perfect for both the wedding and the reception. No doubt a lower budget than her parents would choose, but that was Rachel. She didn't bend to Shamus or her mother the way she did. No matter how defiant she was with them, when it came to what truly mattered to her, she usually caved.

Tonight would prove no different. Once the reality of what she'd done hit her, she was going to change her mind. As much as she wished she was stronger, the past had proved the extent of her ability to stand up to her parents. Leaving the folds of her family would mean walking away from everything. The only thing she owned was her flat, which she was still paying for. The car she drove belonged to the company. The financial decisions she made up to this point were based on her relying on her trust fund. Looking back now, it was stupid, given her father's propensity to change his mind to cling to control.

Most people in her circle received their inheritance at twenty-five. Not her and Michael. No doubt her father had a hand in that decision.

Like a fool, she'd set aside her original plan in uni to pursue an interior design business. To her surprise, running the charities took up more of her time than she anticipated, not to mention the changes she wanted to make with them with a more hands-on approach. Silly her. She'd thought showing her parents her dedication and ability to run the charities would prove her capable and mature enough to handle the charities—and her own life.

She'd lost her mind and forgot who her parents were. At least, her dad.

Although her mother had released the reins with most areas related to their charities, she held on tightly when it came to events, where they were held and the setup. As if Regan hadn't helped with almost every charity and family event since she was ten.

Connor pulled into the hotel parking lot, turned off the car, and shifted so he faced her. The concern in his eyes made her ache.

"Want to have a nightcap to silence that nasty judge Shamus put in your head?"

Regan managed a real smile. "I think I've had enough to drink, but I don't want to be alone tonight." Her hand clasped his.

"Anything you need, Regan." He kissed her hand before getting out of the car and walked around her side to help her out.

Anything you need. He'd said those words to her father. Unlike her parents, who still saw her as a child who required their guidance, Connor saw her as no one did: a capable woman who didn't need saving. No, he saw her as the woman he'd loved and wanted to support. The last tendrils of hurt from his betrayal had melted away, along with remembering his earlier words that night when he begged her to make things right between them.

Overhearing Connor defend her tore down the last of the wall she'd put back up against him. Reminding her that he always backed her when it came to her parents. He never coddled her but tried to show her she was strong enough to handle them. Hearing his words was a strong reminder of why she loved him and didn't want their story to end.

Their hands linked as they strolled inside.

As they headed to the elevator, Regan imagined they'd attended the wedding together as a couple and they were returning to their room. There was no argument with her parents, only an evening filled with family and fun.

"Your room or mine?" he asked as the elevator door closed.

"Yours." If her parents decided to visit her room later to "talk," she didn't want them to find her there. Enough hurtful words were said for one night, and her heart and overthinking mind couldn't take any more. A war with them was coming when she returned to Ireland and refused to marry Eamon. So tonight, she planned to avoid them at all costs.

Regan stood behind Connor as he opened the room to his suite. The room was enormous and tastefully decorated, with a seating area inside and on the large balcony area visible through the glass doors.

"Why don't we sit on the balcony? It's too dark to see the ocean, but you can see the stars, even if they aren't as bright."

She nodded and headed to the doors and stepped outside after Connor opened them. A numbness settled inside her when she sat and gazed out at the night and the area below, which provided lighting from the pool and bar area. The room was too high up to hear the people, but she observed them moving around and interacting, and was stung with jealousy for their lives. A stupid notion but she doubted anyone below was battling their parents against an arranged marriage or contemplating leaving the only life she'd ever known behind.

"How are you doing with everything?"

Regan fake laughed. "You mean about my father trying to marry me off or my boyfriend lying to me?"

"Both."

She avoided his gaze, knowing she'd crumble if she did. It'd be so easy to fall back into his arms and for their relationship to continue where it left off, but deep down, she couldn't. Instead of sharing those words with Connor, she stood and took his hand and led them to his bedroom.

"We don't have to do this, Regan." Connor squeezed her hand before turning her to face him.

"I know, but I just want to be held tonight."

"I'll hold you until those fears and doubts stop swirling and you understand with certainty how wonderful and loved you are."

This was why she came back to the hotel with him. Connor always had a way of making her feel better, whether it was with his words or in the way he touched her.

CHAPTER 37

Regan watched Connor sleep. She wanted to touch his face one more time but didn't want to risk waking him when she was trying to sneak out. Last night, she realized what she needed to do, and it had to be alone.

More than anything she wanted to crawl back into bed next to Connor, wake up tangled in him before having breakfast together like they did so many times when she was in university. But those days were gone, and she had to face her parents and Eamon alone. If she didn't leave, Connor would convince her they could do it together.

As much as she wanted to stay with him and be with him, her life was a mess. One she had to clean up herself. In that moment, she understood why Connor wouldn't accept her help all those years ago.The mess was his family—his—and he wanted to fix it without dragging her into it. That's exactly how she felt now. Except his parents didn't dislike her and weren't trying to keep them apart. Then there was Eamon. She couldn't understand why he didn't tell her about the arrangement. They were friends for years and understood the complicated family dynamics their wealth and obligations came with. Was he being forced into his arrangement by his family? The reason didn't matter. Their marriage was never going to happen.

Regan snuck out of the room, closing the door quietly behind her, and headed to the elevator and to her own room to pack up her things. Once downstairs, she asked the concierge to order her a ride back to where her car was parked, hoping that Connor remained sleeping until she left the hotel, or longer.

When she got back to her car, she drove to the airport, praying the ticket counter would be opened when she got there. The sun was rising as she drove, the sky melding from purples and oranges to bright blues and scattered clouds.

Her phone buzzed on the seat. She hadn't checked it since she woke up, not wanting to deal with what she was certain would be tons of messages from her parents and maybe even Eamon. Connor's name was bound to pop up, whether it was on her call list or text messages.

Regan was relieved when she saw someone behind the ticket counter. She changed to an earlier flight and headed to the waiting lounge. After she'd had a cup of coffee, she finally unlocked her phone and read through her messages.

There were no messages from Connor. *Was he still sleeping? Was he upset to find the other side of the bed empty? Was he angry because of what we shared last night, only to find me gone?*

Regan sent him a quick text, hoping he'd understand.

The other messages were angry ones from her father. Pleading ones from her mother. And "we need to talk" ones from Eamon.

Now he wanted to talk? Not before he and her family dropped the bomb of their arranged marriage in the middle of brunch?

There were no texts from her brother or Rachel. Not that she expected any considering they were officially on their honeymoon.

The plane boarded and she took her spot in first class, buckled up, propped her pillow against the window and closed her eyes. It would be hours before she was back in Ireland and in her own bed, and she'd barely slept because she and Connor spent most of the night talking and holding each other. It was as if he suspected that if he fell asleep, she'd be gone when he woke up. He wasn't wrong, but not for the reasons he thought.

As she listened to Connor share stories about the bookstore, how his gift worked, and how he used it to help people, she sensed his complete happiness. He was content lying next to her in bed, talking and sharing stories about his life and listening to her crazy stories about her parents during the time they were apart and how proud she was about the changes she'd made to the charities.

The absolute joy on his face as he spoke and listened to her blew her away and caused her to uncover something about herself and her own life. She wasn't happy. Was she proud of what she'd accomplished and achieved over the years. Definitely! Happy? Content? Full of joy?

The answer was a resounding no. Connor was the only bright spot in her life and the reason she was so hurt and angry with him for lying. He'd taken away the one true happiness in her life. One that was her own and not connected to her family or work.

As the night progressed, the reality that her life was not one she wanted hit her with the force of a storm—dark, brutal—and shattered the perfect little bubble she'd been living in. It was one thing to know you wanted to escape, imagining it was solely to remove your parents' control, but recognizing your life was held up by crumbling, rotting sticks was troubling.

As the realization of it unraveled, she was grateful Connor couldn't read her thoughts or sense her emotions the way he did with other people. The last reaction she wanted from the man she loved was pity. Connor would back whatever decision she made and happily support her financially if she needed it. Another person funding her life was no different from the situation with her family.

If she was going to stand on her own two feet, she needed to do it alone. As much as she'd fooled herself into thinking she was independent, everything about her life was tied to her parents and their charity foundation. She loved the work she did, but the strings that came with them had kept her stuck in ways she didn't realize. In university, she had a strong plan to be completely independent, both personally and financially, from her parents. But somewhere along the way, she got tangled in everyday life and all the responsibilities with running her family's multiple charities and the events that came with them. To say she'd lost her way was an understatement. Being sidetracked cost her everything that was important to her.

Waiting for her inheritance kept her spinning financially. And now, being forced into an arranged marriage? Connor was always a wild card her parents would never approve of, but if she'd been free from them when she planned, it wouldn't have mattered.

Maybe if she and Connor had rebuilt their lives together, they and their relationship might be in a better place. They might be married and have kids by now. Regan's heart sank. No. Her father would've found another way to sabotage them if Connor hadn't agreed to walk.

The years proved some things did change. Connor was no longer financially vulnerable and she was finally ready to leave the life her parents chose for her behind.

Last night, lying in Connor's arms, reminded her of everything they had so many years ago and how deep a connection they had. Not just physical, but the ease in which they fell back into each other. In those moments, she wanted nothing more than to stay with Connor for more than just one night or whenever they could fit time into their schedules.

Being with Connor again unraveled her desire to have the life she wanted before she entered uni. Getting there wouldn't be easy, and would take time, but starting over would be worth it. Pain pierced her heart, thinking about losing her parents. It might be for weeks, months, or forever. They could be controlling but she loved them and planned to hold onto every happy childhood memory she shared with them. She might lose them, but she'd have Michael, Rachel, and best of all, Connor—if he forgave her for walking away from him tonight.

Hopefully the text she sent him comforted him and assured him that she loved him, wanted to share her life with him still, but none of that was possible until she stood on her own.

CHAPTER 38

Sunlight streaming through the half-open blinds burned his eyes when he opened them. He covered them with his arm until they adjusted to the blinding light. Last night's events were a disaster and a revelation. Confronting Shamus and defending Regan was the best feeling. She didn't need him to stand up for her, but Shamus needed to know how amazing his daughter was and that she wasn't a pawn for him to move around the board of the life and status he was trying to build or maintain. She was a human being who deserved to live the life she wanted, and to love and be with the man she wanted. Him.

The encounter was necessary because it hadn't sunk in since their argument at his home, and one he'd do again in a heartbeat. The expression on her face when he saw her and Moira standing in the doorway was priceless. As if she couldn't believe he felt that way about her. How could she not? Her parents, that's how. Parents who made her feel like she had to earn her place in their family by following a certain path. One they laid out for her.

The moment he woke up, he knew Regan wasn't in bed next to him—and not because she wasn't pressed against his body. It wasn't the coldness of the sheets on her side of the bed, either. Her presence was gone. Her vibe whenever she was near him was missing. It was different from everyone else, and although he couldn't read her like other people around him, he sensed her presence and vibe that was uniquely her. At least to him.

Disappointment hit him deep in his bones that she left without saying anything, making him feel like all the moments and secrets they shared last night meant nothing to her. The ping of his phone stopped him from spiraling.

It was Regan. He knew it before checking his phone. Fear coursed through him and his hand trembled, wondering whether her message would mean she would push him away again like she had the day after she forgave him. He unlocked the phone and read her message.

I love you. Never doubt that. But I must do this alone. You've had years to build the life you want. I need time to do the same. Time to create the life I thought I'd have all those years ago. I lost sight of that. Thank you for reminding me and showing me I'm strong enough to claim it.

Connor stared at the message; myriad emotions ricocheted through his chest like a ball in a Ping-Pong ball. He read it more times than was healthy, but he had to dissect every word and figure out her thought process behind it.

The years they'd spent apart showed him Regan had settled into the life they wanted for her and had forgotten everything she wanted for herself. At the time, he figured she had abandoned her dreams because of how much she loved working with her family's charities.

The light hadn't died out in her eyes when he saw her, even though it had dimmed, but he had no right to ask her or confront her when they ran into each other because he'd lost that privilege when he broke her heart and walked away from their relationship. Walked away from her.

But, at the same time, as he and Regan returned to the hotel, he sensed a shift in her. One that was reflected in her eyes as they laughed and talked through the night. Something was different. Unlike other times she'd argued with her parents and returned to her normal life.

The faraway expressions on display in her eyes and on her face spoke volumes. She was about to take drastic action. Last night, he wasn't sure what that action was, but her disappearance and message answered the hunch percolating in his mind.

The tightness in his chest released a bit that she loved him. He hadn't doubted it last night, but waking up to an empty bed flooded him with past fears. He reminded himself that her departure wasn't about him, but her need to find the freedom that she'd longed for. *Was pushing her dreams aside my fault?*

When they broke up, emotionally he was devastated, but concentrating on his work allowed him to become successful sooner. His drive was getting to a place financially where her father couldn't prevent them from being together if the opportunity presented itself.

Regan's resentment lasted longer than he anticipated, although he couldn't fault her. He'd broken her heart. In the past few years, he'd watched her come into her own, thriving in her family's charities. She appeared happy. Content with the life she was living.

Not being able to read her emotions proved him wrong. Guilt coursed through his blood, making him cold. He should've paid closer attention, told her how he felt sooner. Helped her sooner.

The words he told her father echoed in his head like a bad song. Regan didn't need him to save her. Her journey was her own. Her text had said as much. The changes she wanted for her life had to be made by her. For her.

Going back in time and changing what happened between them wasn't possible, but he could support her now and be there for her when she needed him. He opened his phone and typed her a message.

I love you, too, sunshine. You're a badass and will build the life you want. I'm here for it and you. Always.

No response came. Not that he expected one. Not yet.

He checked his watch; he had three hours before his flight. He showered, dressed, and headed downstairs in search of coffee and breakfast.

The trip back to Ireland was a long one, and he was eager to return to his flat, the bookstore, and the life he and Regan would soon create. Together.

CHAPTER 39

Two Months Later

"What the hell do you mean, you're tendering your resignation?" Shamus bellowed.

When she called a meeting with her parents this morning, she knew sparks were going to fly—and not the good kind.

Her pep talk before leaving the house was worthy of a Manchester United team coach. This meeting was with her parents, so she needed every inspiring and "you got this" word in the vocabulary.

Leaving was never going to be an easy decision, especially with her mother hinting at retiring, but she found a suitable replacement. Were they good enough for her father? Probably not. Once her mother approved, that's all that mattered to her. Departing on a good note was never going to be an option.

Her father's involvement with the charities was limited but because he was a board member, and her father, letting him know was a courtesy. Not to mention he'd have to alert the board of her resignation. The sting of guilt she felt putting him through that passed quickly when she remembered the hell he'd put Michael and Rachel through when she was a consultant with the company.

Moira sat calmly, hands in her laps as if she were expecting her announcement. As much as her husband thought he was the smart one, her mother was shrewd and paid attention more than people gave her credit for. She had to keep up with her husband and being in their world. Her mother ran multiple charities and events. A skill that took patience, dedication, and a whole lot of backbone when dealing with a male-only board of directors.

What Regan had yet to learn was whether her mother would remain silent, which meant her support in a weird way, or be vocal with her father.

"You can't resign from your family obligations!" His face grew redder by the minute. "I won't allow it. First breaking your engagement and now this?"

Regan had the urge to laugh in his face. A forced engagement that was never her idea. Not to mention she didn't agree to marry Eamon in the first place.

Meeting with him was the first thing she did when she returned to Ireland. He was unhappy because the wedding benefited him but came around when she offered him a business opportunity instead.

"Running those charities isn't family obligations, Da. They're a job and I've found a replacement. I will continue to be the face of the charities, like Mother, but I won't be involved in the daily operations."

"This is ridiculous! You can't just hand over your job. What will the board say?"

"Tell them the truth. That I've decided to pursue other opportunities but will still fulfill my family obligations by being the face of the charity arm of the company."

Shamus glared at her, making her wonder whether he'd grab her by the shoulders and try to shake sense into her. Her mother was still silent. A good sign in the big picture of things.

"What will you do?" Moira finally spoke, straightening a crease in her blouse.

"Open a business." She knew better than to say more. Sharing would leave her, and what she was trying to create, exposed to her father's sabotage.

"This is Connor's influence, isn't it?" he blistered. "This is why you didn't belong together. He's determined to ruin your life by pulling you away from your family."

Regan fisted the edges of her dress under the desk. "This has nothing to do with Connor. This is about me and what I want for my life."

His laugh was mirthless and his expression disappointment. "But you're already running a business."

She didn't miss how her father ignored her statement about wanting something for her own life away from her family. "No. It's a family business. Your business." The fact that they were charities, in her mind, was a temporary bonus for her. The likelihood of her working with her family otherwise was unlikely to happen. "And I'm not running it. I'm just your employee."

"What kind of business?" Moira probed.

Regan glanced at her parents, the people who she shared some of the best and worst memories with over the years. Years where they suppressed almost everything she wanted to express that didn't fit into their perfect family mold. The harder she fought them, the more they squeezed, until she'd just given in without even realizing it. Convincing herself that the changes she made with the charities that Connor had challenged her with was what she wanted. That the life she'd created after he left was the one she wanted.

The anger and heartbreak Connor left in his wake had pushed her to lose herself in work, convincing herself it was better that way. Her mother loosening the reins on events they hosted gave her the illusion she had control over the decisions in the charities and therefore her own life. They'd known what they were doing to draw her in, just like her father did with Michael.

When she learned about her father sabotaging her relationship with Connor, the pieces started to fall into place. Each time she tried to pull out of areas of the business around the charities, they dragged her back in with more responsibilities and the promise of more control. All lies meant to keep her in the folds of the family and continuing to control her life. Looking back now, she was surprised her father didn't try to force her into an arranged marriage sooner.

"Does it matter?" Regan answered her mother.

Moira and Shamus glanced at each other before their eyes settled on her.

"Who have you chosen as your successor?" Moira tugged on her husband's shirt to sit back down next to her.

Regan knew hosting them in her office wasn't the best idea. A conference room might've been a better choice, but a more formal setting would've raised their alarms, and she wanted to have the advantage as long as possible.

"Sharon."

Her mother knew the woman she'd chosen to replace her because she'd worked with the company for many years and knew more about the charities and was excited when Regan rolled out the changes she did. That, more than anything, was the reason Regan chose her. Having someone keep the personal touch she'd implemented was her legacy, and she wanted it to continue after she left.

"And events?" her father blistered, clearly not happy with her choice.

"Nora has been shadowing me for a while and is interested in more responsibilities. With Mother's guidance, she's the perfect fit." Regan wasn't about to tell them the long-term plan she had for events.

"Your mother wants to retire and you're giving her more work?"

"It was your idea I retire," Moira said with pursed lips.

Interesting. Regan hadn't realized that.

"I need you by my side for business events. Those are more important than those silly charities."

Moira's back stiffened and her expression grew cold.

Regan knew her mother was proud of the charities her family had cultivated over the years, along with the time and effort to expand them into areas that also benefited her father. A fight was coming, and Regan took the opportunity to leave while she still had her skin before her father's temper redirected to her about her resignation.

"I'll leave you to discuss the candidates I've chosen." Regan pushed her chair away from her desk and stood. "Stay as long as you need. I'm going to take lunch now." She grabbed her handbag from behind her chair and headed to the door.

Both parents glared at each other before they realized she'd spoken.

"We'll talk about this more," her father said quickly.

Regan opened her office door. "There's nothing more to discuss. The decision is made. Let me know if you want me to meet with the board," she offered, even though her father was already on thin ice with them after what happened with his attempt at a merger.

"We'll do lunch tomorrow and talk about your candidates." Her mother's eyes softened, a glint of admiration there.

"I look forward to it." Regan closed the door behind her, feeling lighter than she did before meeting with them.

The meeting didn't go exactly as she planned, but her mother was on her side and, in her mind, half the battle was won.

She longed to call Connor for lunch but decided against it, keeping her plan in place. Although she kept physical distance between them since Cayman, he was relentless about sending her cute text messages and pictures from the bookstore. He respected her distance, but always made sure she knew he was thinking about her. Flowers and gifts were delivered to her office weekly, and the occasional lunch or snack when her day was busy, as if he sensed she needed it.

As much as she wanted to see him and be with him, the sooner everything was lined up in her life for them to be together, the better. If she allowed him in now, he'd want to help and save her, and that's not how she wanted their relationship to start.

Eamon was an investor in her business, which might be strange if not for their years of friendship beforehand. The arrangement was financially beneficial to them both and pacified his family about their broken engagement. Connor investing wouldn't be the same.

Another month and her storefront office space would be ready to move in. Everything was going according to plan.

CHAPTER 40

One month later

Regan glanced around her office space. It was small but quaint, with a waiting area consisting of two high-back leather chairs, a glass front desk, and a large open space with a conference table and built-in cabinets stocked with samples of events ideas. She had no staff at the moment, but she planned to hire once she signed a couple more clients.

When people in her circle found out she was opening an event-planning business, their reactions were mixed.

Ciara thought she was crazy for going out on her own when she could work with her parents. You'd think her and her brother's experience would be an eye-opener, but nope.

Businesses that contributed to her family's charity events in the past were ecstatic and eager to work with her considering they witnessed her event-planning skills firsthand over the years.

Her father hadn't tried to sabotage her, but he wasn't exactly on board either. No doubt he was waiting patiently for her to fail. She couldn't wait to prove him wrong. He obviously forgot about all the business associates who asked why she didn't have her own business since she was so good at planning the family's charity events. Undermining her wasn't an option and would make him appear petty and cruel. Ruining people outside of family and their business circle was one thing, but family? That would make even him look bad.

She still expected behind-the-scenes sabotage from him, but she'd worry about it if the time came.

Her mother had stopped by when the crew were outfitting the space. She didn't say much as she walked around and asked questions about the layout.

The open house was in a couple of hours, and she was scrambling to finish. She considered hiring a company, but it seemed a moot point, and she couldn't imagine Ciara getting her hands dirty.

A knock on the glass door pulled her away from the centerpiece she was perfecting.

Outside the door was her brother, Rachel, Connor, Arlene, and Skylar. *They came all the way from Cayman?*

Excitement ricocheted through her when her eyes settled and held Connor who held a plant in his hand. She hadn't seen him since their time in Cayman. Even though they spoke or texted almost every day, she still missed him—his eyes, and his smiles...things she couldn't see just talking to him on the phone.

"I knew you wouldn't ask for help, so I brought everyone," Connor said with a brilliant smile that made his eyes sparkle. He handed her the plant. "From my mum's garden. She sends her best."

This man knew her too well. She placed the plant on top of the front desk.

"We weren't about to pass up a free trip to Ireland." Arlene pulled her coat closer to her petite frame.

"And help a friend," Skylar scolded, and rolled her eyes.

"My sister is opening a business. Of course I'm not going to miss it." Michael held the door for Rachel, his hand on her back.

"As Connor said, we're here to help, so put us to work." Rachel beamed as she glanced around the space.

Connor was the last one through the door. He gave her a quick hug and kissed her on the forehead. "I'm so proud of you."

Pride shot through her like a sparkler igniting. No one had said those words to her. Not even her brother, who had shared her excitement at stepping into something she wanted outside of their parents.

Not her mother, who showed her support in her own way. And definitely not her father, who thought she was making the biggest mistake of her life and was waiting on the sideline for her to fail and come crawling back.

As she watched them walk around the room, getting a feel of the space and seeing what she'd already done, Regan's heart swelled. She was so blessed to have so many people who loved and cared about her. Even if her father wasn't one of the people who supported her, she had others who did, especially Connor.

"The caterers will be here in ninety minutes, so everything needs to be in place by then."

Everyone gave her their undivided attention as she called out each task and let them choose the one they wanted.

Arlene opened her phone and put on music. Shrugging, she said, "I need it if I'm going to work."

"No complaints here." Michael pulled Rachel into his arms and moved her around the room.

Connor rolled his eyes. "You two just had your honeymoon."

Rachel kissed Michael quickly on the lips. "The honeymoon is never over."

Michael wiggled his eyebrows.

"Eww! I don't need to know that." Regan shivered.

"Me either." Arlene stuck her finger in her mouth to fake a gag.

Skylar rolled her eyes before laughing.

"All right, slackers. Back to work," Regan teased.

Over the next hour, everyone helped finish with the setup, from decorations to an area for people to learn about the business, while leaving space for the caterer. Thankfully her space was small enough, so she didn't need to hire anyone to serve. Someone from the caterer would stay to make sure the plates were refilled and drinks poured. Drinks were a must when it came to events like these.

Fifty people were invited, and only thirty-five RSVP'd, although people showed up even without confirming. She'd experienced that firsthand with all the parties she'd hosted over the years.

This event was the smallest one she'd ever hosted, but she was by far the most nervous she'd ever been.

Thirty more minutes, and she'd see if all her hard work and planning paid off. The event was more than just an open house. It was connecting with new people she'd reached out to and invited as well as people who knew her from her charity events. All of whom she hoped would hire her tonight or sometime in the future.

The caterers arrived, and right behind them, Eamon strolled through the entrance. The tension in the room shifted. Not everyone was aware of her and Eamon's history; however, Michael was, which meant Rachel and her friends did, too, because they shared everything.

"What's he doing here?" Arlene whispered.

"He's her business partner," Connor answered, his posture shifting from relaxed to stiff.

Everyone's gaze shot to Regan, disbelief etched on their faces.

"You'd rather he be my future husband?" She regarded them tightly. No explanation was needed. The choice was a good one, even after what happened with their engagement. They were friends for many years, and they'd both benefit from the arrangement.

"You had other options," Connor grumbled.

"I did, but this solved both our problems." When she told Connor about her business partnership with Eamon, he was unhappy and even insulted she hadn't come to him. She reminded him that he'd refused her help years ago, and that silenced him.

Before the conversation could continue, the first guests started to arrive. Her parents. No doubt arriving early and expecting the event to be in chaos. She greeted them politely and showed them around the space, including her office, which she locked after leaving.

"It's small," Shamus observed with a sneer.

"It's prudent for me to start small, Da."

The response didn't appease him. "How do you expect to attract larger clients?"

"My experience, not the size of my office," Regan countered.

Shamus snorted. "What experience?"

Sorrow layered with disappointment gutted her that her father knew nothing about her—or he did and chose his words to hurt her. Either way, she had enough.

"You might think I'm not good enough to start and run a business, Da, but I am. I've always been. Just because you can't see that I'm a capable adult who can create amazing things doesn't mean I'm not. I've spent too much of my time and energy trying to please you. Make you see my worth."

Regan squared her shoulders. The eyes of everyone in the room were on them, including the caterer, who pretended they weren't listening.

"As of this moment, I'm done. I don't need your approval for anything else in my life. That includes dating Connor."

Her father's face blistered. He appeared more upset about her last statement more than anything else, but she was done caring.

"I've loved that man since I was eighteen, maybe even younger, and you've kept us apart for so many years for your own selfish reasons. We've lost years because of you, and I don't want to waste any more years. I plan to live my life exactly how I want. That means creating the business I've always wanted and being with the man I love and want to spend my life with. If you don't like it—tough shite!" Regan left her parents standing by her office door and strolled over to Connor, pulled him by the collar, and kissed him with everything she felt since the moment she realized she loved him.

Cheers and then "Get a room" echoed in the distance, but she didn't care.

Connor's arms were around her waist, pulling her closer against him before he broke their kiss. "You're crazy, you know that?"

"Crazy about you." She gazed deep into his stormy eyes, her heart swelling with so much love she thought it would burst.

"I love you so much," his lips whispered against her ears. "But if you don't step away from me soon, I'm going to end up embarrassed in front of your family and our friends."

Regan laughed when she got his meaning.

Connor squeezed her tightly. "I'm serious, sunshine."

"I love you too." She kissed him quickly before he shoved her away, both grinning like idiots.

Her father stormed out the door, but her mother stayed, albeit in a corner of the room, observing everything like a spy who'd report back to her father at the end of the evening. Staying was her showing her support, even in a small way.

Regan grinned at her mother, who returned her smile and tipped her head. Her presence and reaction were her way of saying she agreed with everything Regan told her father, including choosing Connor.

The rest of the night was a blur of people, business cards being exchanged or scanned into phones, food, drinks, and tons of laughter. All in all, a success. Her mother had stayed in the background, moving about the room to speak with people she knew and offering support for her business when asked her thoughts.

Connor and Michael embarrassed her by bragging unnecessarily to everyone they spoke to, while Rachel, Arlene, and Skylar socialized and kept guests entertained until she could speak with them.

By the end of the event, she was delighted by the success but also exhausted because she'd been up and going since five o'clock this morning and it was almost midnight. The caterers were long gone, and Michael, Rachel, and everyone stayed to help her clean up because her office officially opened on Monday and she wanted to be ready to greet clients. She had the weekend to relax and spend with Connor. She was looking forward to that more than anything else. They hadn't seen each other in three months. Talking on the phone wasn't the same. Tonight was the best reminder of that. Being able to touch him, kiss him, and just be near him was everything.

Being apart was difficult, but the choice was worth it. Could she have accomplished everything she did with Connor? Absolutely. But doing it alone was necessary for her, or so she thought. Having her brother, Rachel and her friends, and Connor here tonight was perfect. A lesson she wouldn't soon forget.

"Tonight was a success." Her brother hugged her. "I'm so proud of you, Re." He kissed the side of her head.

"Thank you. And thanks for showing up tonight." She turned to look at everyone who stood around her. "Thank you all. You being here was...appreciated." Those words didn't express her emotions enough, but they were the only words she could find in the moment.

"Anytime, hun." Rachel hugged her. "That's what family is for."

"And friends," Arlene added.

Tears beat at the back of her eyes. She was about to push them back, but she let them flow instead. *No more hiding*. "That means a lot."

Everyone in the circle around her closed in and formed a giant hug circle, embracing her. In that moment, she felt loved, appreciated, and seen in ways she'd never been before.

CHAPTER 41

Regan closed the front door of her flat and turned to watch Connor hang his coat as if it belonged there. Like he belonged in her home.

He did.

After everyone left the office tonight, she insisted Connor follow her home. The surprise on his face made her smile.

On the drive home, all the perfect words she'd planned for weeks to say to him vanished like vapor in the air. For the past three months, she thought the physical distance she kept between them was necessary, that she needed to do everything alone. She was wrong. Tonight showed her that, making the perfect speech she had to explain seem meaningless and no longer fit.

She wrapped her arms around his waist from behind, resting her head against his back. "Stay the night, Connor." Asking wasn't necessary. He'd stay if she asked.

His hands gripped her tightly before he turned around to face her. "You sure? Why now?" He searched her eyes, because she knew he couldn't sense her emotions, a fact that still blew her mind.

"Because I was stupid." Well, not exactly those words, but that's what came out of her mouth. "I thought I had to do this alone.

Find my own investor, space for my office. Plan my opening. Everything."

"But?"

"Everyone showing up tonight showed me it doesn't have to be that way. That it's okay to rely on friends and family." Not something that was easy for her to say, considering depending on her parents in the past had proved heartbreaking.

His hand slipped into her hair as his thumb caressed her cheek. "Not everyone is Shamus."

Her mother was left off because, unlike her father, she had shown up. Had been showing up for her and Michael in ways she hadn't in the past, so couldn't stay in the same category anymore.

"I know that. It was something I had to prove to myself I could do alone. I spent too many years using my inheritance as a reason for not moving forward, whether it was with us or the life and business I wanted to create. Doing it alone was like saying I could do it without anyone, but I don't want to live that way, Connor."

"And you don't have to." He kissed her forehead. "I know better than anyone the desire or need to have to do everything alone because relying on others meant disappointment and heartache. But that's not us, Regan. We were never like our parents."

She slid her hand in his and walked them to the living room and sat on the couch. Connor took the spot next to her, still holding her hand as if he were afraid if he didn't, she might change her mind about him staying.

Not a chance.

"You're right. But after what happened to us the first time, I needed you to know I didn't need my parents. That I could build a life with you, without them. But I realized tonight by keeping you at a distance, I was telling you I didn't want you. Didn't need you. And that's not true."

"I must admit I was hurt when you chose to do it alone, but that's because I want to help you in all areas of your life. That's what you do for the people you love. But I understand why you started your business this way, Regan. I'm just glad you kept in touch, even if it was just by phone. But I missed you." He pulled her into his lap. "So much."

She wrapped her arms around him as her legs sat on either side of him. "I missed you too, and staying away from you or not asking you to come over was killing me."

"I never want to be parted from you again." Connor's hand slipped into her hair as their foreheads touched.

"I start work on Monday, so I'll need to be there," Regan joked.

Connor squeezed her frame tightly before he started to tickle her. He continued until they were both laughing and he was hovering above her when she tried to escape his tickling torture.

"I meant it, Regan. I want you with me. Always."

The depth of emotions in his eyes brought tears to her eyes as his meaning sunk in. "Really?"

"I've wanted to marry you for a long time, Regan. You are the love of my life and have been since you brazenly kissed me at your eighteenth birthday party. I love your passion, and your kind heart, but especially that sarcastic mouth. I love everything about you. Even when you're pissed at me."

Regan grinned up at him like an idiot. "And I've loved you since you kissed me when I turned sixteen. Perve."

Connor groaned. "You don't know how guilty and pervy I felt after that kiss."

"Well, it's a good thing I made the first move, then. Once I was legal, of course."

His stunning blue eyes that never ceased to make her weak in the knees when they were directed at her, like they were now, burned into her.

"I want everything with you, Regan. Every laugh. Every tear. Every joy. A home. Kids. I want to build a life with you. One I know won't be perfect because we're human, but one that is full of love for each other. And when we fight, because we're us, I promise to fight fair and fight for us. Our life and our family."

Tears pooled in her eyes, and her throat tightened like it was full of cotton balls. "I want everything with you, too, Connor. All the late nights working. The happy and sad moments with each other and our kids. The moments with just us being silent and together." Her hands cupped his face. "I want it all with you. The best man I know. The one who showed me I can be myself, and go after what I want, even if it doesn't fit the box everyone wants to put or keep me in. The man who loved me even when I hated him for breaking my heart. The man who never gave up on me."

"On us."

"I can't wait to spend the rest of my life with you, Connor."

He kissed her, long and deep, as they clung to each other.

"And I can't wait to start our lives together, Regan."

There was no ring for her finger, but she didn't care. This moment was spontaneous, and she didn't need a ring to know that Connor was hers for life. He'd been hers almost as long as she was his.

They'd belonged to each other, even while they were apart.

They had a future together. Forever.

AUTHOR NOTE

I started this series more than twenty years ago. It looked completed different from how the series turned out. For one, there was only supposed to be one book, but I loved Regan and Connor so much (as did my beta readers), that the one book quickly turned into two. And when Arlene didn't fit the mold of the best friend I had in mind, Skylar was added to the story.

When I decided to write this series, I wasn't sure how readers would like it because it strayed from my usual genre, but the response was amazing and I'm so grateful to you all!

What I loved most about this series is the way the character's gift morphed into something unexpected and so much more than I originally envision and sparked ideas for new characters (heroes and villains) with crazy gifts and stories that I can't wait to share with you in the spin off series for my original Deadly Series.

Where the Gifted Ones series is focused on spiritual healing, personal growth, and deep love connections (with family drama of course), falling in the Psychic Romance genre, the Deadly Series returns to my romantic suspense roots, although this time around with a psychic romance subgenre.

I hope you enjoy reading the Gifted Ones series as much as I loved writing it. It was a labor of love that took years to write but was definitely worth the wait.

ABOUT THE AUTHOR

She once dreamed of becoming the next Nora Roberts, traveling the world on book tours. These days, she's just as happy channeling her imagination into writing stories and compelling characters across multiple genres.

A mother of two, she loves superhero movies just as much as romance and thrives on structure, deadlines, and systems. Without them, her overactive brain tends to run wild.

Elke writes for readers who believe love is powerful, intuition is real, and hope can exist even in the darkest moments. Her stories blend romance, suspense, and spiritual depth— where love is tested, truth is uncovered, and healing is always possible.

When she's not writing, she enjoys connecting with readers at book events and sharing her love of storytelling. Elke loves connecting with readers like you! Find her on:

Instagram| Facebook| Goodreads | BookBub

www.elkefeuer.com | Email her at elke@elkefeuer.com.

ALSO BY ELKE

"Tell me what you thought! I read every email from my readers—send me a message at elke@elkefeuer.com and let's chat."

Want behind the scenes of my writing life, book launches, giveaways, specials and more? Join my newsletter and get Persuading Lola for FREE.

For the Love of Jazz
Book One - Deadly Bloodlines
Book Two – Deadly Race
Book Three – Deadly Family
The Renovation
Persuading Lola
The Trouble with Soulmates
The Trouble with Empaths
The Trouble with Healers

www.ingramcontent.com/pod-product-compliance
Lightning Source LLC
LaVergne TN
LVHW020702110826
845149LV00012B/2084

* 9 7 9 8 9 8 9 6 5 1 7 8 8 *